SURVIVAL IN ANOTHER WORLD WITH MY MISTRESS

NOVEL 6

WRITTEN BY **Ryuto**

ILLUSTRATED BY **Yappen**

Airship

Seven Seas Entertainment

Goshuzinsama to yuku isekai survival Vol. 6
©Ryuto (Story) ©Yappen (Illustration)
This edition originally published in Japan in 2021 by
MICRO MAGAZINE, INC., Tokyo.
English translation rights arranged with
MICRO MAGAZINE, INC., Tokyo.

Seven Seas press and purchase enquiries can be sent to
Marketing Manager Lianne Sentar at press@gomanga.com.
Information regarding the distribution and purchase of
digital editions is available from Digital Manager CK Russell
at digital@gomanga.com.

Follow Seven Seas Entertainment online at
sevenseasentertainment.com.

TRANSLATION: Elliot Ryouga
ADAPTATION: Harry Catlin
COVER DESIGN: H. Qi
INTERIOR DESIGN: Clay Gardner
INTERIOR LAYOUT: Jennifer Elgabrowny
COPY EDITOR: Meg van Huygen
PROOFREADER: Jade Gardner
LIGHT NOVEL EDITOR: Callum May
PREPRESS TECHNICIAN: Melanie Ujimori, Jules Valera
EDITOR-IN-CHIEF: Julie Davis
ASSOCIATE PUBLISHER: Adam Arnold
PUBLISHER: Jason DeAngelis

ISBN: 978-1-68579-635-8
Printed in Canada
First Printing: July 2023
10 9 8 7 6 5 4 3 2 1

CONTENTS

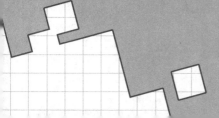

SURVIVAL IN ANOTHER WORLD WITH MY MISTRESS

MADAME ZAMIL stood outside the Dragonis Order's gathering hall with her Shooting Star cross lance rested firmly on her shoulder and a mithril alloy short spear on her back. She was fully equipped and ready to go.

"When did you get here?" I asked.

"After I left the lord's manor, I followed behind you, on guard," she replied. "The harpies are over there, in fact."

"Whoa."

Following Madame Zamil's gaze, I spotted a pink-feathered harpy waving her wings at me—Bron. I hadn't even noticed her. This was all probably because I got kidnapped in Arichburg, huh? Even when I was just going out to run a quick errand or two, security around me had grown more intense.

"Hey, uh, I'm sorry for all the trouble I'm causing you guys."

"Think nothing of it," Madame Zamil insisted. "You are an incredibly important individual to us, Sir Kousuke."

"Ugh, that's a lot of pressure for one guy, you know? I mean, I get that I don't really have a choice... Anyway, how do you feel about those guys? In your expertise as a lizardman, I mean. Can they be trusted?"

"Well..."

Madame Zamil went quiet in thought for a moment.

"I believe that we have no reason to suspect the Dragonis Mountain Nation or the Dragonis Order," she said. "It would be no overstatement to say that their belief and respect toward dragons and their riders is absolute."

"That's scary in and of itself."

"There is no reason to be afraid. To them, you and Lady Grande are essentially royalty. At least in the sense that you are both walking the path of their ancestors from the Dragonis Mountain Nation."

"Do you have any connection to them at all?"

"I do not. I was born and raised in the Kingdom of Merinard, after all. However, as a lizardman, it is a place I would like to visit one day."

"Gotcha..."

So if nothing else, they weren't our enemy. I'd have to report this back to Sylphy and Melty.

"The Dragonis Mountain Nation, eh?" Melty replied after hearing the reports from myself and Madame Zamil.

She placed her hand against her chin and began to think. Sylphy, on the other hand, wore a complex expression on her face as she folded her arms.

"I understand that you and Grande are targets of worship for them," Melty went on. "However, when it comes to matters between two nations, there is no such thing as selfless support. The problem is we don't know what they want in exchange for their help."

"In the absolute worst-case scenario, they might request that we hand over Grande and Kousuke," said Sylphy.

Melty shook her head. "I cannot imagine that would happen... It would risk angering Grande and Kousuke, not to mention potentially lead to war. I imagine their requests will be things like having the two of them visit their country, be granted permission to visit Grande's home as a kind of religious pilgrimage, getting a chance to hang with Grande once a week or once a month at her home, or even permission to fly on her back.

"Put simply, they might want to form a defensive alliance. Regardless of what Kousuke himself thinks, if he were to be put in danger, Grande would absolutely join the battle. For them, being able to battle alongside her would be the greatest honor imaginable. And then there are the elven products. Their nation uses flying dragons to import and export goods, so in addition to their combat prowess, they're also very competent merchants."

"Literal flying merchants, eh?" Sylphy mused. "They certainly seem worth partnering with. As far as I've heard, lizardmen make up the majority race of their country, yes?"

"Correct," said Melty. "It is said that many lizardmen call Dragonis home. However, there are humans and other races there as well. The royal family is composed of demi-humans with dragon characteristics. They're called dragonfolk, or dragonians."

"How are they different from lizardmen?"

"Their appearance, apparently. Imagine Grande in her human form but with more human features. There are quite a few scaled beings there said to be half human and half lizardman."

"Scaled beings?"

"A race with scales on their legs or bodies, as well as a lizardman-like tail."

"I see."

So rather than the full beastlike appearance of Madame Zamil, they were a more humanlike reptile race. I was pretty curious to see what they looked like in person.

"All right," said Sylphy. "I think I have the full picture regarding Dragonis. So did Grande okay the trip to Merinesburg?"

"Yup," I replied. "It was no problem whatsoever. Though she is apparently thinking about what she'll do while I'm over there."

It would be best if she just stayed with Lime and the others.

"Is she going to be okay?" Sylphy asked.

"I'm going to be staying with Lime and the girls, right? It'll all come down to how they get along and if the location works for her."

"Right..."

Sylphy nodded her head, seemingly understanding what I was implying. Since the slimes were deep in enemy lines, they hid in the stinky sewers. As long as I sucked it up while heading into their hideout, I'd be fine. But Grande had a much more sensitive nose than I did.

"Oh, and we're leaving early in the morning tomorrow," I added. "We want to try and get over there by the time that Lime is scheduled to get in touch with Elen."

That way I'd be able to let her know that I'd arrived directly, and Elen could begin making the necessary preparations to meet up with me ASAP. At the end of the day, my only means of getting info to her was when we were both using golem communicators; Lime and the others also only communicated with her through them. *But wait, didn't they say they were guarding her from the shadows? Were they not?* I had no way of knowing. Either way, there was nothing wrong with being early.

"I see... How are your preparations proceeding?"

"I've got everything I need in my inventory."

I had the scripture and its copy in there so that nobody could steal them. The translations were stored in there as well. This way, there'd be no chance of losing anything at all.

"All right. Then I would say we're done for today?" asked Sylphy.

"Er, wha—?"

"Good idea," Melty agreed. "It's still rather early as well."

"Wait. What are you all going on about?" I asked.

Sensing something unpleasant on the way, I attempted to secure my exit, only to have Melty block my path with extreme speed. I shot a look at Danan in the hope of assistance.

"In terms of government affairs, that should be fine," he said. "I will handle any emergency topics."

That bastard averted his gaze to look at some paperwork!

You jerk! I'm not going to forget this! When the time comes, I'm abandoning your ass! Actually, I'll kick it right into the fire myself!

"Madame Zamil, I'm sorry, but could you tell one of the harpies to gather everyone together?" Sylphy asked.

"Understood."

Madame Zamil shot me a look of pity before leaving.

Could you not abandon your security detail? Please? No? Okay.

"Calm down! Let's talk this over! I have to infiltrate enemy territory tomorrow, which means I should really conserve my— hey, stop it! Don't pull that! GYAAAAAAAAH!"

Things turned out less awful than I expected. They were all just worried about me. Yup.

CHAPTER 1

Reunited in Merinesburg

THE NEXT MORNING.

Thanks to the girls taking it easy on me, I found myself with my health and stamina only 25 percent depleted. Their compassion was enough to bring me to tears.

By the way, was it possible for them to not deplete my health or stamina at all? Probably not? Right?

A proper meal and some rest would be enough to refill my bars. Ha ha ha. I was sure I'd recover fully while getting a ride from Grande.

"Kousuke, do not let your guard down," Sylphy warned me. "I do not believe many over there know your face, but Cuvi has not been caught yet. I don't think it's been discovered that we have contact with the saint, but if it has, it's possible they've cast a net out for you. Again, do not let your guard down."

"Got it." I nodded my head earnestly as I listened to her words of caution. If I messed up and got caught again, I'd be causing trouble for everyone in the Liberation Army. Melty could end up cutting her horns off again to go undercover, and I didn't want a repeat of that.

"I won't tell you not to enjoy your time with the saint," Melty added. "It's too late for that. As far as I've heard, we might be able to use that whole Apostle of God idea she brought up. That being said, Kousuke, do not forget that we are your home."

I nodded again. "I know."

I had told Elen how I felt when we spoke before. I would always prioritize Sylphy and the other girls. If the time came where I had to choose, I would choose them.

"I have nothing in particular to add," Ira said. "Just come back safely."

"Of course I will."

"I shall be with him, so fear not!" Grande declared. "Should things take a turn for the worse, I shall burn it all down and flee with Kousuke in my arms."

"Mm. Thanks, Grande. Please watch over him."

"Aye!"

I felt warm and fuzzy watching Grande and Ira nod to each other, especially considering they were the same height. Last night, they formed a tag team and came at me together. Ha ha ha... I was glad to see them getting along so well.

"Master, you better come back in one piece."

"Looking forward to the souvenirs, Master!"

"P-please come home safely... We'll be waiting."

"Don't get yourself hurt, okay?"

The harpies surrounded me, each offering me a few words while gently brushing me with their wings and nuzzling me with their heads. I was super grateful that they held back on me last night. I would've been even happier if they did that just a wee bit more often.

"All right then, ladies. I'm off. I plan on getting in touch every day, though."

"Right," said Sylphy. "Take care. Try not to get wrapped up in anything crazy."

"Don't raise a flag like that..."

That kind of talk would absolutely lead to me getting wrapped up in something. Nobody here knew what I meant by a "flag," but they all stared at Sylphy anyway.

"Wh-why am I at fault?!" she sputtered.

Melty grinned at the panicked Sylphy. "You're not. But I will say this might make for some fun ribbing."

That was the grin of the devil, for sure.

"Don't tease her too much," I said with a smirk.

I pulled out my solo gondola and hopped in. I'd made it so I could travel together with Grande.

"See you all later!" I called out.

"Take care, Kousuke! Hurry back!"

"We are off!"

Grande flew into the air as Sylphy and the others saw us off. At our current speed, we'd be arriving in the outskirts of Merinesburg around noon. I was just going to be delivering the scripture, the copies, and the translation, so with any luck we'd be back before long.

But if I really let myself believe that, I'd end up getting caught in some crazy mess... Or at least that's the feeling I was getting. I couldn't help but feel like I could now sense the will of some being—the very same one that brought Elen and I together.

What was going to happen this time? I hoped it'd be something manageable and simple.

Thanks to Grande, we quickly and painlessly passed over the Sorel Mountains. On the way, a few wyverns spotted us and tried to make a move, but when Grande shot out some magical energy and destroyed some stuff, they quickly fled.

Maybe it was just my imagination, but wyverns kind of struck me as being like dogs that were all bark and no bite. Your average person wouldn't stand a chance, but if you got strong enough, you could take one down. They were perfectly capable of being mid bosses in a story, and the stuff you could get from them was fairly good, but that was about it. How sad for them.

But it was time to move past these poor creatures. We descended into the woods near Merinesburg and made our way on foot to the place Lime and the others called home. Grande was covering her whole body with a robe. It'd be unlucky if any hunters or adventurers in the woods saw Grande's full form—unlucky for them, since we'd have to make sure they kept their mouths shut. Dead men tell no tales.

"So this is where those slimes reside?" Grande whispered, looking at the cave entrance in the shadow of a huge boulder.

She was furrowing her brow, possibly because her strong senses had already picked up an unpleasant scent.

"This is just the entrance," I replied. "The path to where they live is a bit smelly."

"Mm, it already smells quite a bit, but I shall press on. Fear not."

If we got to where Lime and the others lived, it'd be mostly scent-free. But the path to get there was just a normal sewer, so, of course, it stank.

After traveling through the cave for a bit, we finally entered the sewer.

"...Gebleh."

"Hang in there."

Tears flowed from Grande's eyes as she covered her nose with one powerful hand and my hand in the other. Meanwhile, I lit the way with a torch as I led her through the sewers. Any critters or giant rats that saw Grande immediately fled at full speed, so it was an entirely safe journey. Monsters had excellent survival senses.

Eventually, we passed through the sewer area and emerged in the slime girls' territory. At this point, the awful scent had more or less dissipated. Grande still wasn't having a blast, but she wasn't in tears like she was earlier.

"Hrm, so this is where the slimes resi—hm?"

Grande seemed to notice something, as she cast her gaze deep into the sewer tunnel toward the darkness. It felt like she was on guard...

"Eeee..."

"Er, that's terrifying."

It sounded like something was closing in on us. But wait, if something odd was happening down here, there were only three possibilities—it had to be the work of one of the three slimes.

Grande was about to step forward when I put a hand on her shoulder and held her back. I moved in front of her and lit the area with my torch.

It would be safer to have me leading the charge, but I'm sure the three slimes would wait and see before doing something rash.

"...Sukeeee..."

"Ah, well, I'll be," I muttered.

"Kousukeeeee!"

"Eeek!"

"Wha—?!"

A sticky blue liquid covered the entire path as it drew near us. Given the color, this had to be Lime, but the sheer quantity was insane. If she collided with us like this...

"G-Grande, get out of—URGH?!"

"Kousukeeee!"

SQWOOSH!

The blue liquid swallowed us entirely, and I couldn't tell up from down anymore. I felt like I was in a laundry machine. The powerful water current—er, slime current—was impossible to resist. Wait, was she actually cleaning me? For some reason it kind of felt like I was being licked all over and gently squeezed. I also couldn't breathe! I was going to suffocate at this rate!

"Let him go, you fool!" Grande barked, pulling me out of Lime's grip at the last possible moment. "He's going to suffocate!"

"Aaah, give him back!" protested Lime, reaching out for me with her tentacles, but Grande just swiped at them with her sharp claws and powerful tail.

"Y-you saved me," I panted.

"Is she really safe to be around?" Grande asked.

"Probably... Long time no see, Lime."

"Looong time, Kousuke!" she chirped. "How ya beeeeen?"

"Good, good, but I was about to be very not good just a second ago, Lime."

"Sorry." Lime shrunk down and dropped her shoulders sadly. Wait, wasn't she just large enough to cover this entire waterway? Now she'd become about the same size as Grande, and in an instant at that. Did she actually have a super high density or something?

"Well, I won't get any madder as long as you understand what you did wrong," I sighed. "Grande, forgive her, okay? And thanks for saving me."

"Mm, if you say so, I shall," Grande agreed. "Slime, reflect on your actions."

"Ugh, I will." Lime earnestly nodded, clearly regretting her own failure.

After traveling on Lime with Grande for a bit, we eventually arrived at her home. The red slime, Bess, and the green slime, Poiso, were already waiting for us, illuminating their home with some kind of magic.

SURVIVAL IN ANOTHER WORLD WITH MY MISTRESS

"Welcome," Bess said. "I'm glad to see you doing well."

"Sorry about Lime, by the way," added Poiso.

"Long time no see. How've you ladies been?"

"Doing well, of course!" Bess smiled warmly. She was the slender red slime with the sharp eyes and unyielding spirit. "We can't get sick or hurt, after all."

"Thanks to the saint, nobody has been dumping oil down here and lighting it on fire anymore, so it's been quite nice." The one who brought up that startlingly violent scenario was the green slime, Poiso. She had sleepy eyes and a kind of ditzy personality.

They'd actually mentioned something about oil and fire before. And being shot with magic, too.

"You certainly got here quickly... Lime, you mustn't keep him all to yourself," said Bess.

"I'm sure he made the decision," Poiso said. "If anyone was going to come here, nobody would be a more perfect fit than him. But you're right, that was fast. No fair, Lime."

"Juuust a little more," said Lime.

Having carried us home, Lime now morphed into a chair large enough to seat myself and Grande together. She was huge. Her lower body was currently a massive sofa or bed, but her upper body made her look like a giant. She was even bigger than Shemel. The round things pushing into my back were huge as well. This was a brand-new sensation. But since she was a slime, big jugs weren't really that much of a big deal.

"This is so comfy..."

Meanwhile, Grande was on the verge of falling victim to Lime Sofa. It was impressive that Lime could take down even a Grand Dragon like this.

"I don't have to explain why I'm here, right?" I said.

"Of course not."

"We're aware of all conversations between the Liberation Army and the saint."

"That's a little frightening in terms of security," I admitted, "but you guys are on our side, so..."

"We're Princess Sylphy's allies," said Lime.

"Right," agreed Bess. "And since the Liberation Army is under her command, we as the royal guard are undoubtedly Princess Sylphyel's allies."

"Obviously," concurred Poiso.

"Yeah." I nodded my head and decided to explain things nonetheless.

"And so during the afternoon meeting, I'll let them know that I've arrived here, and we'll make plans so I can meet up with Elen," I concluded.

"Gotcha! Will you be here until then?"

"That's the idea. I'm in your hands."

"You certainly are."

"Leave everything to us!"

"Please take it easy on me."

They were literal bottomless pits. If they went full blast on me, I'd completely dry up. Fortunately, the three of them were more than aware of this, so I'm sure they'd take it easy on me.

"Tell us about heeer." Lime looked down at Grande sleeping atop of her and tilted her head. Now that I thought about it, there was no way they knew much about her.

"Her name is Grande, and she's a grand dragon," I told them. "She might not look the part, but..."

"A dragon, huh?" said Lime. "She certainly has enough magical energy to prove it."

"Mm, bad match," said Poiso.

"Indeed," Bess agreed. "She's a bad match for us."

"Really?" I said. "I was hoping you guys would get along."

"When we say a bad match, we don't mean it like that," Bess said. "We mean in terms of combat. The three of us might struggle against her."

"Seriously?"

Grande was scared of Melty, but the three slimes could take Melty together.

"None of our attacks would affect Grande. On the flip side, I imagine many of her attacks would work on us."

"If we caught Melty, we could win. If we caught Grande, it'd be impossible."

"I see..."

They had formed a kind of awkward triangle. Melty had the attack power to break through Grande's tough scales, but her defenses were weak and she'd fall if caught by the slimes. However, while Grande couldn't be harmed by the slimes' attacks, Melty's power would breach her defenses. At the same time, Melty's attacks couldn't finish off the slimes, but the slimes couldn't win against Grande's overwhelming defense.

"Would you girls lose against Melty's magic attacks?" I asked.

"It's possible," said Bess, "but if we caught her off guard or managed to trap her with a single attack, we could win. We could sneak attack Grande, but nothing we did after would hurt her, so we'd have no way of winning."

"On the flip side, Grande's attacks probably couldn't hit Melty," Lime added. "She'd dodge them all and beat her up."

"Ah."

I thought back to when Grande lost against Melty. It really was incredibly one-sided.

"In other words, Melty's tremendously powerful because she could theoretically win against you girls and Grande?"

"She's basically a type of monster," said Poiso. "Her species aren't called overlords for nothing."

"As far as I'm concerned, all of you are impossible to beat."

The same went for Sylphy, Madame Zamil, Sir Leonard, Ira, Danan, and Shemel and her girls. I didn't stand a chance against any of them. I could come out on top if I set traps and stuff, but that wasn't anything to brag about.

"Kousuke, you're also a monster," giggled Lime.

"Indeed," said Bess. "I'd be terrified of fighting you. Who knows what would come flying at me."

"Our best bet would be to strike first," said Poiso. "Wanna train? It's been a long time."

"Nah, I'll pass."

It'd be tremendously sad if we fought every time we reunited. Plus, I'm the only one who would end up getting beaten up and hurt. Never again.

"More importantly, I've got gifts for everyone," I said, "so let's enjoy those, okay?"

"Gizma meat?"

"What did you bring?"

"I'm super curious."

First and foremost, Lime asked for gizma meat, so I handed her a chunk of it. Some for Bess and Poiso as well, of course. A giant chunk of gizma meat was like candy to these girls.

"I basically have anything and everything, but I don't really know what would make you all happy."

As I spoke, I pulled out a bottle of mead, some candy, block cookies, and other stuff. I also pulled out things I suspected they wouldn't be all that interested in, like gold and silver accessories, fake flowers and beautiful cloth for interior decoration, rugs, and perfumes and scent bags sold in Arichburg as well.

"Delish!" Lime was particularly pleased with the food, as she was practically vibrating while picking from whatever she could get her hands on. She seemed especially fond of the mead and candy. Did she have a sweet tooth?

"I'm quite interested in this." Bess, on the other hand, was drawn in by the beautiful cloth, rug, and fake flowers. She had already begun to decorate their home.

"Hrm, I see..." Meanwhile, Poiso was fascinated by the perfumes and scent bags. She had taken them into her body and was investigating them with great interest.

Lime was into the foods, Bess was into the decorative goods, and Poiso was delighted by the perfumes and medicinal herbs.

"Absolutely delish."

Without me even noticing, Grande had woken up and was happily munching on some candy. Just when did she even get up? Eh, it didn't matter. She must've been hungry after flying over the Sorel Mountains. I decided to pull a burger out for her.

And so we spent the time chilling out and enjoying some good times until our call with Elen and the army.

While I enjoyed an early lunch (basically candy) with Lime and the others, we talked about what happened after we parted ways and I went home. After killing time for a bit...

"You suuure have a wide strike zone," said Lime.

"More like he has no sense of fidelity," said Bess.

"Call it charm..." I sighed. "Most of the time I'm the one who ends up being pounced on."

"You're easy... I mean kind," snickered Poiso.

"What did you just say?"

Poiso was spitting some hot aether at me, that cursed slime. Did she want me to splash her with some antidote? Actually, that probably wouldn't work on her. Poiso wasn't a poison slime so much as she was a medicinal one. She could apparently refine and handle poisons and medicines at her will. She also had the best digestive abilities out of the three girls.

"But when it comes to myself, I am in fact a monster, and so are you all, no?" said Grande. "Yet he accepts us with no resistance even though we are not demi-humans like Sylphy and the others. What is that if not a lack of fidelity?"

"Why're you putting yourself down like that?" said Bess. "Don't you have any self-confidence?"

"Urgh... I do! I'm quite cute and super duper pretty."

Grande attempted to fight back against Bess's piercing blow, tapping her sharp claws together. I'd never seen her behave like this before. Did she have a complex over this kind of thing?

"What do you think, Kousuke?"

"I think she's legit cute," I answered, rubbing Grande's horned head. "Her magnificent horn, partially transformed hands and feet, cool wings, thick and powerful tail; everything about her is cute. And to be honest, she was plenty cute before she took on her humanoid form."

The way she reacted to things was adorable, y'know? Sure, it was impossible to feel lust for her when she was in her dragon form, but I was sure there were folks in this world who probably could. Even if they weren't me. Just had to make that clear, twice.

"You're the real deal," Lime nodded.

"Suuuper wide strike zone," giggled Poiso.

"You don't really fuss much over outside appearances, huh?" said Bess.

"I don't think that's true..." I protested. In my opinion, the slime girls, Grande, Sylphy, and everyone else were all immense beauties. And then on top of that, they were slimes, dragon girls, elves, cyclops girls, harpies, weirdly strange demonic beings... It was awesome.

What about Elen? She was the type of beauty I desperately wanted to get close to, but she felt so far removed from someone like me. Though I suppose that went for all of them.

I continued to pet Grande's head while thinking to myself, which resulted in her turning bright red as her eyes darted all over.

"Uurgh..." She was violently smacking her tail against the ground as well. The stone fragments that broke off were planting themselves inside of the slime girls, one of them bouncing off of Bess's face and stabbing into Poiso. That tail of hers sure was powerful.

"...ve," she mumbled.

"Hm?"

"LOOOVE!"

"GAH!"

Grande came jumping at me while swinging her tail about. What was she thinking?! She made my wyvern armor look like paper! Ow, ow! Her horn was grinding against my chest, and it hurt like hell!

"Mm... Snff, snff... Mm..."

Grande nuzzled her face (and horn) against my bare chest while breathing loudly through her nose. She was tripping out. All I could see from my position was her head and horn, but

I was certain her eyes probably had heart marks in them. And that horn of hers hurt!

"Head over heels," said three voices in unison. Lime had... divided her body?! And now she was observing us from different angles.

"What an easy dragon," Poiso smirked as she watched the two of us.

Bess, on the other hand, looked fed up with the whole thing but seemed uninterested in stopping Grande. "And she doesn't even care that we're still here..."

It took about five minutes for Grande to finally return to normal before things got too bad. My chest hurt from that horn of hers, but I wasn't bleeding. We were all good.

"..." Grande was currently sitting on her knees in the corner of the room facing the wall, covering her body with her wings to hide her shame.

"Grande?"

"..."

I tried calling out to her, but her tail only twitched. She was totally ignoring me.

"Are you embarrassed?"

"Noooothing to be ashamed of!"

"Kousuke would never get angry over thaaat."

The three Limes were all trying to comfort her. She seemed to really regret destroying the wyvern armor I was wearing, but if I fixed it at my smithing station, I could repair it fairly quickly. I wish she wouldn't worry herself over that.

This had all resulted in her taking fairly significant psychological damage. It really wasn't a big deal, though. Nobody got hurt.

"Monster instincts and impulses are strong," said Poiso. "It's not her fault."

"And Grande hasn't been interacting with humans for all that long," said Bess. "Don't worry, you'll both get used to each other as time goes by... Ah, it's time."

Bess headed over to the golem communicator. She was apparently in charge of the relay today. Lime's main body had also come beside the communicator, leaving her clones to handle Grande.

"Is Elen already at the meeting spot?" I asked.

"She is," said Bess. "Want me to tell her something?"

"Yeah. Tell her I'm already here and that I want to see her soon. Is that okay? And I'd be grateful if you told her that the Liberation Army has some stuff to tell her regarding you-know-what."

"Understood... She's asking when you're coming."

"As soon as she's ready on her end. She just needs to tell me where to go. She can let me know tomorrow, or sometime in the morning of the day after, using one of you as a relay. Ah, but wait, you guys are guarding her right now, yeah?"

"Correct. She could just tell one of us when she's alone, no?"

"Right, right. Let her know."

"All right... She says she understands."

"Cool. Thanks a lot."

"You're quite welcome," Bess responded with a smile.

Shortly after, the call between Elen and Sylphy and her people began. I thought it would end quickly because there wasn't much to talk about today, but Elen had a proposal.

"There's someone I'd really like Kousuke to meet."

"Kousuke? What's this about?"

I could hear Sylphy's suspicious tone over the communicator. Hell, I felt like I could even see her expression.

"I got the message this morning, but in five days' time, my boss, a leader of the Nostalgia-sect, will be arriving in Merinesburg. I would love for Kousuke to meet her."

"Her...? So she's a woman."

"She is, but she's close to fifty years old. Of course, you never can tell when it comes to Kousuke."

I couldn't help but interject. "Even I have my limits, ladies."

Even I wouldn't go after someone who was the same age as my mother... But if we were talking about numbers specifically, Sylphy, Ira, Melty, and Grande were all about that old... Wait, no, that's not what this was about. We were talking about outside appearances. I'd already proven age was just a number so long as they looked to be about my age. But wait, a nearly fifty-year-old human woman wouldn't be interested either, right?

"Anyway, let's leave that pointless conjecture to the side and stay focused."

"Right," said Sylphy. "So you want Kousuke to meet your boss, yes? What's your objective here? Depending on your answer, I might have to reject your proposition."

"I want Kousuke to wear the Crown of Radiance and prove that the apostle is on our side," Elen replied.

"The Crown of Radiance... If I remember correctly, it's supposed to make the blessing of God visible, or something to that effect? What is there to gain by doing this? Don't tell me you plan on getting Kousuke wrapped up in the church's internal power struggle?"

"Depending on how things go, that is entirely possible. Within the Church of Adolism, one with a powerful radiance has immense influence. Quite frankly, the only reason a weak branch like the Nostalgia-sect can face off against the main one without being crushed is because of my presence as the saint. Kousuke's radiance is on par with my own. If he supports the Nostalgia-sect and brings with him old Adolist scripture from before it was modified, this benefits them and not the main sect. It would put us in a much more advantageous position."

"And you would put Kousuke in danger to accomplish that? Madness. I will not let him be put in harm's way."

I'd fully expected Sylphy to reject Elen's idea out of hand. But Elen didn't back down so easily.

"Sooner or later, the Holy Kingdom and church will become aware of Kousuke's existence," she said. "And when that happens, it would be safer for him to be widely recognized as an apostle. Neither the Holy Kingdom nor the church would be able to easily assassinate him at that point."

"I believe making his existence public would be far more dangerous than any of that."

"Kousuke is already famous within the Liberation Army for being your partner, is he not? I believe the Holy Kingdom has been aware of that for quite some time. They are not nearly as incompetent as you all believe them to be. Consider this: I managed to meet him. Am I wrong?"

"No, but... Didn't you say that you were not aware of where Cuvi was based?"

"That's correct. If nothing else, the fox demi-human is not a member of our Nostalgia-sect. However, it is difficult to imagine that he belongs to the main one. They would never use a demi-human spy."

Now we were discussing the very man who kidnapped me.

If he wasn't part of the Nostalgia-sect or the main church, then who exactly was he? He was likely allied with some unknown third force, but even Elen had no idea what that might be.

"Then could he be a part of the Empire that the Holy Kingdom is at war with?" I asked.

"I cannot deny that possibility," said Sylphy.

"I see," Elen said. "It does seem more realistic than him being a part of the main sect."

I initially said it as a joke, but they both responded to me positively. That would mean that, three or more years ago—before Danan and his crew began their revolt—the Empire sent Cuvi into the Kingdom of Merinard. It was possible that he was sent in far before that, even.

I didn't know if this was fact or fiction, but I'd heard that spies on Earth could sometimes stay undercover in their target countries for dozens of years... Not like ninjas who wore their black garbs, possessed ninja swords, and threw shuriken. These spies just quietly lived in their target nation, collecting information.

It wasn't impossible that Cuvi was in the same position.

"Either way, as long as it is made clear that the Nostalgia-sect possesses another member with a similar or greater radiance to my own, that's all we really need," said Elen. **"When we make this public, he doesn't have to reveal his name or face. There will eventually come a time when he needs to appear before others, but I will take great care when we cross that bridge. I would like him to meet my boss face-to-face, though, if possible."**

"Hrm, and why is that?" asked Sylphy.

"Showing her his radiance isn't enough to gain her trust. It is different than showing him off to the masses."

"Hrm... I suppose that is fine."

Sylphy looked hung up on something, but she clearly decided not to press the matter further. On a personal level, even if they wore that crown, I don't think I could trust my fate to someone wearing a mask and hiding their face.

From a commoner's point of view, however, they might just see them as a super elite beyond their reach and be fine with it.

"Anyway, I permit Kousuke to meet with your boss in the name of strengthening the ties between our Liberation Army and your Nostalgia-sect," Sylphy concluded. **"I will leave the actual decision to Kousuke. However, do not forget that our objective is to retake the Kingdom of Merinard. We will not hesitate to offer our support so that**

the Nostalgia-sect holds the power in the church and gives us back our remaining territories, but if you cannot do that, we will be forced to take them back by force like we did the southern regions of Arichburg. As we have not signed any formal peace treaties, we are currently simply acting as two separate entities who share the same foe. We are, on a fundamental level, incompatible. Kousuke is only acting as a bridge between us. Take care not to do anything strange to him. Should that happen, I will do anything within my power to kill you."

"Understood," said Elen. "I do not wish for more blood to be spilled. While their beliefs are different, the followers of the main sect are still fellow believers of Adolism. Comrades. At the same time, I do not wish to go to war with the people that Kousuke holds dear to his heart. I plan on doing everything within my power to resolve this without bloodshed."

"Do not forget those words. Now then, if anything happens, contact us via the slimes. When do you want to hold our next call?"

"If nothing out of the ordinary transpires, we shall speak in five days' time, my boss included."

"Understood... Kousuke, do not let your guard down."

"Got it. If anything happens on your end, let me know ASAP."

"Of course. I shall talk to you later."

And so the call with Sylphy ended.

"She speaks to you with such a kind voice," Elen mused.

"I suppose she does."

SURVIVAL IN ANOTHER WORLD WITH MY MISTRESS

"Should I speak like that to you as well?"

"A little late for that, isn't it? I don't mind it, but I like the vibe you and I have right now."

"I was thinking the same thing. Let's keep that for when it's just the two of us."

"Y-yeah, sure."

"I'll check my schedule regarding the scripture pick up, so please give me some time. As soon as I make a decision, I'll tell one of the slimes. Sooner is better, so I'll try to let you know by tomorrow if possible."

"Got it. Just don't push yourself too hard."

"I won't. Farewell."

"The saint has left the meeting area," Bess told me.

"Really? Whew..."

I couldn't help but sigh in relief. Listening to Elen and Sylphy go at it was more exhausting than I expected. It wasn't the worst thing in the world, but I could feel the weariness building up in my heart. The way they spoke was completely different from when Sylphy spoke to Ira, Melty, or the harpies. I could feel the wall between them. Maybe that was just to be expected, considering they had yet to even meet face-to-face.

"Oil and water?" asked Lime.

"I wouldn't say it was that bad. It was like...they were trying to figure each other out."

"Well, they only really know each other's voices," said Lime. "I don't hate her, you know? She's pretty interesting."

"Samesies!" said Poiso. "She's really nice!"

"She has a strong sense of curiosity," Bess said. "I noticed she seems to have no misgivings over touching us, either."

"Really?"

But thinking about it, that was the sort of thing Elen would have no problem doing. She traveled her own path, so to speak.

"Is that it for today?" asked Lime.

"Let's see... I can just leave the armor to repair itself, and there's nothing I need to make today, so—gah?!"

By the time I realized what was happening, it was too late. I made a mistake.

Made a mistake made a mistake made a mistake made a mistake made a mistake made a mistakebvdqbdq—

"Forgive me."

"We'll be nice and geeentle."

"Just leave everything to us."

"G-give up."

Bess's arms wrapped around me, holding me in place. Ah, Lime's clones were carrying Grande over here. She'd be going down with her captain. Hah, hah, hah.

"Look, just have a little bit of self-restraint, okay, Poiso?"

"I'll consider it!"

Poiso grinned. Nope. Not a lick of self-restraint to be found. Her medicinal production skills were insane. Like three times more insane than Ira's. Like, make your speaking ability evaporate levels of insane.

Grande was my only hope. I had to believe her instincts and abilities as a dragon would save me.

"Garrrgh..."

Nope, it was no good. Poiso's medicines worked on dragons. After going through unspeakable things, Grande was now in the corner of the room muttering to herself. How sad. If I ever put Poiso and Ira in the same room, I was afraid it might end in some kind of horrific scientific tragedy.

Hm? Why wasn't I in the corner, eyes dead, mumbling to myself? Because I was used to this kind of thing! Ha ha ha! Ha ha ha... Or maybe I was already dead inside.

"Poiso, you really need to show some self-restraint," I told her. "Seriously. Poor Grande's been mind-broken."

"She was weaker than I thought."

"Poiso, do you really want to get into a fight with me?"

"I'm sowwee..."

I was genuinely annoyed, so when I flashed some real anger her way, she immediately apologized. It was times like this that I wish she'd just do that from the get-go.

"He got mad at Poiso!" said Lime.

"Please forgive her," Bess said. "She sometimes gets ahead of herself. I do think she regrets her actions."

"I'm willing to put up with a certain amount of craziness, because I owe the three of you the world, but Grande's different."

"I'm really sorry..." Poiso said quietly, as if she really regretted what had happened. When I glanced over at Grande, she wandered over and began to apologize to her. Good.

As for what actually happened, I'll keep that to myself. For Grande's honor.

"What time is it?" I asked. "It's hard to tell when you're down here for so long."

"Still early in the morning," Lime replied. "The sun's just barely come up."

"Gotcha. Wasn't Elen supposed to get in touch?"

"She told us to come to the castle just before noon with the appointment document in hand."

"Ah, right. That."

When I last parted ways with Elen, she gave me an appointment document that would allow me to come and see her. In exchange, I gave her a bullet pendant.

"Then I suppose we should hurry and get going after breakfast. We've got time to take a leisurely walk over."

"Breakfast!"

"I'd like something other than gizma meat today."

"Then wyvern meat it is!"

And so a brand-new day began in earnest. The wyvern meat was a hit with the slimes. Poiso was particularly fond of the poison tails. Was she going to make another strange medicine from its poison?

"I told you, I regret my actions," she insisted. "You don't need to worry anymore."

Or so she said, but could she be trusted? I'd have to keep an eye on her going forward.

"Will you be okay alone?" asked Grande. She had managed

to bounce back after eating breakfast, but she was still putting distance between herself and Poiso.

"Yeah," I assured her. "And either way, bringing you along is kind of an impossible ask. It'd become a huge deal."

"Gr... Even though nobody cares in Arichburg?"

"The Holy Kingdom and church's influence in Merinesburg is strong. It is what it is."

"Look, just be careful," she told me. "If anything were to happen to you, I would go on a rampage."

"That'd be bad news, so I'll do my best to keep safe."

If Grande went crazy in Merinesburg, that'd be one hell of a shitstorm. Politically speaking, it would be a catastrophe, so I genuinely had to be careful. After all, Grande was a dragon. If she lost her cool, human lives were like ants beneath her feet.

With breakfast done, I finished getting ready for my outing. I had milk and block cookies this morning. As for what kind of milk I drank, well, I'll leave that to your imagination.

Oh, and this was unrelated, but the milk circulating in regions heavily populated by demi-humans tended to be about 35 percent breast milk from cow demi-humans. Apparently there were a lot of folks who naturally produced milk even when they weren't pregnant. That included mountain goat people and horse people, even camel and alpaca people as well. Not that this had anything to do with anything.

Ah, and about 40 percent of all edible eggs that made the rounds in said regions were from harpies or other races with wings—demi-humans who were capable of laying unfertilized eggs. Though at the end of the day, eggs in general weren't widely available, so the percentage was high.

In my case, when I put something into my inventory, I could see exactly where it came from in an instant. Not that it matters! Ha ha ha, what were we talking about again? I sure had gotten used to this world, huh?!

"All right. I'm off!" I announced.

"Take care!"

"Be caaareful."

"Don't let your guard down."

"Please, be careful."

The girls saw me off as I exited the sewer and emerged in the forest. The light from the sun felt brighter than ever.

"Let's do this, Kousuke," I told myself.

Today I was equipped with the wyvern armor I repaired, a steel helmet, a round shield on my back, a short sword and knife at my hip, and a short spear in my hands. I was rocking the mercenary style today. I wouldn't normally walk around so heavily equipped, but this was enemy territory, and a guy traveling alone would look suspicious otherwise. If I appeared to be a merc or an adventurer, nobody would question me.

Apart from that, I had some spare underwear, dried meats, and bread in a bag, plus my wallet and a water bottle.

As far as my skill with the spear or sword went, well, I was passable, I suppose. The last time I was here, Lime and the others worked me to death, and when I got home and told Madame Zamil about my training, she started working me four times a week. Whoops.

Her training regime wasn't that bad, but as of right now, I was strong enough to beat a new recruit in the Liberation Army. Nothing to brag about? Yeah, I was well aware.

Of course, a new recruit in our army would be a demi-human, and they typically had much higher physical abilities than humans did. A new demi-human soldier could beat your average human soldier in close-range weapons combat. In other words, that meant I was a little bit better than your average human soldier.

If nothing else, thanks to my practical training, I was good enough to take down goblins with no problem. Any more than three or four of them at a time and I wouldn't be having a good day. At that point, I'd switch to my shotgun or submachine gun and riddle them with holes.

No matter how hard I trained, at the end of the day, I was still just a weakling. When I'd said that to the new demi-human recruits training with me, they looked at me as if I had lost my mind. Huh.

I pondered these pointless things for a bit as I walked through the woods, occasionally bumping into goblins and fleeing from them using my strafe jump. Eventually, I succeeded at exiting the forest.

Why didn't I fight? Well, they might have given me EXP, but I didn't think it was worth putting myself in danger. If I wanted to grind, I'd be better off going up to the Sorel Mountains and shooting down wyverns. If I could bring Grande or Madame Zamil as bodyguards, it'd be perfect.

But quite frankly, I didn't see the need to raise my level in the first place, which was why I didn't do anything like that. If I unlocked new recipes or something, I'd be on it posthaste, but all I ever got were skill points to raise my physical abilities or shorten my crafting time... Or I could upgrade my mining abilities, but they weren't really giving me any problems at this point. If anything, my mining was too effective.

Plus, whenever I was in Arichburg, I was always busy. I didn't have the time to grind levels.

I eventually found the road and casually made my way toward Merinesburg. As always, there were plenty of people coming to and fro, but it felt like there were slightly less of them than before. It didn't look like there were fewer farmers who had come here to sell their goods, but there were definitely fewer merchants and travelers. Or maybe I was just imagining things? I could certainly tell that there were fewer wealthy folks trying to flee the city. In fact, I didn't see a single one. Maybe they'd all already gotten out.

I was inspected at the same gate I entered from last time and crossed over into the city. It was a different soldier from before, and when I introduced myself as "Kou," he didn't react one way or the other. He did, however, jot down my physical features, such as my eye and hair color. I guess black hair really was rare around here.

Entering the city proper, I once again found a group of somewhat dirty looking children near the entrance. One of the boys approached me.

"Wait, aren't you the guy from last time? Radical! You came back?"

It was the same boy who had led me around the city during my last visit. As far as I could tell, he hadn't gotten himself hurt or sick in the time since I was gone. I was glad to see him doing well.

"Long time no see, eh?" I said.

"Need a guide again?" he asked.

"Hrm..."

I was just heading to the castle, so I didn't need a guide this time around. Since I was in the big city and all, it'd be a good idea to buy souvenirs, but that wasn't number one on my to-do list. My first objective was the castle, after all.

"I have some business to attend to, so I'm good for now," I told the boy. "But once I wrap that up, I am planning on doing some shopping. Where might one go if they were looking to grab some souvenirs?"

"Hrm, either the marketplace, the artisan's district, or the general store off the main street."

"I know about the artisan's district, but I'm not familiar with the marketplace. Where is it?"

I showed the boy a piece of copper, and he raised two fingers. Two pieces, eh? That was fine, even if he was pushing it a little. I handed him two coppers, and he smiled broadly at me.

"Take a right on this street, then you'll see it on your left after walking for a while," he said. "During this season, I'd say dried apricots and prunes are a good bet."

"Gotcha. Catch you later, kid."

"If you need anything, come back and ask me!"

I waved back at the boy and started my trek to the castle. It was visible from anywhere in the city, so I couldn't get lost. I wasn't exactly used to wearing such heavy armor, but I nonetheless kept moving.

CHAPTER 2

The Lonely Saint

O N THE WAY to the castle, I asked a few elderly folks the precise way to get there, and after walking for a bit—a little under an hour—I finally arrived in front of the massive building. What, I took too long? C'mon. Merinesburg was a lot wider than Arichburg, and the way the streets were laid out, you couldn't just walk there in a straight line. Plus, the closer you got to the castle, there were sentinels guarding the gates asking for appointment documents and such. It took a while, okay?

The guards seemed on edge, to boot. When I asked why, they said there had been multiple assassination attempts on the saint. One guy tried to charge her headfirst only to trip and fall over, another tried to use magic but got knocked out by a stone from out of nowhere. One assassin attempted to shoot her with an arrow, but he suddenly caught fire and fell off the roof he was perched in.

This was clearly the work of the slime girls.

Eventually, I came face-to-face with the knight guarding the castle gates.

"You are...? Hrm, a glum face and black hair. You're exactly as described."

Well, sorry for looking glum! You big jerk!

I hid those words behind a smile and let the knight say what he wanted. It wasn't as if I thought I was some hottie or whatever. No damage taken here. Nope...none at all.

"Your documents are the real deal. You're free to enter the castle, but we'll have to confiscate your weapons."

"Yeah, that makes sense."

"Sorry, but you have to take your armor off as well."

"Okay."

This was no biggie. If things got bad, I could always just reach into my inventory for whatever I needed.

I left my short spear, short sword, knife, round shield, and wyvern armor with the knight, and I took my wallet and documents out of my bag and handed it to him. After he'd made sure I was unarmed, I was allowed into the castle.

When I was being checked for weapons, I got the strange feeling that my crotch and butt got felt up, but I decided not to think about it too much.

"I sent out a messenger just now," he told me. "A guide should be coming shortly. Wait here."

"Roger that."

There were all kinds of folks in the castle. The ones who stood out the most were the soldiers, equipped with short spears, and the knights. When everyone shared the same armaments, the aura they gave off was something else. People really did seem on edge.

And then there were the men and women busily running around wearing robes. I kind of expected to find maids in here, but they must have been deeper in the castle with their masters out of fear of the assassins. But wasn't it those masters who had ordered the attempts in the first place?

I'd been waiting for my guide for a little while when a familiar sister walked up to me. Uh, what was her name again?

"Amalie?"

"Yes, that is me," she said, flashing me a warm smile. "It has been some time."

This was the very same sister who had been forced by the saint to wear the crown so her radiance would be visible, eventually resulting in her breaking down in tears. When I was stabbed by the poison sword, she looked after me a great deal.

"Lady Eleonora is waiting. Right this way."

"Right. Thanks for showing me the way."

"It is nothing. You see, Lady Eleonora cannot wait to see you again. She's been jittery since yesterday."

"Huh."

I was hoping Elen would be more careful. People were going to question how she got in touch with me... But maybe she had let Amalie in on the details? As far as I could tell, she didn't seem at all suspicious of the saint...

"Lady Eleonora has been blessed with quite a few revelations as of late. In fact, she saw that you were coming in one of her visions."

"I-I see."

So Elen had been explaining the info she received through Lime and the others as divine revelations. Was that okay? From, like, a religious perspective?

After walking down the hall a bit, we went up some stairs and eventually arrived at a large, decorated wooden door. Amalie knocked on it.

"Lady Eleonora. You have a visitor."

"Please come in."

For some reason, Amalie positioned me directly in front of the door, then, after making sure nobody was around, opened it.

I was puzzled, but as the door opened, an unidentified golden object leapt into my chest.

"Wh-whoa!"

I couldn't help but yell as I tried to catch the thing in my arms, but it wrapped itself around my body before I could. These were arms, and the golden object was a person's head.

"You really caught me off guard there, Elen."

"Who cares? Right now you should be holding me."

"Ah, jeez... There, there."

Elen nuzzled her head into my chest, so I embraced her in my arms and gently stroked her back. After we'd been doing this for a while, Sister Amalie cleared her throat.

"Lady Eleonora, Lord Kousuke, there's no telling when someone might spot the two of you, so could you perhaps leave it at that for now? Should you wish to continue, I recommend entering the room."

"Fine," Elen conceded. "I guess I have no choice."

Elen shifted her body a bit, so I let go of her. Despite her neutral expression, she gave off the aura of someone who did not wish to let go as she backed away. As for me, my heart was

palpitating like crazy, and I felt like I wasn't in my right mind. Sure, I was surprised by the way she embraced me out of nowhere, but it seemed like I was incapable of keeping my thoughts steady while I was touching her. What was this?

I did my best to contain myself as I entered the office-like room. It was fairly spacious, and right in the front was a desk. To the left was a rather nice lounge suite, and in the back was a door. Apparently, there was another room back there.

There were absolutely no furnishings otherwise. It was an unnatural state, for sure. It was almost as if what furnishings were here had been deliberately taken away.

"Is something the matter?" Elen asked me.

"Nah, it's just... I was thinking about how little you have in here despite it being so spacious."

"I thought you might say that. This office formerly belonged to the white pig bastard who called himself a bishop. The furnishings were so tacky that I had them all disposed of."

"Lady Saint, watch your language, please," said Amalie.

"My, I apologize. You must understand, the furnishings were so tacky that I spent many days here, troubled by their existence," Elen explained without a lick of emotion on her face.

She walked over to the lounge suite and set herself down on a comfortable-looking couch. She patted the space next to her, but I opted to sit across from her instead.

"And why are you sitting over there?"

"I have some stuff to give you, so this is more convenient."

"Please. You need not put on airs."

Elen continued to pat the space next to her, so I gave up and sat myself down by her side. Elen gave off a satisfied aura as she leaned in close to me and began to nuzzle her cheek against my right arm. What was she, a cat?

"Are you good?" I asked.

"Not yet."

"I see... Well, you're adorable, so I'll allow it."

After I let her satisfy herself for a spell, she then laid her head down in my lap. With little to no choice in the matter, I gently caressed her head, being careful not to mess up her beautiful blonde hair.

"You're coming on real strong today..." I murmured. "I don't remember you being this kind of character."

"I do not know what you mean by 'character,' but I have been waiting eagerly to see you again ever since the day you left me. I believe God will forgive at least this much."

Elen rolled over so she was staring straight at me with her crimson red eyes. If nobody had been watching, I would have kissed her right then and there. She was that adorable. But even I knew that would be a bad idea. Considering our positions, it would be a huge problem. Though at this point it seemed a bit late to be worried about that.

"Lady Saint," Amalie interrupted, "please restrain yourself from going any further."

"Fine, fine... I suppose I am satisfied for now, so shall we begin?"

"Gotta say, I love how quickly you can flip the switch like that." I couldn't help but feel warm inside watching Elen put on airs.

Elen lifted her body from my lap, and her scent passed my nose, causing my heart to race. What was happening?

"Um, so about the thing we talked about..."

I glanced at Amalie.

"What is it? Are you ogling Amalie? In front of me?"

"No, of course not! I was just wondering if it was okay to talk about this in front of her."

"In that case, it is fine. I have already spoken to her about the scripture."

Specifically the scripture, eh? So she hadn't yet told her what group I was affiliated with, then.

"I see... In that case, here's the stuff."

I pulled the Adolist scripture from the Kingdom of Omitt from my inventory, along with the copy and the translation, and placed them on the table. Since this was her first time seeing my abilities, Amalie was stunned.

"I see," said Elen. "As far as I can tell, both the scripture and copy are quite old."

"They had protective magic cast on them and were being saved in an underground library of sorts," I explained. "This is the original scripture, this is a copy, and this is the translation I did while Ira, a friend of mine, transcribed it for me. I used my ability to translate it, so there shouldn't be any mistakes, but I still think it'd be best if you did your own research and translation as well. The tags mark the places we found that are different from the teachings of modern-day Adolism. Feel free to use them."

"I see. May I?"

"Of course."

Elen grabbed the original scripture and began to flip through it, doing a quick read-through. She could read old Omitt?

"You can read that?" I asked.

"Yes. Reading scriptures is a part of my job. Hrm, the wording here is certainly a little antiquated. Interesting."

As she read through the text Elen's crimson eyes narrowed. Had she come across a part that was different from what the main sect preached? She seemed to be primarily checking the modern scripture's parts that focused on anti-demi-human sentiment.

"Amalie, please search through the copy."

"Understood."

Amalie sat across from us and, with a gentle touch, began to check the contents of the copy. Eventually, she furrowed her brow, having come across something different herself.

"What do you ladies think?" I asked. "As professionals?"

"Well, I am now quite certain that the current beliefs of the main sect were heavily modified in the past," Elen replied.

"Any concerns over whether that scripture is the real deal or if it can be trusted?"

"I do not believe there to be any problems in that regard," she said. "The publisher of the original scripture is a famous cathedral that existed in the Kingdom of Omitt at the time. The seal is also genuine. Of course, if we presented this to the main sect, they would most likely destroy it to keep it under wraps."

"Then what do we do?"

"We shall have to come up with a plan, but that is our job. This scripture is a powerful weapon that puts a massive crack in their position. This might be the trump card that allows us to burn that shithead pope and those cardinal pigs at the stake."

Elen began to cackle in an unsettling fashion. Amalie wore a pained smile, but didn't seem particularly rushed to lecture her about it. Usually she'd step in at a moment like this, but maybe she had her own thoughts on the situation.

"We shall take good care of these three texts," Elen assured me.

"Please do," I said. "Make absolutely sure nobody steals them."

"Of course. Only Amalie and I know that they are here, so it will be fine. Something must be known for it to be stolen, after all."

Elen placed the scripture on the table and turned her gaze toward me. "Now that that is dealt with, I would like to discuss matters four days from now."

"Oh, right. Your boss is coming, yeah?"

"Correct. I would like you to meet—"

But before she could finish, there was a rushed knock at the door.

"What could it be?"

Elen tilted her head, and Amalie quickly stood up and made for the door. There was no telling who this could be, so I quickly rose to my feet and stuffed the texts into my inventory before moving to sit across from Elen.

"What is it?" Amalie asked. "Lady Saint is currently with a guest."

"Yes! There's an urgent message from the Archbishop's group. The messenger is headed this way."

"An urgent message?"

"Correct. Would you like me to pass them through?"

Amalie looked to Elen, who thought for a moment before nodding.

"Please do."

I wasn't sure what was going on, but it seemed like something had happened to Elen's boss. This timing didn't give me a good feeling.

Knock, knock.

"Please enter."

I could hear Elen's cold voice above my head.

Where was I, you ask? Underneath the table, of course! I thought she would have me hide in the other room, but no, she stuffed me under her table and promptly sat at it.

Which meant that in front of me were her bare legs... Not. It was her lower body dressed in her saintly robes.

"Pardon the intrusion! I came here on behalf of His Highness, Archbishop Dekkard!"

"Well done. What tidings do you bring?"

"The home country has launched a subjugation force of sixty thousand soldiers to eliminate the rebel forces in the Kingdom of Merinard."

"Sixty thousand..."

Whoa, quite the number. I wasn't sure if that included the

transport corps or not, but still. I knew the Holy Kingdom was big and all, but did they really have the resources to send out that many men? What about the war with the Empire?

"The details are written down here. Also, I have a message from the Archbishop that he wanted me to deliver without failure."

"What is it?"

"Prepare yourself."

"Prepare..."

Elen whispered to herself as she began to confirm the contents of the message. I could hear the dry sounds of rustling papers above me. Did Elen put me here so I could hear all of this?

What did her boss mean by "prepare?" Sure, there was lots of work to do if sixty thousand soldiers were on their way. There would have to be a place for them to stay, drinking water, food... If they were suddenly going to get an extra sixty thousand soldiers here, they'd also have to worry about pandemics, because they would be deadly in this scenario. Hell, could Merinesburg really afford to support that many troops?

I was endlessly curious about the contents of the message.

"I see... Thank you for delivering the message. Please rest."

"Yes ma'am! Thank you very much. However, I would like to return to my master as soon as possible."

"Right. Then, if there's anything you need, please let Sister Amalie know. Also..."

I thought Elen had gone quiet, but she stood up from her seat in silence instead. What was she doing? I tilted my head, when suddenly, her legs in front of me, or more specifically her robed lower body, began to glow. What was happening?!

"A miracle of invigoration. Since you seem exhausted."

"My word... It is an honor to receive a miracle from the saint herself!"

Once the light faded, I continued to listen in on the conversation above me. So that was the sign that one had used a miracle, eh? It sure stood out. If she used one at night, she'd give away her position immediately, no?

"Please tell His Highness the Archbishop that I understand entirely. And thank you very much."

"Understood. Please excuse me!"

I heard the sound of footsteps followed by the opening and closing of a door. It sounded like the messenger was gone, but Elen showed no signs of moving from where she was, which meant I couldn't get out. I poked at her knees and she moved about half a step back, but it wasn't enough.

When I poked my head out in the space between the desk and her seat to look up, I saw Elen staring down at me with her crimson eyes.

"I thought you might have wanted to indulge in my lower body for a little while longer."

"I don't have that sort of fetish, plus your robe is covering everything so there's nothing to enjoy..."

"So you want me to do this instead?"

Elen slowly began to raise her robe up, revealing her bare legs. Ah, they were so slender and white... No, focus!

"Stop it. A holy woman such as yourself can't be that lewd." I grabbed the rising hem of her robe with both hands and brought it down. That was a close call.

"I have no chance of beating your elf princess if I do not resort to such tactics."

"There's no need to rush it. Just take it nice and easy, okay? Plus, this isn't a competition."

That being said, Sylphy and the others totally seduced me, and I fell for it hard every time. I was weak against this kind of stuff, and I was well aware of it. Hell, I was learning! Go, me!

Elen finally stepped back, so I crawled out from under the table. Free at last!

"Sixty thousand troops, huh?" I said. "That's a crazy number, but I guess I should've expected as much from such a massive nation."

"Indeed. It means they've finally decided to eliminate everyone in their way."

Elen took the message on the table and handed it to me. She clearly wanted me to read it for myself.

I read for a moment before uttering, "What?"

I couldn't believe it.

"Is this for real?" I asked.

"Unfortunately, yes," Elen answered with a shrug.

The message itself was written in difficult-to-follow language, but it basically read as follows: "The objective of the subjugation force isn't just the elimination of the Liberation Army but the assassination of the Saint of Truth Elen as a witch." What the hell?

"What the hell is going on?"

"While I was away from central, all of the reject shitbags I used my eyes on managed to regain their power. As much as I hate to admit it." Elen sighed deeply. Was that even possible? "They want to paint me as a witch and say that all the sins I revealed using my eyes were actually plots of my own making, most likely. It certainly isn't beyond them to think of such a plan."

"Isn't that crazy?" I said. "I mean, it's not like you used your eyes and just denounced them on the spot, right?"

"Of course not. When I use my eyes, I can very easily figure out what evidence there is and where it can be found. During every interrogation, I made sure to nail down such evidence."

"And they still managed to flip the script...? I don't even know what to say."

I had words for the Nostalgia-sect for just letting this happen while Elen was away, but since I didn't know what was actually happening on the inside, I knew it would be irresponsible to voice my opinion. In other words, within the Church of Adol, the Nostalgia-sect was so small that it couldn't even push back against the main sect's hard-to-believe motions.

"Then won't it be dangerous to stay here in the castle?" I said.

The main sect had already denounced Elen as a witch and sent out a subjugation force. They would likely arrive later than Elen's boss, but even if this Archbishop got here, there would be no way of stopping the armed forces now that they were on the move. Staying here would mean letting Elen get put to the stake as soon as they arrived.

We were now long past the idea of arguing that modern Adolism had been modified and was the incorrect version. There would be no stirring up internal strife within the Holy Kingdom or Adolism at this point. If we stayed the course, Elen would be eliminated, and the Nostalgia-sect she stood for would likely be eliminated before long as well.

"Indeed. At this rate, I likely do not have even a month left. I will be captured, interrogated, made to confess to all of my 'sins,' and then burned at the stake." Elen turned her back to me and cast her gaze out through the window of the office. Was she looking at the sky? At some point, dark clouds enveloped it. Rain was on the way.

"I won't let that happen," I told her. "I'll kidnap you myself beforehand."

"Is that how you plan to make me yours?"

"Sounds good to me. And then together with the Liberation Army, we'll destroy the Holy Nation. No matter what."

"Sixty thousand troops, Kousuke," she reminded me. "You would kill that many innocents?"

"If necessary, yes," I replied. "At the end of the day, the weight of sixty thousand faceless lives of the Holy Kingdom's military is nowhere close to the weight of your life, Elen. And let's face it. Even if you weren't an issue here, I'd end up having to fight them anyway."

After all, they were sent to eliminate the Liberation Army as well. We were always going to have to meet on the battlefield.

"So I'm just extra, then?" Elen asked.

"In the grand scheme of things, yeah. But to me, you're a top priority."

"I see... Right. They called me a saint and raised me up on a pedestal my whole life, but at the end of the day, I was only ever just a young woman with a somewhat special power."

"Maybe so. But you have the power to save lives, no?"

Elen turned to me and nodded. "You are right. If I use my miracles, I might be able to save a few lives. A few dozen lives, even."

But that wasn't what I meant.

"That's not it. If you and the archbishop publicly side with the Liberation Army, then that might open up the ability for us to speak with the Holy Kingdom. No matter how weak the Nostalgia-sect's position might be, even you guys have connections all over the place, right? Not just within the Holy Kingdom itself but abroad."

"Hm, that is true. Both myself and Archbishop Dekkard are fairly well known abroad."

"The Liberation Army desperately needs those kinds of connections. If we can make appeals abroad for peace, we'd be able to lower the number of casualties in this conflict."

"I wonder..." Elen whispered to herself. She was as expressionless as always, but a sad aura surrounded her.

I understood. She was feeling as though everything she had ever worked for had been turned on its head. She was barely responding to what I was saying at this point.

"When you're down in the dumps, I recommend something sweet," I said. "Let's go sit over there."

I pushed Elen from behind and sat her down on the sofa, then pulled out her favorite dessert from my inventory: fluffy pancakes covered in strawberry jam with whipped cream and strawberries on top.

"Here, say, 'aaah.'" I cut a piece of fluffy pancake out with a fork and knife and guided it to Elen's mouth.

"Mm... Tasty."

After I had repeated this process multiple times, life finally returned to her crimson eyes.

"I want something to drink," she said.

"Roger that."

I pulled a ceramic cup filled with milk out of my inventory. I wasn't about to reveal where said milk came from. It didn't matter so long as it tasted good.

Elen took the cup from me and began to drink it down.

"This is delicious. I believe you served me this milk last time as well."

"Hahaha, the environment is good over there, you see. Results in higher-quality milk."

The rear base was far away from the front lines and rarely ever got attacked, so the stress was low. And there was tons of food, to boot.

"I doubt you'll do anything stupid," I said, "but I'm warning you. Any funny moves and I'm kidnapping you and making a break for it."

"Right, right. And when that happens, I shall not struggle."

"Good. Now, we need to figure out what our next move is."

I didn't have the brain to come up with a plan, but considering how things were advancing, it would be best for the Liberation

Army to take back Merinesburg before the subjugation force arrived. This place was massive, and its walls were thick and powerful. And perhaps most importantly, the royal family—Sylphy's family— were asleep in the castle, frozen.

Ultimately, Sylphy was the type to do battle even if her family were taken hostage... But I didn't want her to have to make that choice. We had to send troops here. The problem was whether they could take down the fortresses and checkpoints on the way here before the Holy Kingdom arrived.

Sure, we could take Merinesburg itself, but if our supply route got cut off... Well, I supposed things would be fine so long as I was here. If anything, holding up in Merinesburg and bleeding out their forces might actually be the best strategy. And while they surrounded us, we could continuously attack them from Arichburg as well.

Mass produce the airboards, create a high-speed mobile unit, and take down Merinesburg while ignoring the villages and fortresses on the way here. Our main forces could then capture the towns and fortresses that the mobile unit had ignored while moving forward. Then we'd use a portion of our mobile unit to make intermittent attacks on the Holy Kingdom's forces, bleeding them out and slowing their advance. If our main forces arrived in Merinesburg before theirs, we could hold up in the city. If they didn't, the mobile unit could protect the city while our main forces struck at the Holy Kingdom's back. Hrm, this had a real chance of working.

The harpies' airborne bombing runs, mini-guns mounted

on airboards that could move faster than horses, select airboard attacks, golem ballistae and goat's foot crossbows as defensive measures... If we used what we had effectively, it didn't seem like it would be that difficult to push back sixty thousand enemy troops. And in the absolute worst-case scenario, I could always make gleaming magic jewel bombs.

"What is this evil aura I am feeling?" Elen asked.

"How rude! I was just thinking about ways we can take down the Holy Kingdom's forces." Granted, the ways in question involved a one-sided massacre. The saint sure had a good nose. "In any case, I'm pretty sure we can handle sixty thousand troops no problem, so don't worry too much."

"I am extremely jealous of the fact that you can look at this situation and say, 'no problem.' Is your head perhaps filled with nothing but flowers?"

"Oh ho ho, back to your usual self, eh? That's what I like to see."

I rubbed Elen's head, now that she was back to her normal, biting self, and continued to think of strategies to take down the Holy Kingdom.

I was all too aware that Sylphy and the others would have to go over things, because my plans were likely filled with holes. That meant I needed to get in touch with them ASAP.

Which also meant that I needed to search the room for the Lime clone that was undoubtedly hiding in here. I began to look around.

"You called?"

As I glanced around the room, it was Poiso who caught on first and emerged from the cracks in the wall.

"So you're on guard duty today?"

"Yup! We swap roles every day."

The green slime that emerged from the wall quickly took the shape of a human, though from about halfway down her thighs, it was all slime.

"I'd like to put in an express call to Sylphy and the others. Is that doable?"

"Absolutely!" Poiso cast her gaze toward the door. "But wouldn't it be dangerous to do that here?"

She wasn't wrong. All that stood between her and being spotted was a single door. She could probably act as a relay without showing herself, but there was nothing to gain from having someone unrelated see or hear me talking to Sylphy.

"We shall use the back room," Elen said.

"Ah, right. That door."

I looked at the door past the couch. I'd been wondering where it led, and I finally had my answer. It was something of a private space.

"Let us be on our way," Elen told us.

"You too, Poiso," I said.

"All righty!"

With Elen leading us, we walked over to the door, and she unlocked it with an expensive-looking key. Talk about weirdly high security.

Since she opened the door for us, we proceeded inside.

"Huh?"

It appeared to be a bedroom. Not only was the window small, but it was placed high on the wall, so it was rather dark inside despite it being midday. The walls were also quite thick. What stood out the most, though, was the rather large bed. King-sized, even. And there was this scent that permeated the entire room... Like some sort of perfume.

"Hey, Elen?"

I heard the door lock behind me, Elen's crimson eyes glistening in the darkness.

"H-hey, uh..."

An unspeakable aura surrounded Elen as she trotted right over to me and pushed me forcefully.

"...Why won't you go down?"

"I mean, no offense, but your thin arms aren't going to get me down. I'm not that weak."

"Would this not be the time to go with the flow?"

"No, no, no. What exactly are you planning?"

"I was thinking of perhaps teasing you a bit."

"Stop it. And isn't it supposed to be the opposite? Why do all the women in this world try to push me down? Isn't that weird? Shouldn't the guy be the one doing that?"

"Is that a tradition of your home? Please, be my guest."

"Don't 'be my guest' me! Now is not the time for this."

Elen stood with her back to the bed and her arms spread out, but I simply pushed on her forehead and got her to sit down.

If we weren't in the middle of something I might've actually leapt on her, but now really wasn't the time.

"Coward," she said.

"Hey."

"Spineless."

"You're not going to trick me. There's something called timing, you know. Plus, when it comes to this kind of thing, I'm way more experienced than you. If you keep taunting me like this, who knows what might end up happening to you? I suggest you watch out."

"Boo." Elen puffed out her cheeks unhappily. "I find it terribly rude of you to bring up your experience with other women at a time like this. You man-whore."

"Lady Saint... Please watch your words."

"My apologies."

Where in the hell did she learn that term? Elen could be quite the weirdo when it came to that kind of thing. Maybe instead of revelations, she was getting sketchy radio broadcasts with her brain.

"Are you finished?" said Poiso. "If you like, I could leave the two of you alone for an hour or two."

"We don't need your consideration."

"I could even offer some delightful medicine that would get Kousuke in the mood."

"That sounds fascinating, but I would like for my first time to be gentle."

"I'm not sure that's possible. He becomes quite the rabid beast. If anything, I can give you the same medicine."

"Stop it, you dummy. Quit joking around." I forced myself into their terrifying conversation in order to put a stop to it. At her current rate, Poiso the evil poison slime was going to trample all over us.

"Fine, fine," said Poiso. "But it is pretty rude to keep her waiting, you know."

"I get it, and believe me, I'm trying to show some self-restraint! Don't make me spell it out for you."

"I understand. Now then, I'm gonna get you connected, so hang on a moment."

Poiso's eyes went vacant, and my eyes met with Elen's as she sat on the bed.

"What is it?" I asked.

"Self-restraint, is it?" she said.

"Yes, okay? And consider your position."

"Valid point, though I suspect that will cease to be a problem very shortly."

"Do you really think things will work out so easily? Not that I would mind."

A familiar voice came through Poiso; it was undeniably Sylphy.

"You wouldn't?" I asked.

"Not at all. What is another woman or two at this point? Though once we hit ten, I will have to start asking people to show their own self-restraint so Kousuke does not collapse."

"Please stop, I don't wanna die."

"It must be tough being the king of a harem."

"He is only one person, after all. Now then, as much as

I am enjoying this conversation, I imagine this is not why you called?" Sylphy said, pushing the conversation forward.

She was right to do so. We didn't have much time as it pertained to this specific topic. We had to be quick.

"Okay, so I handed over the scripture and additional documents, but Elen's boss sent us an urgent message," I explained. "The Holy Kingdom has dispatched an army of sixty thousand troops toward the Kingdom of Merinard with the express goal of taking out the Liberation Army."

"Sixty thousand... Three times as many soldiers as twenty years ago. I imagine, with those numbers, they've undoubtedly dispatched their mage squad as well."

"Twenty years ago, huh...? You'd think a lot would have changed since then."

In terms of human life spans, that was easily an entire generation. Hell, maybe even two. They had been consistently at war with the Empire for these past twenty years, so it was likely they were much more skilled than before.

"I am not well versed on military matters," Elen said, "but I have heard that the Holy Kingdom's mage squad is their ace in the hole as it pertains to the battlefield. The other group we must be wary of are the Order of the Holy Knights."

"The Order of the Holy Knights... They are made up of those who possess magical aptitude, yes?"

"Correct. They are a group of knights who are far more powerful than your average soldier or knight. Their blades are capable of cutting soldiers in two, armor and all, and even magical attacks seemingly have little effect on them as they cleave through enemy mages."

"They're the group that have been distinguishing themselves over the last few years..."

The voice coming through Poiso seemed somewhat gloomy. I tilted my head, unsure of why that was.

"Yes. When they were first formed, they were a small group of ace knights, but now their numbers are much, much greater. I imagine they are part of the sixty thousand on their way here."

"I assume many of those knights come from noble houses or clergy households."

"...?" Elen blinked. "Um, yes. Is that relevant?"

"There are barely any elves left in the Kingdom of Merinard. Demi-human numbers in general have dropped in the last twenty years to large and small degrees, but elves are the only ones that barely remain. Meanwhile, the Holy Kingdom has amassed a great deal of magical power. I do not need to say any more than that, surely?"

"No... It cannot possibly..." Elen looked as though she had been hit with a brick. Sylphy had described such atrocities to me in the past, so this wasn't as shocking as it could have been, but Elen was not me.

"I have not seen this with my own two eyes, so I cannot say for certain. However, I can't imagine these are unrelated. And we'll have to battle against those people... But that is fine. There is nothing we can do about it now. It is about how we act going forward, correct?"

"Yeah," I said. "And so I have an idea..."

I then went on to describe the strategy I came up with earlier to Sylphy. Put simply, we would establish a separate high-speed strike unit that would use its mobility to ignore any obstacles on the road and occupy Merinesburg, the Holy Kingdom's stronghold in Merinard.

By putting Merinesburg down first, we would destroy the chain of command for the Holy Kingdom's military within Merinard and prevent them from being able to cooperate. The Holy Kingdom's Merinard forces would potentially try and take back the city, but I would repair the city walls, and we could counterattack from within the city, preventing it from falling again. We would hold up in the city and use harpy bombs to blow up their forces as they surrounded us.

Also, if they tried to take back the city, our regular forces could much more easily take over their checkpoints and fortresses on the road. After all, their forces would be divided. The perfect chance to put them down.

"I believe Elen's cooperation is necessary for this strategy to work," I added.

"I do not think there is much I can do to help," she said. "Surrendering swiftly is all that comes to mind."

"That is fine. We can handle the people in the main faction, so make a list of them for us, all right? That is the best way to protect both you and Kousuke, so don't skimp out."

"Understood," said Elen. "However, I will not accept any unreasonable treatment of the innocent. Please keep that in mind."

"Of course. We would not inflict harm on someone just because they are a human. The Kingdom of Merinard was a nation in which humans and demi-humans alike lived together in peace, after all."

Elen paused for a moment. "I just wish to keep the casualties at a minimum. That is all."

These two just didn't seem to pair together well. I could have cut the tension in the air with a knife. But at the end of the day, we were talking about a former princess who had her kingdom stolen from her and the saint of the nation that committed said atrocity. Maybe there was no way around this.

"To be honest," I said, "I'm not crazy about getting you involved, Elen. Sylphy, why don't we just go all in and pretend to kidnap her so we can force them to surrender?"

"The move of an evildoer. If we were to do that, the hatred from the followers of Adolism would be overwhelming."

"Damn, no good then?"

"Absolutely not."

"I certainly would not mind," Elen spoke up. "At this rate, I am going to be burned at the stake by the followers of the main sect."

"We might end up going in that direction in the end, but not right now. We want you to keep the masses under control. The more important question is, how much time do we have until this army of sixty thousand arrives?"

"True," I agreed. "It'd be easier to put together a plan if we knew what our time limit was."

"My superior arrives in Merinesburg in five days' time, and this emergency message arrived after we were alerted to that fact," said Elen. "Considering all of that, I would say we do not have much time available to us. It is entirely possible that they are already near the border."

"Even if they've already reached the Kingdom's border, how long would it take for them to get here?"

An army of sixty thousand cannot move particularly fast. Half a day's worth of walking over twenty-four hours, give or take. But that is if they are in enemy territory. Within the Holy Kingdom, they wouldn't have to worry about restocking supplies, and once they enter Merinard, they won't have as many problems as they would if they were coming into truly undisputed enemy territory. From the border, it takes about ten days on foot. We are looking at two weeks if we're lucky. I shall send out recon harpies with golem communicators.

"That's a great idea," I said. "Just remember, safety first."

"But of course. I'll order them to make their lives a priority. You're coming back to us, right?" Sylphy asked me.

"Yeah. There's a lot I need to prepare. If possible, I'll be heading back today."

"All right. Be safe on your way home. I shall get the details from you then."

"Right. Anything you want to add, Elen?"

She shook her head.

"Nothing, apparently," I told Sylphy. "Okay, I'll be back tomorrow at the latest."

"Right. I'll be waiting."

"The call is over," Poiso said, having served as the relay this entire time. Her body shook gently.

I had a lot I needed to think about and a whole lot more to do. It felt like my head was about to pop.

First on the agenda was taking care of the gloomy-looking saint in front of me.

"That shocking, huh?"

"Of course... It is disgusting..." Elen said, letting out a deep sigh.

In order to increase the number of magically gifted children, the Holy Kingdom annexed Merinard, made the elves into slaves against their will, and forced them to give birth. This was a real, likely possibility, and the realization of that fact colored Elen's face. She looked like she had seen a ghost.

"I cannot believe they would do such evil things for the sake of mere power... Do they not have hearts? What of the families? Their loved ones?"

"As far as the main sect are concerned, they're nonhumans, and therefore, they exist only to serve humanity as cattle," I said. "They probably think cattle have no gods to speak of."

Elen went silent. While she belonged to a different sect, the followers of the main sect were members of the church. She probably didn't want to believe that there could be such a gulf between their beliefs.

"Personally, I've heard endless stories about the horrible treatment the demi-humans have undergone at the hands of the Holy Kingdom," I added. "Hell, even I thought those who followed Adolism were all the same, right up until I met you and learned about the Nostalgia-sect."

"I...see... Then I suppose the demi-humans must truly hate us."

"Of course." I shrugged. "Did I ever tell you about how when I first popped up in the elven village in the Black Forest, I was surrounded and nearly lynched by dozens of demi-humans just because I was a human? Humans equal followers of Adolism equal people deserving death. That's how deep that hatred runs, and how could you blame them?"

Elen went silent yet again, but I understood. Anyone would get like this, hearing just how deeply they were hated. But this was something she was going to have to learn one way or the other, so I thought it best to make her aware sooner rather than later.

"But hey, no worries," I told her. "It'll all work out."

"Do you really believe that?"

"Absolutely! Just leave it to me. Hell, I was on the verge of getting my ass lynched, and I still managed to gain their understanding. We have options."

If we could publicly cooperate with the Nostalgia-sect in all of this, we'd be able to plant the seeds for their acceptance. After all, we had shared enemies in the main sect and in the Holy Kingdom. It theoretically shouldn't be too hard to join hands. Hopefully.

"Anyhow, you just need to take care of yourself. And there's a strong possibility that we'll be seeing a lot of injured folks in the near future, so you should prepare for that. It might be a good idea to stock medicinal goods and food if you can."

"Understood... So you are leaving already?" Elen turned her unsteady gaze toward me, making it so very hard to leave her behind. I wished she would stop.

"Yeah, I am," I admitted. "The sooner I get moving, the better chance we have at minimizing casualties."

"I see..."

The downtrodden Elen was so lovely that I had to turn my heart to stone as I extended my hand to her where she sat on the bed.

"Let's head back."

"Okay." Elen took my hand, stood up, and embraced me. "We can afford at least this much, right?"

"Just a little. It'll be bad if I can't hold myself back anymore. Plus, we've got an audience."

I pointed at Poiso, who was grinning in the corner and making some kind of foam from a suspicious-looking pink gas.

With Elen still in my arms, I quickly exited the bedroom. Whatever she was making couldn't have been any good.

"Poiso, make sure you throw out that suspicious gas of yours," I said.

"Fiiine. I think you would've been fine banging once or twice."

"Young women such as yourself shouldn't use language like that," I lectured Poiso as she gooped out from the cracks of the door.

Out of the three slime girls, she really was the most dangerous. Poisonous in more ways than one.

"I'm a total newbie when it comes to strategy and tactics, so I need you to stay in close contact with Sylphy, okay?" I told Elen.

"Understood."

"Don't worry. We'll see each other again soon. Just take good care of yourself. Poiso, I'm counting on you girls to keep her safe."

"Gotcha! I'll let Bess and Lime know."

"Thanks. Well then..."

"Yes... See you later."

And so I left Elen's office, and a sister, not Amalie this time, led me back to get my equipment. After putting everything back on, I departed the castle.

There was absolutely no time to take it easy. The enemy was already on the move, so we needed to quickly create equipment, form our mobile unit, and give them the bare minimum training that was required. I also had to brush up on as much battle strategy as humanly possible.

I could come up with all kinds of ideas using the things I'd created, but actually doing any of those things would require a proper brush-up from the pros.

Using my ability, I could brute force my way through maintenance issues or logistics, but organizations didn't work like that. The lives of our soldiers were on the line.

Unfortunately, it didn't appear as though I'd be able to keep my promise with the guide boy by the front gate.

I exited out into the main street and started to head toward the city entrance. After getting checked over, I finally left Merinesburg behind me. When it came to mercenary types like myself with little on them, there wasn't much to go through in terms of security, though they did check my weapon to make sure I hadn't used it to cut anyone down.

After I walked along the road for a bit, the forest came into view and I moved off the path. That was when I peeked behind me and noticed that a group of three was tailing me.

But why? Because I made contact with Elen? Or was I being targeted simply because I was alone? If it was because of Elen, these could be people from the main sect.

This was a problem. What was my move here?

Losing them would be easy enough. I'd just enter the woods and use my strafe jump to move at high speed and out of their range. But if I did that, I'd leave behind tracks and a load of broken branches. If any of the three following me were good at tracking, they could find their way to the slimes' home.

Could I stay hidden by crouching and sneakily moving? I'd probably be able to outlast them, but it wasn't 100 percent guaranteed. I doubt I'd show up if they used magical tracking, thanks to my weird body, but they'd probably find me the old-fashioned way.

My best chance here was to wipe them out with one of my guns, dump their bodies into my inventory, and use my skills to erase all traces that anything happened. But could I pull the trigger? I had no problem pointing a gun at gizma, goblins, kobolds, wyverns, ghouls, or even liches, but what about humans? I had a feeling it would be no problem, but who could really be sure until the moment arrived?

As I made my way toward the woods, I racked my brain over how to deal with my pursuers.

"Striking first and taking them all out would be simple and easy, but..."

It seemed clear as day to me that the people following me probably meant me harm in some way, but in the unlikely event they weren't hostile, this could develop into a huge problem. Ultimately, I could just stuff the bodies into my inventory, and nobody would know any better. I wouldn't feel good about it, though.

As soon as I entered the forest, I used my command action sprint to dash my way through the woods without using my strafe jump, intentionally leaving a trail behind. After a short while, I came upon a clearing. I cut through it and looped back around to just before the area where I entered the woods, using my jump and command jump to perform a double jump to the top of a tree.

"When did I become so inhuman?" I sighed as I leapt from treetop to treetop, circling the opening I stumbled upon and eventually hiding myself in a tree right off to the side of the space.

"I present to you...my silenced sniper rifle," I whispered as I pulled the rifle out from my inventory. Most of the gun was covered with a large suppressor. It had an effective range of about four hundred meters, which wasn't particularly long, but it was nice and compact and could fire specially designed large caliber subsonic rounds, making it the perfect stealth weapon. It could also use ten and twenty round magazines. This thing had a rapid-fire function, to boot, so it was quite the handy weapon.

Since being able to use golem workbenches, I could now take on more complex and precise work such as making rifles like this one. They cost a lot, and mass production was impossible, but the price I was paying bullet-wise was the same as before.

By the way, I discovered that polymer and rubber materials could be swapped with slime. After figuring this out, I'd been quietly hunting the slimes in Arichburg's sewer system. Heh heh heh heh. This also allowed me to collect powder and other materials as well! I didn't exactly want to head to the sewer too often, but slime materials were just too good. I wondered if I could get Lime and the others to share some stuff.

I loaded my first magazine into the silenced rifle and waited for a bit. The three men who had been trailing me appeared in the clearing. They must've realized this was a perfect spot for an ambush, as they all seemed on guard. They weren't moving forward into the open.

"...should wait. Something..."

"At this rate... ...lose sight..."

They were speaking to one another, but I couldn't make out what they were saying. If Sylphy or Melty were here, they'd probably be able to figure it out, but I didn't have long animallike ears.

Eventually, the men seemed to prioritize trailing me over the potential dangers ahead, as they stepped into the designated kill zone. Well, not that I was planning on killing them. At least for now.

My targets were within fifty meters. The bullets this gun used had heavy tips, so they naturally dropped in height over a long distance, which was something I needed to take into consideration. But at this range, not so much.

I looked through the optic scope and lined it up with the knee of one of the three men. This was going to hurt like hell, and if it didn't get healed, it'd be way worse than taking an arrow in the knee. If it turned out he was friendly, I would immediately sprint down and heal him.

POOF!

The sound of the rifle's internal mechanisms moving accompanied the very quiet sound of it firing. Shortly after, the area around the knee of the farthest back pursuer erupted in a flower of blood.

"Gah?!"

"Huh?!"

The two men in front turned around upon hearing their companion's cries. Gotcha.

I pulled the trigger once again, and as the rifle's mechanisms quietly shifted again, a 16g bullet head launched out of my rifle at about 300 meters per second and cut through the clean air of the woods, right into the second pursuer's thigh just above his knee.

The bullet pierced his leather armor easily, ripping through his skin and diving into his muscles. The rotating nature of the bullet wreaked all kinds of havoc inside of his thigh, from his muscles to his blood vessels.

"GAAAH?!"

The second man gripped his leg and collapsed in place.

The final man had no idea what was going on beyond that they were under attack. He lowered his posture and scanned his surroundings.

But it was no use. He didn't know what guns were, so he didn't think to lay flat. That said, it wouldn't allow him to flee from my rifle.

The gun let out its quiet sounds a third time, and the third man collapsed to the ground.

"That was less trouble than I expected," I commented to myself while observing my targets through my scope.

The third guy must've gotten lucky, as he was already standing up again on his own, so I unloaded another shot into his opposite leg.

"AAAAAAH!"

He let out a tremendous scream of pain. Yeah, that had to hurt, but there was no guarantee there weren't others trailing them, so I couldn't pop out immediately. They might've been lying there to lure me out. Hell, they could've had life potions like the ones I made, and they were just waiting for a chance to heal once I got close.

I kind of felt like this was worse than killing them, but it was all in the name of staying safe.

After waiting three minutes, nobody else appeared, so while it might've been a bit too soon, I decided to reveal myself. I slipped my rifle into my inventory and held up my short spear and shield, slipping through the dense woods toward the men before calling out to them.

"Yo. Let me get straight to the point. Why were you guys following me?"

They appeared to have already noticed me. The guy I shot first was still on the ground, and the other two were gripping their wounds. They were all staring at me, and I could see the pain on their faces. As far as the men with thigh wounds were concerned, I had thought I'd busted their arteries, but it turned out they weren't fatal. Or maybe they used some kind of healing magic or something?

"Don't think you're gonna get away with—"

"Yeah, see, I don't care about any of that. Didn't I tell you I wanted to get straight to the point? But I guess judging by your reaction, you're not here to be friends."

I stabbed my spear into the ground and pulled a handgun from my inventory. It was .45 caliber, and each magazine could hold seven rounds. I wasn't sure why, but I seemed to be fond of the .45 calibers when it came to handguns and submachine guns. Sorry, but I was a true believer in them. Add to that the fact that they were subsonic and suppressors worked well with them, and, well, they ruled.

"And what if we're not? Do you really think we'll just talk?"

"Nope. I was just thinking that there's no reason for all three of you to be here. It's fine if there's only one or two."

I turned the barrel of my gun toward the man trying to pick a fight and pulled the trigger.

BANG!

Along with the sound of the gun firing, the 15g bullet collided with the man's shoulder, ripping through the surface of his skin and shattering his bones. The man screamed in horrific pain and began to roll around on the ground. I was surprised by how easily I was able to pull the trigger. Maybe my Genocider achievement was dulling my nerves or something.

The remaining two men looked at their comrade screaming on the ground and turned pale.

"I'm going to ask once again. Why were you following me?" I interrogated, quietly pointing my gun at the third man's shin.

"I-I have nothing to tell—GAAAAAAH!"

BANG!

This time I made it a point to miss, but the man passed out from terror nonetheless. Then I pointed my gun at the man with a bullet hole in his thigh.

"What's your move? Want me to give you another hole?"

"I-I'll tell you everything! Everything!"

The man covered his thigh as he shrunk down in an attempt to avoid the barrel of my gun. I could see the fear in his eyes. Fear of being harmed by a weapon that he did not understand. Fear that gripped his heart and soul.

"Then start."

It was possible he'd lie, but I could always just take him to the slimes, and they'd figure the truth out. They told me before that they could slip inside of brains, so... Was it just me, or were they closer to being shoggoths than slimes? Though I suppose the very concept of a living slime originated with the shoggoth, so it didn't make much of a difference.

The man spilled the beans. Fascinating beans, at that.

To put it shortly, the main sect suspected that Elen was in contact with the Liberation Army, so they were intelligence agents sent to keep tabs. But they weren't the main sect's own agents. They were part of an outlaw group within the Holy Kingdom—kind of like a bandit guild or something.

"I see," I said. "That's unfortunate. For you guys, anyway."

The fact that they ended up trailing me, the greatest secret within the Liberation Army, was incredibly bad luck.

This probably happened because I went to see Elen so directly and out in the open. Now that they had seen me and my guns, I couldn't let them live.

While thinking about the remaining bullets I had, I glanced at the other two men. Both of them were unconscious. I pointed the barrel of my gun at one of their heads and pulled the trigger.

BANG!

The unconscious man's body twitched, a hole appearing in his head and a pool of blood forming on the ground. The second man who had surrendered saw this and began to tremble in fear, grinding his teeth.

BANG!

The other body twitched. I slipped both corpses into my inventory. When doing interrogations, it was normal to use multiple accounts to determine their veracity, but since we could see directly into their brains, we only needed one man. It'd be a pain to carry two or three living dudes all the way to the slimes.

I pulled some metal handcuffs from my inventory and placed them around the wrists of the terrified survivor.

"I'll heal your wounds. Follow me, and don't cause a fuss."

"I-I don't want to die..."

"If you listen to what I say, I'll think about it."

But *only* think about it, as I knew the reality in my heart. I poured a little bit of life potion on the man's thigh, then had him drink the rest of it. It wasn't long before he was totally healed.

Man, this stuff worked so well that it was actually creepy.

I stood the man up, grabbed the spear sticking out of the ground, and put it back into my inventory along with my gun and shield. I also collected the bullet casings, just to be careful. Then, I pulled out a submachine gun.

"Walk where I tell you to," I told the agent. "I still have questions for you."

"H-hey! I'll tell you everything you want to know, just save me! Please!"

"Shut up and walk. Do you want your brains blown out? Do you wanna join your friends in the afterlife?"

"E-eek..."

I kicked the man's ass and got him walking. I hated this, quite frankly. But it was too late to have regrets. I'd blown away thousands of men with explosive blocks or harpy bombs. And in the end, I was handing weapons to my allies and making them fight the Holy Kingdom. What was a little blood on my hands? It was nothing. Nothing at all.

I mentally repeated that to myself while kicking the guy's ass and heading toward the slime girls' home.

"Wh-where are you taking me? What is this place?"

"Shut up and keep walking or else I'll fill you with holes like those goddamn goblins."

"O-okay, I get it! I get it, so stop pointing that thing at me, please!"

I kicked the man forward for about another hour. We were attacked by goblins on the way (which I riddled with holes), but otherwise there were no problems on the way to the slimes' home.

The agent seemed confused as to where we were going, but I led him down the sewer path. He eventually lost his cool and began to look around the area in a panic.

"H-hey, it's dangerous to go any farther! We're in the Merinesburg sewers, r-right? I heard there are super strong slimes down here!"

I silently kicked his ass again, and he began to move once more. The disgusting scent of the sewers had largely faded, proof that we had entered the slimes' territory.

"H-hey—"

"Welcome hooome! Who is thaaat?"

Just as the agent, in tears, was about to say something, Lime appeared and spoke to us. The man in question was so baffled that he went completely silent.

"He's a Holy Kingdom spy who tried to capture me... I want you ladies to check if what he says is true."

"Huh, an enemy?" There was a coldness to the voice that came from Lime's jiggly body. I honestly never thought I'd hear such a tone from the usually happy-go-lucky Lime. The contrast was incredible.

"E-eek..."

The agent crumbled to his knees after seeing Lime take her female form. How could he react like that to someone so adorable? What a bastard. Slime girls *were* adorable! No, I didn't have weird turn-ons. Shut up.

"So I hate to ask you girls for help on this, but if I recall, you can look directly into people's minds, right?" I pointed to my own head.

Lime smiled and giggled. "Yup, yup! But what do we do with him after?"

"I'll think about that when we come to it."

"Okaaay! Want me to do it?"

"As long as I get the info I need, I don't mind who does the job. But I do want you to prioritize accuracy and details."

"Then Poiso would be good! I'll bring her."

"Thanks a bunch."

Lime changed forms and enveloped the agent in blindingly fast fashion, restricting his movement and sealing his mouth shut before taking him deeper into the sewers. The man was of course panicking, but no one could hear his screams. There was no way to physically escape her grip. Though maybe Sylphy or Melty might've been able to use magic to get free.

I walked behind them for a bit until eventually I saw light. We had arrived at Lime's home.

"Oh my. Welcome back... Um, who is that?" Bess asked.

"A prisoner?"

Bess and Poiso immediately spoke up upon our arrival. Grande, on the other hand, was fast asleep atop of Bess, who had spread herself out like a bed. Had she slept the entire time I was gone?

"Exactly," I replied. "Apparently the Holy Kingdom's main sect had suspicions that Elen is connected to the Liberation Army, so they sent out spies. According to him, he's more of a spy for hire than he is a direct agent of the main sect."

"I see. And so you want us to see if he's telling the truth or not, correct?"

"Bingo. And if he dies in the process, he dies in the process. He's seen me and my guns, so it's not like we can just send him home anyway."

"Nngh?!"

His mouth still sealed shut, the agent looked at me with wide eyes and began to resist as best he could, but Lime's body wouldn't budge.

"Sorry pal, but you ran out of luck the second you and your dudes trailed me."

"Then I'll take a quick look into his brain," said Poiso. "Can I assume you're okay with me taking charge?"

"Yeah. The only thing I won't allow is for you to let him outside alive. Even if you mess with his brain or alter his memories, there's a chance someone might be able to get info out of him the way you girls do."

"Got it. Then I'll take him! It shouldn't take much time."

Poiso took the agent from Lime and dragged him along. I thought he would resist more, but as soon as she touched him, he lost all the strength in his muscles and stopped fighting back. Did she inject him with some kind of drug the moment she touched him? Poiso really was terrifying like that.

"We can leave him to her," I said, "which means it's time to wake Grande..."

Just as I moved to awake Grande from her Bess bed, I suddenly felt someone wrap themselves around me from behind. Since Bess was in front of me, it had to be Lime.

"What's up?" I asked.

"You have wrinkles on your face."

Lime suddenly extended multiple tentacles and began to massage and touch my brow. She then moved on to my cheeks, neck, shoulders, and entire body.

"You seem stiff. It's times like this you need to rest."

Lime had seemingly picked up on something I didn't, as she took me into her body without waiting for my reply. Eventually, the only part of me not inside of her was my neck and head. There was nothing I could do.

"So how many of them were there?" Bess asked me.

"Three."

"Three, I see. Well, I can't imagine that felt good. But I do think it best you not concern yourself with it too much. There's nothing to be gained from that."

"Is that really how it is?"

"It is. Though it would also be a problem if you didn't care at all."

"Would it?"

"It would."

"This is all so tough…"

Lime continued her full body massage as Bess offered a little bit of counseling. Perhaps because I was still amped up, I still wasn't as stunned by what I'd just done as I thought I'd be. I couldn't help but feel like my achievements were doing some work on that end. Also, at some point, I'd been stripped down to my underwear.

"Lime?"

"Relaaax."

Apparently, she just wanted me to be comfy. Her massage felt so good that I had started to get sleepy. This really did feel wonderful.

"It will take some time before Poiso gets everything out of the prisoner," Bess added. "I know you're mentally and emotionally exhausted, so take a nap."

"All right… I will."

It felt like Bess's calm tone was echoing directly in my brain, but since this world's magic didn't work on me, it had to just be the power of her voice.

"Good night."

Lime's bell-like voice reached my ears. Also, something smelled good. It felt…familiar. The thought crossed my mind, but my mind was starting to switch off, and my consciousness slipped into the darkness.

◆ ⬢ ◆

"Ah?!"

"Eeeek."

I woke up and tried to sit up, but I found my hands buried in something soft. Or to be more specific, my hands were now inside of Lime's body, which had formed a bed beneath me.

"Sorry, I didn't mean to do that."

"Mm, it's oookay! Feeling better?"

"Yeah, I'd say so. My head feels clear."

I was feeling good. Killing my pursuers on my own had an emotional effect on me for sure, which led to some discomfort, but now I felt oddly calm. It wasn't as though I'd had pleasant dreams or anything, but maybe Lime's full-body massage had allowed me the best possible sleep imaginable, giving me the chance to truly relax. Actually, wasn't there something I was curious about just before I fell asleep?

"You are quite the sleepyhead, Kousuke."

"I don't want you of all people telling me that, Grande."

"I am no sleepyhead. If anything, I am quite the early riser by dragon standards. I only happened to oversleep just a wee bit today."

"You dragons have quite the long time scale if you consider sleeping from the morning past noon to be a 'wee bit.'"

I looked around for a moment, but only Lime and Grande were home. Bess had apparently gone out.

"Poiso's still not back?" I asked.

"She caaame back a second ago," Lime replied.

"Indeed," said Grande. "She said that she wanted to see if she could find anything else useful in his mind and that it would take some time."

"I see... Then I'll leave the interrogation to her, and you and I can head back to Arichburg first," I decided. "We could always get the results delivered over golem communicator."

"That is true."

"Mm, thaaat might be a good idea. You should head hooome as soon as possible."

"Right, right. Though I feel bad about not getting to say bye to the other two."

"I'll leeet them know!" Lime's entire body morphed into a big hand that gave me a thumbs-up. I bet it'd hurt, getting punched by a hand that big.

"All right. Then sorry, but let them know I said thanks for everything."

"Will do! Cooome again!"

"I'll make sure to be back soon. Grande, let's go."

"Leave it to me!"

After saying goodbye, Grande and I proceeded through the sewers to the outside. On the way there, Grande kept glancing up at my face for some reason.

"What's up?" I asked.

"Hrm... No, it's nothing. I was just thinking about how the slimes, er, spirits truly are something else."

Grande shook her head and gave me a considerate pat on the back.

Her odd behavior had me curious, but I continued to walk on, nonetheless.

I'm sure it was nothing I needed to concern myself with. It was essential that we get back to Arichburg ASAP, after all. I felt bad for making Grande work so hard, but we would probably be able to make it home by the time the sun was beginning to set.

CHAPTER 3

Getting Prepared

THE TRIP BACK to Arichburg was fairly uneventful, since there were no monsters in the Sorel Mountains that could catch up with Grande's flying speed. We left a little late, so she pushed herself a little harder than normal.

Even so, we got back to Arichburg just as it was getting dark, so I'd say it all worked out. Since it had turned into the home base for the Liberation Army, Arichburg and its surroundings were safe enough, but the city still closed its gates at night. Not that Grande and I couldn't get in anyway, thanks to both our position of power in the organization and literal physical power.

"Well done getting home," said Sylphy.

"Good to be back," I answered. "It...wasn't particularly harrowing to be honest."

"Liar."

Sylphy glared at me and pulled my cheeks.

"Oufies."

If she put her full power into it, she could literally pull my cheeks off, so she was clearly taking it easy on me.

While I was having my cheeks pulled at, Ira appeared out of nowhere to wrap her arms around me. "Welcome home."

"Thanks."

She looked up at me, her head at the height of my chest. It was in the perfect position, so I gently stroked it, and she narrowed her one large eye happily.

It was crazy to think that someone so small was older than me.

A little distance away from us was a horned devil with a broad smile on her face.

"I'm glad you're doing okay," said Melty. "How was the saint?"

"Use some common sense," I told her. "You know nothing happened."

"You didn't leap at her like an uncontrollable beast?"

"No!"

In fact, she tried to pin me down. She failed.

"Look, I'm glad everyone's happy I'm back, but time isn't our ally right now. We need to get serious."

"Wha—?!" The harpies, who'd been waiting for their turns, began to boo me. There were over ten of them, and if I gave each of them a chance to do their bit, the sun would set on us.

There wasn't much to talk over at this point... If anything, there were way more effective uses of my time, such as adjusting and producing equipment. Leaving the talking to Sylphy and the others made sense.

I had more to do than just make things, though.

"This gets very loud, so if you're sensitive to loud noises, be careful, got it? All right...I'm going to fire it."

I pulled the trigger.

GATAGATAGATAGATAGATA!

The relentless sound of bullets firing filled the air, colliding with the target—that I'd wrapped with armor plating—and cutting it in half. The machine gun, known as the man with a tiny mustache's buzzsaw, had a very short firing range.

In other words, what I needed to do was teach the right people in this world how to use the weapons from my world.

"This weapon is an extension of the bolt action rifle. It's called a machine gun. As you can see for yourselves, it makes shields and armor about as useful as paper. It also uses the same rounds you use in your bolt action rifles."

I pulled a small arms round from my inventory. At this point, it probably made more sense to refer to them as machine gun rounds.

"This thing can fire twelve hundred rounds in a single minute—an absurd rate of fire, quite frankly. That said, if you keep firing at that speed, the barrel will overheat, so normally you'd swap out barrels. But since this barrel is made of black steel, you probably won't have to worry about that. Still, it'll be necessary to keep replacements on hand."

While explaining this, I opened the hatch to the side of the air-cooled gun barrel cover and pulled out the heavy barrel.

"Hot, hot!"

I panicked and returned it into the cover out of fear of burning my hands. I should've worn gloves.

"What are you even doing?"

The captain of the rifle squad, the panther demi-human Jagheera, grimaced as she watched me. She had her ears tucked down tightly to prevent the loud sounds from bothering her. I was impressed, to be honest. Demi-humans had so many unique, useful features. My ears were still hurting.

"So, um, that's quite the weapon you have there, but..." Jagheera kept her ears down as she searched for the right words.

"You think it's too powerful to use on human opponents?" I asked.

She nodded her head. "Well, yes..."

The rest of the rifle squad wore similarly serious expressions.

"Yeah, I get it. The bolt action rifle is basically an extension of a bow and arrow or the crossbow. A tool to kill another being. I think it's fair to call it a 'weapon.' Juxtaposed to that, the machine gun is designed so that a small number of people can one-sidedly take down a larger force and finish them off. An anti-personnel machine, so to speak."

Seeing that Jagheera was listening to my explanation with her full attention, I continued, "Quite frankly, bolt action rifles included, all the weapons I show you should never have existed in this world. Any combat encounters in which we use them cease to be battles, instead becoming one-sided massacres. Despite that fact, I will continue to have our forces wield them for the purpose of killing our enemies. Why? Because it's necessary."

We'd be utilizing the mobility of my airboards in the coming battles. But just that wouldn't be enough. We needed the power to stop the enemy in their tracks. An overwhelming power that could apply guaranteed damage every time.

"As for the rifle squad's coming mission, you'll be hearing from Sylphy or Danan soon enough. But this weapon *will* be required to make that mission a success. That's why I want you all to at least learn how to use it."

"Understood," said Jagheera. "Get it, everyone?"

The members of the rifle squad all nodded.

If Hell existed in this world, I'd be bringing Jagheera and her troops along with me. If possible, I wanted to limit that to just Sylphy and myself. We were the ones forcing Jagheera and the others to do this, so I felt they had room to be forgiven.

"What are you spacing out for?" Jagheera asked. "C'mon, teach me how to handle that thing."

"Right, my bad."

I then began to explain how to reload and swap out the gun barrel.

The plan was to issue a warning to the Holy Kingdom's forces first, before we used these to attack them, but I doubted that would lead to them complying. Then again, I'd already used bombs to blow away thousands of their troops, and all other manner of means to kill their people within the Kingdom of Merinard, so why was I worrying? My primary goal now was to make sure none of the rifle squad got themselves hurt when using this new gun.

I'd have to be an all-powerful god if I wanted to save the lives of our armed enemies as well. In games, when you beat the enemy, they usually just vanished. There was no reason to feel guilty. But in the real world? Unfortunately, things weren't that simple.

Even with my ears covered, I could hear the endless sounds of bullets being fired, almost like the roars of a wild beast.

"FWAAAAAAAAH!"

Like a beast—

"GWAAAAAAAAH!"

Roaring—

"YAHOOOO!"

"You guys are *actually* just roaring like beasts!" I shouted, stomping on the ground.

Look, I felt bad about using my weapons to force our people to one-sidedly massacre the Holy Kingdom's military forces. Seriously, I did.

"THIS IS SOOOO FUN!"

But these guys told a very different story. It seemed the members of the rifle squad weren't completely satisfied with the firing rate of their bolt action rifles, as they were now unloading like crazy with the new weapon. And all of them were standing and shooting without the bipods equipped. Were their shoulders going to be okay? Could they control the recoil? Oh, they were totally fine? I guess that's all right, then.

I had forgotten that compared to the people of my old world, the folks here had near superhuman abilities. Even someone as slim as Jagheera was far stronger than I was. She could easily swing around a machine gun weighing over 11 kilograms.

"Walking around with a full mag swinging from this thing is kind of a pain."

"Yeah." In response to her complaint, I pulled a drum magazine from my inventory and handed it to her.

"Hrn? And how am I supposed to use this?"

"Like so..."

I quickly taught her how to use a drum magazine, which could be loaded with fifty shots. To describe it visually, it was a round bullet container that could be utilized by a machine gun. Inside the container was a bullet belt, and loading it was the same as before.

"Hrm, they've both got pros and cons," she said. "If you're gonna settle down, it'd be best to just pull bullet belts right from the ammo box. But if you're gonna be moving around and fighting, this drum magazine thing makes more sense."

"Exactly. If you're crawling on the ground, you'll be dragging the bullet belts around and could get dirt in them, causing misfires and such."

"Right, right. So, I take it since you're teaching us how to use these crazy weapons, you have an enemy you want taken out."

"I'd say so."

Regardless of how I answered her, these weapons made the situation clear as day, so there was no point in beating around the bush.

"Put it this way: I'm not just going to stand here and send you guys into dangerous territory on foot," I said. "I'll be going with you, too."

"Seriously? I guess if you're with us, things'll work out one way or the other."

"Leave the ammunition to me!"

I was actually in the process of crafting said bullets. There was a host of raw materials in a cave I found near Arichburg, so we wouldn't have any powder shortages for a while to come.

What raw materials? Well, let's just say... Okay, it's the giant poops from the bats that lived there. It was good for fertilizer, too!

As for the metal, while I was on standby waiting for the bullets to finish, Grande would be taking me to the mountains for some mining, so we were good there as well.

"I want you and your people to pay attention when learning how to swap out the gun barrels and loading cartridges," I said. "Next up is this bad boy."

The next object I pulled out of my inventory was an airboard. This wasn't the prototype I built but rather the mass production model that R&D had put their heads together to create.

"The hell is this thing?" asked Jagheera.

"A vehicle called an airboard. With a single magic crystal, you can get all the way to Arichburg from the rear base in a day. It has an extremely high speed."

"Wha?! A day to get here from the rear base?!"

"Yup. Plus, it can travel across pretty much any kind of terrain. Weedy fields, badlands, you name it. Not the woods, though."

It looked like a pickup truck with the bottom half cut off, placed on a board, and with propulsion tubes attached to the left and right sides. Only the driver's seat was surrounded by armor plating.

"It does somewhat resemble a horse and carriage... What of the wheels?"

"This baby doesn't need wheels."

I then attached the machine gun to the mount on the back of the airboard. It was designed to hold an ammo box of up to 250 rounds, allowing the wielder to fire the gun smoothly without needing help loading.

I'd wanted to attach a revolving turret to it, but on account of both weight and technology, I had to give up. Plus, at the end of the day, the members of the rifle squad could all use machine guns without a stand, so I didn't really need to concern myself with that.

I was fairly certain that I only needed the part of the gun mount for locking the ammo box in place. I could put one on both sides of the airboard and the back. To counteract weight issues, I could either raise the floating devices' output, or I could add more of them. For the time being, though, the priority was having a few of these airboards ready to go, so I put off optimizing the balance between these things for later.

"All right! Let's give this baby a test drive. Jagheera, you're on the turret. Let's get one other person on here for swapping the barrel and reloading. Everyone else, be on standby."

Following my orders, Jagheera and a small squirrel demi-human got onto the back of the airboard. The other members of the rifle squad stood in wait at their designated location. We were about to demonstrate how this thing would move while firing, so I needed them in a place where there wouldn't be any tragic accidents.

"Jagheera, make sure you've got these wyvern gloves on when you switch out the gun barrel," I instructed her. "Once you shoot 250 rounds, that's when you switch. And while she's doing that," I said as I turned to the squirrel demi-human woman, "you handle the reload. I need you to know how the ammo box locks into place and how to reload the gun. We shouldn't be shaking around too much, but when this thing rotates, you'll feel your body being pulled in the opposite direction, so don't get thrown off the airboard."

"'Kay."

"Roger that."

The squirrel demi-human nodded earnestly while Jagheera slipped on the wyvern gloves. After confirming they were good to go, I locked a magic crystal into the fuel slot in the driver's seat, then engaged the starter for booting up the airboard. Soon, magical power flowed from end to end of the board, causing it to float up into the air.

As far as the control system was concerned, we'd argued and exchanged ideas over it in the R&D department. If we were going to use these things for battle, we needed the system I made, which was good for hyper accurate controls. And if we were going to use them for long-range travel, then the current system would be no good because it required the driver to always be paying attention.

I even argued for using a handle and foot pedals like a car. We exchanged all kinds of ideas.

Ultimately, for these mass-produced models, we decided on the first twin-stick system I designed. This was partially because we didn't have much time to spend on development or on the creation of a new control system. We'd investigated having it control like a car, but that system simply didn't pair well with the airboard's use of hover and propulsion devices. Its mobility was closer to that of a marine vessel. And using a handle and foot pedals to control the complex balance between the left and right propulsion while also having a rudder would require a high-grade golem system.

Therefore, we rolled with twin sticks for propulsion and hover and a foot pedal for controlling the rudder. Thanks to the modified rudder and propulsion devices, its ability to rotate and accelerate had gotten better, and its magical efficiency was a good ways better than the prototype.

"Oooh, it's floating," said the squirrel demi-human.

"You can change its height somewhat as well," I said. "It'll float a maximum of 1.5 meters above the ground, but the higher you get, the less stable it becomes, so I'd recommend against it. All right, here we go!"

I set the propulsion low to start with, moving slowly through the air. Despite the lack of wheels, the back of the airboard moved along fine, which caused the two women in the back and the watching soldiers to "Ooh" and "Ahh" in surprise.

"I'm going to raise the speed gradually, so I want you to start shooting the targets, Jagheera."

"Roger that."

I raised the propulsion devices' output and maneuvered the airboard near the targets, turning so that the back of the vehicle was facing them. I could immediately hear shots being fired from the rear. She'd started shooting.

After firing the machine gun, reloading, and repeating this process, we returned to where the rest of the rifle squad was waiting.

"Well?" I asked.

"It's honestly amazing that this thing can run along the ground without shaking at all," said Jagheera. "It's fast as hell—maybe even more so than a horse. If anything, I didn't really need the turret."

"I figured. It only lets you shoot toward the back, after all. It'd probably be better if I set up a bullet box stand that could spin around."

"Yeah, that sounds good. Then we could shoot in any direction comfortably."

"So a bullet box stand, then... I never even considered that."

It was more surprising to me that she could handle the machine gun's recoil and weight with no issues whatsoever. I never even considered that as a possibility. But they were right that a rotating bullet stand would allow them to reload much more smoothly. If I put something like that in the center of the bed, though, it'd be in the way when we were traveling normally, so either I had to make it removable or have it fold down into the bed when not in use.

"I wanna get this feedback to R&D ASAP," I announced. "That said, I don't think the rotating bullet stand will be done in time. For now, I'll have them install bullet box stands on all sides."

"Got it. We should let the other troops practice, right?"

"Yeah. I'm going to need everyone to learn how to drive one of these, too."

And so we spent the day teaching the squad how to use machine guns and drive the airboard.

"Are you done playing the teacher?" Sylphy asked.

It was the night after instructing the rifle squad. Sylphy, Ira, and I were spending time together in the manor's detached housing. We'd finished bathing and eating, and we were just enjoying some drinks together.

"Yeah, for the most part," I said. "Thinking about how much ammo we used up while training gives me a headache."

I took a sip of the mead Sylphy poured for me, then sighed. The sweet scent of the drink tickled my nose. Something about sighing after drinking mead had a sweet, floral feel to it.

Anyway, just because we'd spent a whole day shooting guns didn't mean we were done. I mean, we weren't going to do this *every* single day, but after a day or two, we'd have to do more shooting.

A single ammo box was 250 rounds, so making all twenty members of the rifle squad fire four boxes of bullets each meant a total of 20,000 rounds. I was collecting all the shells, though, so it actually only cost about half of what it normally would. Plus, we weren't using expensive brass for the shells. We were using iron.

You would think reloading into those used shells would be tough, but thanks to my skills, it didn't matter if they had bent rims rolling inward or totally borked bodies, they would be 100 percent fixed like brand new! I only needed to have powder and bullet heads. Of course, it wasn't as if I was able to get *absolutely* all of the casings back. It was hard finding the ones fired from the airboard...

"R&D is working full time," said Ira, looking up at me with her big eye from her position on my lap. Apparently, it was my turn to dote on her today. Sylphy was attached to me as well, so I knew what my role was in all of this.

"Just tell them to make sure to get enough rest," I said. "I'll be helping so we make it on time, too, so pass off anything it'd be faster for me to make."

"Mm, okay. I'll have them make a list first thing tomorrow morning."

"Thanks. But don't push yourself too hard. Same to you, Sylphy. We've gotta be in tip-top shape for what's coming next."

"Yes, I know. That is why I am currently holding on to you and replenishing my strength."

"Mm, Kousuke power," murmured Ira.

They were apparently recovering via some mysterious power. Talk about eco-friendly—all it took was attaching themselves

to me. And I felt like I was being healed by them, too. Was this perhaps a new kind of perpetual motion machine?

"Anything new from Elen?" I asked.

"Nothing about the incoming military," Sylphy replied. "However, she has been working behind the scenes for our take-over of Merinesburg."

"I wonder what that means... I doubt she's planning on open-ing the gates for us, right?"

There were thousands of troops total within the city gates. It wouldn't be that easy to convince them all to surrender to us.

"Apparently she's coming up with reasons to send the main sect soldiers and commanding general out of the city," explained Sylphy. "Something like a large-scale patrol mission or making them climb a mountain as a part of their training. Even send-ing them to the incoming subjugation forces under the guise of a supply run. That kind of thing."

"Is that actually going to work?"

"Who knows. That woman is going to do what she is going to do. And think of it this way; despite the strange relationship with the main sect, she is undoubtedly a saint of Adolism. If she uses her position right, she should be able to brute force a fair number of things."

"Is that how it works?"

Sylphy seemed confident, but I was extremely concerned. Using her title, Elen had collected all kinds of information and cast judgment on a bunch of sinful clergymen while crushing a raging miscreant with her divine miracles like some kind of rampaging general. At least, that was how the stories went. But as far as I was concerned, she was just a delicate young woman who could break under pressure, just like any other.

"It is," said Sylphy. "Anyway, regardless of how things turn out, we won't be able to keep this all under wraps. All we can do is keep the casualties to a minimum."

"That hurts to hear."

"I hate saying this, but such is war," Ira said, before letting out a sigh and closing her eye.

It wasn't as if Sylphy or Ira enjoyed war. Sylphy was in this to get her kingdom and family back, and Ira was working to free her race from the oppression of the Holy Kingdom. Melty and Madame Zamil shared the same desires as Sylphy, and Danan and Sir Leonard wanted revenge.

And, of course, we all shared the larger goal of saving the demi-humans being oppressed by the Holy Kingdom and taking back Merinard.

Was war the only way to achieve our greater goals? Whenever I thought about this question, the only answer I could come to was "yes." The differences in ideology between the Kingdom of Merinard and the Holy Kingdom were just too fundamentally great.

On the one hand was the Kingdom of Merinard, where humans and demi-humans lived together as "humanoids." Then you had the Holy Kingdom, a nation that believed in human supremacy and felt demi-humans were nothing more than slaves to be used. How could these two nations ever come to a compromise?

Even if there were talks, the Holy Kingdom would never truly listen. At least not right now.

"Hopefully, this battle can put an end to things," said Sylphy.

"Agreed," said Ira.

"Yeah, likewise," I sighed.

I guess our only option right now was to fight. We just had to be careful not to use that as an excuse to continue fighting endlessly.

After I returned to Arichburg, a week passed in a flash, and the day of the operation was upon us.

"Feels like we're finally where we need to be..."

Morale among the members of the mobile strike force was high. We had a total of five hundred soldiers split between a hundred mass-produced airboards. All of those vehicles lined up in a row made for quite the sight indeed. We didn't just have airboards built for the strike force—we also had some made to carry the main forces' baggage and supplies. R&D had just managed to fulfill all the orders, and this morning they looked pale as ghosts, but pleased. Now they could finally pass on to the next life. Namu, namu.

I was in charge of the supply train for the mobile strike force. Everyone riding an airboard had a day's worth of water and food, but still, if I were to suddenly drop dead, the strike force would be doomed.

Actually...that wasn't completely true. They had the mobility to flee to Arichburg so long as they avoided fighting. If they could retreat, things would work out. At this point, it'd be worse if we lost Sylphy. She was the de facto leader of our operation, and she was required to free the frozen royal family in Merinesburg Castle.

"Your Highness, Sir Kousuke. Could you please retreat to the rear or to the middle of the convoy?"

Madame Zamil was riding with us, and she was staring at the two of us with her reptilian eyes that gave away no hint of emotion.

"Not happening," said Sylphy. "If anything, I would prefer to be at the very front."

"And considering my abilities, I should be just behind the rifle squad, seeing as they'll be taking heavy damage and using up lots of ammunition," I said.

Madame Zamil sighed in response.

"Don't worry," said Ira, who was also riding with us. "My new barrier can repel even dragon breath."

She was attempting to cheer poor Madame Zamil up, but if anything she was only adding to the chorus of people saying everything would be fine.

"We could break through the Holy Kingdom's main forces with the group of people we have here right now," Melty smiled from the rear seat of the airboard. "If push comes to shove, I can also fight."

Grande, who was lying sleepily in Melty's lap, chimed in, "I have no intention of involving myself in the conflict of humanoids, but should things turn sour, I suppose I could take you all and flee far away from here."

Madame Zamil sighed once again and closed her eyes, giving up entirely.

Our airboard was very close to the front of the convoy. Right behind us were rifle squad airboards equipped with machine guns. If we were to suddenly come into contact with an enemy, it was highly likely we'd be caught in the battle.

However, we had the harpies scouting from the sky above, so it was unlikely we'd be caught off guard. The girls up there all had golem communicators, so they'd let us know as soon as they spotted enemies.

"Roll call for mobile infantry and government support squads complete."

As we all tried our best to calm a worried Madame Zamil down, Sir Leonard's voice came through on our small golem communicator.

The breakdown for our mobile strike force was as follows: twenty harpy bombers, twenty riflemen led by Jagheera, four hundred elite soldiers led by Sir Leonard, Ira's twenty-strong mage unit, and then the required government figures, making for a total of five hundred people. The government support unit was made up of the civil servants we brought with us.

Behind us was the main force led by Danan, composed of crossbow soldiers, heavy infantry, and a raid unit of former adventurers for a total of three thousand soldiers, give or take. Ah, we also had a test squad equipped with prototype maguns as well.

Generally speaking, the five hundred members of the mobile strike force were here to crush the various fortresses and obstacles in our way, with the rear main force taking over enemy territory as they passed through.

We would continue onward without waiting for them, striking hard and fast before the enemy could make a move, destroying the Holy Kingdom's forces at each of their bases.

The plan was to avoid civilian casualties as much as possible, but it'd be impossible to keep them at zero.

"Rifle squad, ready."

"Aerial bombing squad, ready."

After hearing the reports, Ira took the golem communicator into her hand and began to speak. "Mm. The mage squad is riding with the rifle squad, so we're ready as well."

"All right," said Sylphy. "Then, as planned, the rifle squad airboards will take the lead. All units, maintain a vehicle's distance from one another and drive carefully. It'd be shameful if you had to retreat from the battlefield before even encountering the Holy Kingdom's forces. Our first objective is Bobrovsk! Mobile strike force, move out!"

At Sylphy's call, the one hundred airboards floated into the air and began to glide forward. Leading the pack were the riflemen and mage airboards equipped with machine guns. Our airboard was right behind them, and then behind us came the airboards carrying the harpies, and the elites behind them.

It was a real tough time teaching over a hundred people how to drive these things...

In the other world, this would be a whole convoy of amateurs without their licenses. It'd be an actual miracle if there were no accidents.

By the way, I was the one driving our airboard. And, of course, this airboard was unique. On the control stick was a trigger.

"Shall we?" I asked.

I was more than ready to fire on the enemy with my own two hands. It was time to walk the walk.

CHAPTER 4

Blitzkrieg

WE HAD OUR scout harpies kill any suspicious birds that could have been messengers while progressing down the road. There were definitely scouts in the woods, but we didn't have the time to deal with them, and it wasn't like they could follow us, what with how quickly we were moving.

We were on the move for about an hour before we arrived at Bobrovsk, a town under the control of the Holy Kingdom. Since our harpies had been taking care of their messenger birds, they didn't realize we were invading until their defense force saw us coming. The citizens outside of the town walls waiting to be checked were hurriedly rushed inside. They were clearly unprepared for us.

"Kousuke, I'm going to use the speaker."

"Right."

Sylphy took the mic positioned between the driver's seat and the rear seats, then began to speak.

"To all members of the Holy Kingdom residing within Bobrovsk, we are the Merinard Liberation Army! Drop your weapons immediately and surrender. Should you fail to comply in half an hour, we will begin our attack!"

We were too far away from the walls of the town for their arrows to hit us, so we had no way of knowing how they were reacting. If nothing else, though, it didn't seem like they'd immediately settled on violence.

As we waited, the airboards behind us emerged from the road and surrounded Bobrovsk. The rifle squad airboards had their machine guns, but they weren't the only members of the strike force equipped with long-range weapons—Sir Leonard's elites were well trained in the use of crossbows.

It was possible to fire from atop an airboard, so everyone had a means of attacking without dismounting their respective vehicles.

"Do you think they will surrender?" I asked.

A bell began to ring from within the town, perhaps to make everyone aware of the emergency. It was easy to imagine Bobrovsk in a complete panic.

"Doubtful," Sylphy said. "Those chosen to be commanders on the front line are typically stubborn bastards to prevent them from simply giving up the fight without ever taking up arms. Take three rifle squad airboards and circle around to the northern gate to seal it off. Kill anyone who tries to break through."

"Roger that."

This time, Sylphy took the golem communicator mic and began to issue orders.

"Harpy scouts, make sure there aren't any messengers trying to flee the town. Bombing squad, get ready. Cooperate with the scouts and bomb any messengers trying to break through our line. Continue taking down any messenger birds you come across."

"Roger that!"

Sylphy's orders were fairly ruthless, but cutting off the enemy's line of communication was important. Completely preventing any leaks at all would be impossible, but it was nonetheless important to take what measures we could.

Between the Holy Kingdom's might and our Liberation Army, we had more than a few points on them, but the biggest one was our information advantage. We had golem communicators and could deliver intelligence back and forth in real time.

In comparison, the fastest way for our enemy to deliver information was by messenger bird or horse. Since messenger birds could be caught, they were exceedingly unreliable—and as far as messages delivered via horseback were concerned, they moved at about the same speed we did, so it didn't make a difference.

Therefore, incapable of getting information in a timely manner, the Holy Kingdom would always be subject to surprise attacks. Thirty minutes just wasn't enough time for them to get their people in order, especially since they had to evacuate the citizens as well. If they ignored that side of things, they might've been able to put something together, but...

"This is the north gate. A group of possible messengers has appeared and is charging toward us with cavalrymen."

"Kill them," ordered Sylphy.

"Roger."

I could hear the quiet sounds of explosions from afar.

"Cleanup complete. No casualties on our side."

"Well done. Stay on alert."

"Roger."

"You heard her. Unit 2 and 3 with me. I'm leaving Unit 4 in charge of this position. If anything happens, ask the princess for orders."

"Understood."

After the princess gave out her orders, I delivered my own to the many members of the rifle squad and gently tapped on the back window of the driver's seat. The airboard then began to hover above the fields surrounding Bobrovsk. It was amazing to me that we could travel above these fields without damaging them, and so quickly. These new vehicles had more mobility than a horse and carriage, so I had no complaints. It was unfortunate that they provided no cover from arrows or magic attacks, but since we had two mages capable of casting barrier magic, most enemy attacks wouldn't be able to reach us anyway.

The current makeup for airboards carrying riflemen was two riflemen, two mages, and a single driver. The mages also acted as reload support. This was an experimental system, but I felt that it made for a very functional unit.

Circling around to the north, I found that the town road was already quiet. The bell in the town was ringing, so farmers and travelers had been evacuated inside the town walls. But on closer inspection, there seemed to be activity around the gate. I told our drivers to spread out a safe distance away from the town gates.

"Seal off the road and standby," I said. "Prepare the machine guns so they're ready to fire immediately."

"Yes, Captain."

I got my own machine gun ready. Kousuke had seen to their maintenance yesterday, so all we had to do was make sure they worked and were loaded.

After a moment, the town gates opened and a group of twelve cavalrymen emerged, clearly aiming to break through our air-board wall. There were two lightly armored knights among them, likely messengers, while the rest were properly equipped. The cavalrymen would function as shields as they plowed through us, and the messengers would try to get past through the gap the others had made for them. I immediately got in touch with the princess via golem communicator.

"This is the north gate. A group of possible messengers has appeared and are charging toward us with cavalrymen."

Her Majesty's reply was brief and decisive.

"Kill them."

"Roger. Units 1, 2, and 3. Our objective is the group of enemy knights. Let them get closer... Closer... Prepare your firearms... Open fire!"

As soon as I gave the order, I pulled the trigger on my machine gun and began to shower the enemy calvary ahead of us with bullets.

GAAAAAAAAN! GAAAAAAAAN!

Ferocious sounds cut through the air as the group of horseback soldiers transformed into plumes of blood.

A bolt action rifle was powerful enough to pierce enemy armor in a single shot, and these machine guns could fire twenty of those shots in but a single second. It didn't matter if they were armored or riding a horse—these soldiers could do nothing in the face of this kind of firepower.

Each airboard was equipped with two machine guns, which meant that a total of six of these monsters were raining bullets on the squad of knights. In seconds, they were annihilated. Horses included, no survivors.

"If we had our bolt action rifles, we could've just taken down the men."

That was true. There had been twelve riders total. Six people equipped with bolt action rifles could have taken them out before they got close.

"That might be true, but one of the objectives of this operation is to display our strength."

"But killing the horses is such a waste."

"It's unavoidable."

Horses were tremendously useful. You could ride them, they could pull carriages and luggage, they could help plough the fields, and you could eat them. Four completely different uses! Though when you say that to a horse beastman, they'd give you a dirty look.

Not that any of that mattered now. It was time to make my report.

"Cleanup complete. No casualties on our side."

"Well done. Stay on alert."

"Roger."

I then changed channels.

"Drag the corpses to the side of the road. Send one soldier each from Unit 2 and 3. Everyone else, stand guard. Mages, stay on your respective airboards."

Answers quickly came from both units.

"Roger that."

"Aye, aye."

"Well then, take care!" I said.

"Huh?! You mean I have to go?!"

"I'm the captain. I gotta give orders, duh."

"Ugggh, you suck, Jagheera!"

It was wonderful having such loyal men and women under my command. Now then, how was our enemy going to respond?

Some cavalrymen had tried to break out through the north gate, but after their failed attempt, Bobvrosk was much like a shellfish that had retreated back into itself: silent. Well, that wasn't entirely true. We could see soldiers on the town walls that were likely part of a garrison, so I guess my comparison wasn't so apt. But all the same, it did not appear as though they were preparing to surrender.

Sylphy checked the position of the sun.

"It's time," she whispered.

I didn't get it at all, but she could accurately tell what time it was from where the sun was in the sky. For me personally, it felt like we were well past thirty minutes, but I guess I was just in something of a rush.

Sylphy once again picked up the mic.

"It is time!" she called out. **"If you wish to surrender, raise your white flags. If you do not, we will begin our attack!"**

There was no response. That was it, then.

"Harpy aerial bombing squad. Destroy the southern gate."

"Roger that. Beginning bombing run."

The harpy bombing squad was already airborne thanks to Sylphy's orders, so they quickly began dropping bombs from high up. They dove down at great speed, released their payloads, and then just as quickly rose back into the air. A moment later, the town gate exploded. It was supposed to be multiple medium-sized explosions occurring at once, but because the timing was perfectly aligned, it looked like one massive blast.

"Is it just me, or are the harpies in perfect sync?" I remarked.

"That is because they train whenever they have a moment of free time," said a dozy Grande from behind me. "They even used my lovely abode as a practice target. I helped them gather simulated bombs and everything. I also built dirt walls and the like."

Just what were those harpies getting up to?

Either way, their perfect strike destroyed the southern gate in its entirety. The harpies dropped another set of bombs on the remains, clearing the area completely. At this point, they'd used all the bombs they were equipped with, so they'd have to resupply... Wow, they got back here fast.

"Your next targets are the garrison on the wall, the barracks, and the weapons storage building," Sylphy ordered.

"Aye, aye!"

The harpies flew off again, and this time the garrison on the wall was blown away, followed by explosions at a number of facilities within the town walls. All we could do was watch from afar.

"This is really one-sided," I said.

"That was the whole point, no? And since they're attacking from so high up, even the enemy's arrows and magic can't reach them. They have no way of defending themselves."

I could hear Ira's cold analysis from behind me. She wasn't wrong, either. We were out of range, so they were getting their asses kicked.

"Um, so what's the plan after this?" I asked.

"We leave the cleanup to the forces behind us while we move forward," said Sylphy.

"I figured."

We didn't have the time to deal with that sort of thing. Our role as the strike force was to take down enemy strongholds with overwhelming strength and haste, allowing our main forces behind us to easily mop up what was left. There would have been no point to our speed if we had to wait for the others after every attack.

"Status report."

"Scouts reporting. The garrison on the wall has been wiped out, and crucial facilities have all been destroyed."

"Perfect. Come on home, harpy squad. After a fifteen-minute rest, we resume our march forward. Everyone take care to stay hydrated."

"Roger that."

"Fifteen minutes, eh?" I said. "Then I'll take this time to refill their stock of aerial bombs."

"All right," said Sylphy. "I do not think there is anything to fear but be careful nonetheless."

"Aye, aye."

With that, I got out of the driver's seat. It was time to restock.

"Enemy resistance has ceased!"

"Leonard, send in the infantry."

"Roger."

Two days had passed since the strike force was sent out, and we were yet again on the road to Merinesburg, taking down Holy Kingdom strongholds one after the other. Just yesterday, we took down a total of four defense points. Today, we were on our second. The strike force was getting more efficient with each and every encounter.

We warned them, gave them the chance to surrender, and then Jagheera's rifle squad closed off all entry and exit points. Together with the harpy recon squad, we eliminated any form of communications the enemy tried to send out, while Sir Leonard's special forces started to prepare their siege.

Most of the time, the Holy Kingdom's forces didn't choose surrender, instead opting to hole up in their bases. As a result, the harpy aerial bomb squad would go to town on them. After eliminating any enemy resistance, we'd move in to get rid of the rubble and grab our spoils of war as quickly as possible. While that was happening, Ira's mage squad would heal any enemy survivors just enough so that they wouldn't die. Then we'd move on to the next target. Rinse and repeat.

"So, uh, I know we've won and all, but this place is basically falling apart," I remarked.

"Maybe the architect sucked," suggested Ira.

"It doesn't look like they cheaped out on stone materials," said Madame Zamil.

"They stacked the stones up high, but if an explosion hit it from the side, it wouldn't be able to hold up," Grande said. "And if one spot collapsed, the rest would follow right afterward."

"I see," the rest of us chorused.

I shouldn't have been surprised that a grand dragon knew so much, considering how well versed they were in handling dirt and stone. Ira, Madame Zamil, and I all understood her explanation.

"You know those bombs the harpies drop?" Grande went on. "If you are trying to defend against them, you should not build tall walls, but rather vertical and horizontal moats, then fight from inside of them. The bombs might explode on the surface, but you would be safe from the blast wave and shrapnel. Certainly, if a bomb happens to land directly inside, you'd be dead, but you can keep the casualties to a minimum. It would also be easier to hide from rifle fire."

Amazing. Grande had come up with the entire concept of trench warfare despite not having any knowledge of it from my world. Dragons sure were smart as hell.

"Dragons really are hyper intelligent," said Ira. "Amazing."

"Agreed," said Madame Zamil with a nod. "I'm impressed."

"Right? Right?" Grande chirped. She was in a wonderful mood thanks to the others' compliments. I just wished she would stop happily smacking the airboard with her tail. The whole thing was shaking, and it was going to break at the rate she was going.

In fact, we were all in a grand mood, but we were still technically in the middle of battle. We weren't screwing around—it was just that our senses were dulled at this point.

"Kousuke, let's use *that* at the next fortress-type stronghold."

Sylphy, on the other hand, still wore a serious face. Between me, who had been dulled to the violence, and Sylphy, who continued to treat it with the utmost seriousness, which of us were better off I wondered?

"I'm not crazy about the idea, but we do need to experiment."

And so I pulled out the special aerial bomb I'd developed the previous night from my inventory.

It was about the same size as the normal aerial bombs, but it had a folded parachute connected to it. Its detonation was handled by a golem core, making it extremely trustworthy.

Why did I attach a parachute? So that the harpies dropping it wouldn't get caught in the blast.

This bomb was, well... It had no blasting powder in it. Instead, it had a single standard sized magic crystal and two small gleaming magic jewel shards.

Exactly. This was a gleaming magic jewel bomb.

As someone with no understanding of how magic worked, I couldn't begin to tell you the details behind how this thing functioned, but according to Ira, who took it apart and analyzed it herself, the crystal's magical energy was circulated between the two shards and amplified, ultimately causing the two shards to produce far more magical power than they were capable of storing, resulting in a giant explosion.

I didn't get it at all.

"According to my calculations, it should be powerful enough to blow away a small fortress."

"According to calculations, eh?"

If she happened to be a digit off with those calculations, we could potentially be blown away ourselves. That's why we had to make safety a priority here.

"Suppression complete. Collecting spoils of war and providing aid now."

"Well done," Sylphy said. "Mage squad, onward to the fortress. Kousuke, you're up."

"Mm, okay."

"Aye."

Following Sylphy's orders, I put the aerial jewel bomb away in my inventory and got out of the driver's seat. Next, Ira dismounted the airboard, followed by Madame Zamil with her weapon in hand. Sylphy and Melty were staying behind, and Grande had no intention of departing in the first place. She was smart as hell, but she preferred lying about. She was a dragon, after all.

"Now then, time to get to work," I said.

Ira nodded. "Yup."

Just to be safe, I checked my shortcuts—in case I needed to pull out a weapon quickly—then made way for the collapsed fortress.

We were essentially washing away blood with blood, treating our enemy's lives like they were insignificant. This was war. But even with that said, there was one line we didn't cross.

The Holy Kingdom saw us as nothing more than bandits, which meant that between them and the Liberation Army, wartime law didn't apply. Technically, nobody could do anything about us lynching survivors, sticking them to our shields, or anything else.

That didn't mean it wouldn't cause problems. If we got too grotesque, we'd lose the support of the people, and we'd suffer the aftereffects when the time came for political negotiations. And if the enemy learned that surrendering was pointless, they'd resist to the very end no matter what. That would be a huge negative for us. We were currently mopping the floor with them to the point that there was no room to even struggle, but that wasn't wholly a good thing.

Ultimately, this was all in the name of creating an excuse for ourselves when it came down to negotiations with the Holy Kingdom.

To that end, we had three broad stances:

[Send a warning and request surrender before attacking.]

[Provide medical attention to wounded soldiers and those who have lost the ability to fight.]

[Cremate the dead without leaving their bodies to rot.]

Technically, we *could* attack the enemy without warning, and there was no need to offer them medical aid or recover their bodies.

But it would be bad news if the Holy Kingdom used any of these slights as ammo to hit us with later. That's why we made a point of sticking to these rules when interacting with their forces. We weren't pretending to be good people. This was just necessary.

I thought about this as I walked until I felt someone poke at the side of my stomach. I turned to find Ira looking up at me with her big eye. Gosh, she was adorable.

"Feeling bad about using the new bomb?" she asked.

"It's just...a lot. I'd be lying if I said I wasn't resistant to the idea."

This wouldn't cause radiation poisoning or rain toxic material down on the land, but seeing something with that kind of power just didn't feel good. Almost like an allergic reaction.

But at the end of the day, using a plethora of aerial bombs to turn a fortress into a mountain of rubble and doing the same with a single magic jewel bomb weren't all that different.

"We have to test this thing before we use it on their main forces," I said. "It's our only option."

"Agreed."

Eventually we arrived at the busted fortress. Ira waved her hand at me and trotted off to where all the wounded were being held, while I took Madame Zamil with me and collected the rubble and clumps of enemy soldiers into my inventory.

In the midst of doing this, I came across survivors buried alive and corpses in the most horrific states. Whenever one of our soldiers with a good sense of smell located a survivor, I would dash over to get rid of the rubble. I was basically being treated like heavy machinery, but that was fine. What was hardest about this work was having to see so many dead bodies.

This was what it was all about in the end. The bodies missing a part or two were one thing, but I'd even run across corpses split in half, missing parts, and so on. Bodies were just all over the place. I'd gotten used to the sight to the point that I didn't vomit anymore, but it wasn't exactly feel-good work.

After finishing that up, I dug a hole and dumped all the bodies inside of it. The mages used flame magic to cremate them all in one go. Then we buried the ashes and erected a stone monument there, with today's date and a repose for the soul carved into it.

All of the weapons, armor, food, money, materials, and even the busted walls of the fortress ended up in my inventory. This particular stronghold had collapsed due to the bombing runs, so it was basically now a vacant lot. The only proof that this was once a fortress was the cenotaph we put down.

"Shall we move on, then?"

"Indeed."

Sir Leonard had watched me build the cenotaph up close. He then turned his attention to the surviving Holy Kingdom soldiers who had gathered nearby.

After healing them up, we gave them the supplies necessary to get them to the next town or village and let them go. We healed them just enough so that they could walk on their own. Everything else was up to them now. We didn't have the time to look after them all.

"Something on your mind?" I asked Sir Leonard.

"Hmph... I couldn't care less about them. Let us move on."

"Right, yeah."

I followed Sir Leonard's back as he began to walk away. Judging from the way the fur at the end of his tail was oddly poofy, he seemed to have something on his mind, but he was holding himself back. Just like a true veteran.

"The plan is to use the gleaming magic jewel bomb at the next fortress," I said.

"That thing, eh? I almost feel bad for the soldiers who are going to get blown away in the name of an experiment."

And yet I could see his shoulders shaking slightly from behind. It looked like he was laughing.

Sir Leonard was ordinarily a very chill older man, but at the end of the day, his wife was killed by the Holy Kingdom in the war twenty years ago, and his pride and honor were terribly damaged. I wondered if the weight of vengeance felt lighter on his shoulders if he sympathized with the enemy out loud.

◆ ⬡ ◆

"So yeah, that's basically it."

Sylphy poked her head out from the trench that Ira's mage squad had worked together with me to make.

"This might surprise you, but Sir Leonard has mellowed out quite a bit," she said, looking toward the fortress. "Remember, he has spent the last few months as a commander, hunting down the remnants of the Holy Kingdom's forces all over Merinard. I am certain that it opened old wounds for him."

On arriving at our third target of the day, we had immediately requested their surrender. We were now waiting to see how they'd respond. They weren't ready to strike at us when we first arrived, which seemed to imply that we were moving at a faster pace than the enemy's information network.

"They're probably super confused," Sylphy said.

"I bet. A bunch of soldiers riding weird vehicles appear out of nowhere, tell them their fortress will be destroyed in thirty minutes, and then all the soldiers disappear into trenches far away from them."

There was little doubt in my mind that the Holy Kingdom was extremely puzzled by all of this.

However, despite their confusion, they were still preparing to defend themselves. There would be no surrender here.

"Sylphy, it's about time."

"Right... Kousuke."

"Yup."

I pulled the megaphone powered by wind magic from my inventory and handed it to Sylphy. I'd made this at the same time I made the ones for the airboards. It was basically the magic equivalent of a transistor megaphone.

"Members of the Holy Kingdom hiding behind the walls of your fortress, surrender immediately!" she called out. "Should you fail to comply, you will be destroyed along with your fortress!"

But their only answer was a wave of scattered arrows. We were well out of their range, though, so they hit little more than dirt.

"Well, I figured that would happen," Sylphy sighed. "Pirna, begin the operation."

"Roger that. Beginning gleaming magic jewel bomb drop."

"All units, take defensive positions. Be careful of flying debris."

Replies from the captains of the various squads came in quickly.

I had already packed away the airboards into my inventory, of course. It'd be a real pain in the ass if they got damaged by debris.

"Mm, Pirna's flying," Ira observed.

"Yeah. She dropped the bomb. Get down. You too, Sylphy."

"Right."

I pulled at the hem of Sylphy's clothes as she tried to bear witness to the moment of the bomb's detonation, making her hide in the trench with the rest of us.

Just when I was beginning to wonder when the bomb would hit, I was blinded by white light, and everything went silent.

◆ ⬢ ◆

We were supposed to be fine hiding in the trenches, but my sense of balance was all wrong. I couldn't really tell if I was sitting down or standing up. I could hear ringing in my ears, too. Did my eardrums get blown out?

"Kousuke, Ira, are you two okay?" came Sylphy's voice.

"Mm, no problemo," said Ira.

"I'm still a little rattled," I admitted. I placed both hands on the ground and managed to recover after closing my eyes for a bit. I stood up and poked my head up from the trench.

"Oh...man..."

"There's nothing left."

"Yeah, just as calculated."

The area where the fortress had once resided was now completely wiped clean. There could be no survivors.

"Using this is far too dangerous," I said. "We have to reserve it as a last resort."

"I wonder..." said Sylphy. "Well, I suppose we can make a decision at tonight's meeting."

"Good idea."

Neither of the women agreed with my more cautious conclusion.

When it came to the bomb's construction, I was responsible for many aspects of the magic jewels and the creation of the bomb itself, so even if my opinion didn't win anyone over, I could probably still control how and when these were used, but I was going to have to be very careful about it.

The night after the bomb was used in combat...

The final fortress we took down was Berli Fortress. The Liberation Army unit who went in to take over the location was treated to a delicious meal and a single mug of some high-grade mead.

A single drink might've come off as cheap, but we couldn't afford to drown them in booze when there was work to be done the next day. Truth be told, Sylphy also wanted to give them a one- to two-day break, but we didn't have that kind of time. We had to clear the way so that we could do what needed to be done in Merinesburg. And so, while the soldiers were eating and drinking merrily...

"If we're going to kill all of them anyway, we should destroy their fortresses as well," Sir Leonard argued. "Why not use the weapons we have? It saves us both time and manpower."

"The richness of the magical energy in the surrounding area was abnormal after we used the bomb," said Ira. "If we were to keep using them, it's possible we could cause some kind of magical disaster. As a mage, I cannot support the thoughtless use of this new weapon."

"It does indeed save us time, but we're also destroying supplies along with the soldiers and fortresses themselves," Melty pointed out. "It might not be difficult for Kousuke to construct a fortress, but this could have an adverse effect on our governance going forward. Not being able to recover precious supplies is a problem."

"Putting aside whether we should use these bombs going forward, there is no doubting the positive effect its use has had on the morale of our troops," said Madame Zamil. "Even those who were concerned about going to war with the Holy Kingdom now believe we more than have a chance at victory. On the flip side, I imagine the enemy must be terribly deflated."

"I have no objection to their use," said Pirna. "I was able to get away before it exploded, no problem. Give the order, and I'll drop as many as need be."

Sir Leonard's thoughts were reasonable in a sense. We were in a hurry, so being able to just blow up any obstacles in our way would be very effective. However, we could not ignore what Ira said either. In the past, because the elves from the Black Forest performed devastating attacks with their spirit stones, they created the Omitt Badlands, a place that couldn't sustain any life. If we kept using gleaming magic jewel bombs, there was a real possibility we could walk that same dark path. That's what Ira was warning us of.

"Melty, your angle on this is a bit greedy, no?" I said.

"How rude," she huffed. "Fortresses and army posts are typically built in places where they are needed. You then put soldiers there, have them watch the roads, and, if needed, they can be used to take down bandits and monsters. That's why they exist in the first place. In the short term, not having fortresses around won't cause any huge problems, but in the long run, it is highly likely we'll have to build new ones in those same locations. And if that happens, we will need to send you back there. We have a giant list of things that only you can do, Kousuke, and yet we're going to go out of our way to destroy usable facilities and make that list longer? Doesn't that sound backward to you?"

"R-right."

"Plus, we're at war right now. In order to continue this campaign, we need weapons, armor, arrows, medicine, food, money, and all kinds of other supplies. The more we have, the better. You get that, right, Kousuke?"

"I do."

"So I object to being called greedy... That's so mean." Melty began to wipe her eyes with the hem of her clothes. She was clearly exaggerating, but yes, calling her greedy was wrong.

"I get, I get it," I said. "I took it a step too far."

Melty smiled brightly. "As long as you understand." She sure did switch gears fast!

"So, morale, huh? I guess I shouldn't be surprised."

"Indeed," said Madame Zamil. "The rifle squad never seemed particularly concerned, but the infantry were apparently quite worried. Even with the harpy bombs, they thought it would be difficult to emerge victorious when faced with charging cavalrymen or mage squads. The one-and-done destruction of the fortress seemed to put their hearts at ease."

"Of course," Sir Leonard said. "No matter how massive the enemy forces are, one of those is enough to eliminate them."

"Since we haven't signed any war treaties, we can do whatever horrible things we want, but if we take that for granted, it's going to come back to bite us," Melty pointed out.

"We can cross that bridge when we come to it, no?" said Sir Leonard. "Winning is our first priority."

"Thinking like that is only going to cause more issues for Sylphyel, me, and the royal family back at the castle."

"If we do not win, none of that even matters. If we have a means by which to slaughter our enemy without any casualties on our side, we should use it without hesitation."

I could almost see the sparks flying between Melty and Sir Leonard as they made their respective arguments. Pirna was watching them with a pained grin on her face. For her part, she was fine with using them. She would follow our orders, I guess. Or more specifically, in this case, *my* orders.

I glanced to the side, where Sylphy was gazing at the two engaged in a fierce debate. She seemed to be in deep thought. She was more than likely reflecting on the topic at hand.

Soon, her gaze turned toward me. "What do you think, Kousuke?"

At that, everyone at the table turned my way. It felt like their stares were going to burn holes into me.

"Quite frankly, they don't cost much to make," I said. "We could use as many gleaming magic jewels as we wanted, and magic crystals could be replaced with large magic jewels if necessary. So we could use these gleaming magic jewel bombs without taking any sort of monetary hit. But I don't think we should."

"Why?"

"Use a trump card at the wrong time and it can turn into

a noose around your own neck. If we have other options, we should use them even if it means a little extra work and sacrifice on our end. Quite frankly, I'm terrified by this new weapon. I can end hundreds, if not thousands of lives in a single instant. I don't think we should hesitate to use it when we absolutely must, but it doesn't feel right to just wield this kind of insane power with reckless abandon. Plus, when you consider the future, it might not be a good idea to kill more of their soldiers than we have to, no?"

"That is true," said Sylphy. "It would not be wise to draw more animosity than necessary."

"Agreed. Our final objective in all of this is to occupy Merinesburg, take out the army coming for us, and rebuild the Kingdom of Merinard, right? If that's the case, eventually we will have to make the Holy Kingdom recognize us through political means. Am I wrong?"

I glanced at everyone in the room.

"The gleaming magic jewel bomb will be one of our cards in those discussions, which is why I think we need to be very careful about their use going forward."

"Well done, Kousuke," Melty said. "You're nothing like the meathead men I know."

"I was simply thinking about how best to take care of our own. What do you think, Madame Zamil?"

"We should use them when the time calls for it." Madame Zamil cast her gaze toward Sylphy. In other words, she would deliver the final call on this.

"Understood," Sylphy said. "Considering its effects on negotiations in the future, whether we use the gleaming magic jewel bombs will be my decision. All right, Kousuke?"

"Sure."

But in the end, I had the final say. It would be up to me whether to produce a bomb on her command or not. She had no means of accessing my inventory without me, so I was the final line of safety before committing mass murder.

Not a role I wanted.

Seeing my expression, Sylphy grimaced. "Do not make that face."

I must've looked terrible.

"Then this is it regarding the gleaming magic jewel bombs, correct?" she said. "Everyone, rest well and prepare for tomorrow."

The meeting's attendees parted ways at Sylphy's command, leaving behind only me and her.

"What about the others?" I asked.

"Not satisfied by just me?" said Sylphy.

"Please. I was just curious."

We didn't have too many opportunities to be alone like this. At the end of the day, everyone got along well, and it was kind of like I was a feast for them to share. But if I didn't have the health and stamina system I was granted upon coming here, I would have died a long time ago, no joke.

"So, what brought this about?"

I stuffed the meeting table and chairs into my inventory and pulled out the usual couch and wood table, plopping them down.

I was capable of turning a location into a living room at the drop of a hat. Super useful.

"No particular reason," Sylphy replied. "Melty couldn't leave the management of procured supplies to her people entirely, so she went to go look over things. Ira has a meeting with the mage squad. Pirna said that the harpies are super high energy right now due to all the bombing runs and the gleaming jewel bomb today, so she's going to calm them down."

"I see."

I nodded while the two of us sat down side by side. Apparently, this wasn't part of some plan or anything, though I didn't doubt that they were being mindful in their own way, trying to give us time together.

"I know we are only on day two of our campaign, but you must be exhausted," she said. "You have never been okay with seeing a lot of people die."

"You're not wrong."

I'd done all kinds of awful things in video games, but I didn't have that kind of experience in real life, obviously. But compared to when I first came here, I'd gotten much more used to this kind of violence. Hell, I'd murdered Holy Kingdom spies with my own two hands.

"This is what it means to walk beside me," Sylphy told me. "Terrible, right?"

"It ain't easy mentally, but being with you is more important to me."

Sylphy considered my answer for a moment. "I see."

She then leaned her body up against mine. This was normally the kind of atmosphere where I'd whip out some mead, but today, it seemed like she wanted me to dote on her more than she wanted to drink.

"There, there..."

I gently pulled Sylphy down so I could rest her head over my thighs, then began to stroke her hair, prompting her to narrow her eyes like a pleased cat. Despite spending all day on the dirty battlefield, her hair still felt smooth. Was this some kind of power unique to elves?

"You've been working really hard, Sylphy. I know it must be difficult to shoulder everyone's lives and make harsh decisions."

"It is so very difficult."

Sylphy closed her eyes and let out a sigh as I stroked her head.

Liberation Army soldiers could die as a consequence of her orders, and with just one command, hundreds of Holy Kingdom soldiers would be annihilated. For two straight days in a row, Sylphy had needed to make these decisions. I couldn't imagine that was good for the heart and soul.

"You're doing great, Sylphy," I told her. "Everyone knows it, myself included."

"Really?"

"Really. That's why I want you to let me dote on you tonight. I'll do anything you want me to do."

"Anything? In that case..."

Sylphy held nothing back, requesting everything she wanted of me. Yes, yes. Daddy's right here.

"Sylphy?"

"…"

The next morning, Sylphy was back to normal and hiding beneath the sheets in shame.

"What exactly did you do last night?" Melty asked.

"Can I tell her?" I asked.

"If you do, I'll be forced to kill you and take my own life."

Sylphy was totally serious.

"There you have it."

"Then I guess I can't ask. How unfortunate."

Melty gave up quickly, perhaps having sensed that Sylphy was indeed not kidding. That was for the best. I certainly didn't want to accidentally say anything and get punished for it.

CHAPTER 5

Taking the Capital

"**W**E'RE FINALLY HERE."

"Yeah, though it doesn't look like things are going to go all that smoothly."

Today, we had yet again made our way through multiple defense points, crushing them as we passed. A few hours had gone by, and our strike force had finally arrived at Merinesburg.

It'd been three days since we left Arichburg. Considering how many enemy bases we'd destroyed since our "march" began, we got here stupidly fast. If we'd been able to prepare more airboards to carry our troops, we wouldn't have had to crush all the bases on the way over, but that was something to think about later. Hopefully we could find an easier way to make everything work.

"That's a whole lot of people... How many, you think?"

"Well, over a thousand, certainly. Maybe less than two thousand?"

The enemy was in front of us, dressed in matching armor and lined up neatly. On the front lines were heavily armored infantry, while behind them were spearmen. Further behind were bowmen. To the right and left of these soldiers were the calvary.

Meanwhile, we had exactly five hundred soldiers. We couldn't know for sure until our recon harpies reported back, but when it came to sheer numbers, they must have two to four times more people than we did. If we tried to face them in a full-frontal assault, we shouldn't have a chance of winning.

"Normally, this'd be a pretty demoralizing gap in power..."

"They look like fish in a barrel," Sylphy whispered with a pained grin as she looked at the enemy encampment.

From next to her, Ira said something extremely frank: "Should we bother asking for their surrender?"

"Well, just for the sake of adhering to form. I doubt they'll comply, but..."

"Yeah..."

Ordinarily, in this world, numbers equaled power. The side with less soldiers asking for surrender was unspeakable. Even though we were riding unusual vehicles, we had less than half the military might they did. Demi-humans were powerful fighters, but in a battle on an open field, numbers were everything. Or at least, that's what they were probably thinking to themselves.

"Shall we?"

"Yup!"

I handed Sylphy the mic, and she cleared her throat a few times before speaking into it.

"I am the leader of the Kingdom of Merinard Liberation Army, Sylphyel Danal Merinard. To the members of the Holy Kingdom dispatched within our territory: Lay down your arms immediately and surrender! Should you choose not to comply,

you will have sealed your fate. Should you disarm and surrender, we promise to see you safely back to your country."

Sylphy's voice echoed throughout the area, and after a brief period of silence, we could hear laughter from the enemy's encampment. I couldn't make out any words, but I could tell they were making fun of us.

"Doesn't sound like they'll be surrendering," I remarked.

"Sure doesn't," said Sylphy. "Oh well. Rifle squad, begin your attack. We have lots of space out here, so go wild. Harpy bombing squad, destroy their rear forces. Infantry, wait here. Your job will be to take down any fools who try to take to the fields."

After we'd heard back from the various squad leaders, the harpies immediately began to take to the air in front of us, and the rifle squad took off on their airboards.

In response, the spearmen in the Holy Kingdom's army stepped forward and thrust out their spear tips like hedgehogs. They must've judged our airboards to be like chariots. Unfortunately for them, they were not that easy to deal with.

Shortly after, the sound of machine gun fire filled the air, and the spearmen began to collapse in bloody heaps.

"Oho ho, they're firing arrows."

"Meaningless in the face of my Stop Barrier."

Just as Ira said, the arrows raining down on us lost all of their momentum before they could reach the airboards, falling straight down to the ground. The mages aboard the airboards were using Ira's new barrier magic to keep everyone safe. I didn't know how it worked, but it apparently drained the incoming arrows of their kinetic energy. She'd mentioned something about having some struggles with target designations or something like that, but it was all beyond me.

As our rifle squad carved away at the enemy forces, explosions eventually began to erupt from their rear. The harpy aerial bombing squads had arrived above the enemy and were dropping bombs down on them from beyond the range of their arrows.

"This never stops being hard to watch," I said.

"It's a one-sided massacre yet again," Sylphy agreed.

The Holy Kingdom's forces were already in disarray.

And that made total sense. They were getting trounced from the front and back. Those on the front lines were massacred by never-before-seen weapons and were basically in a state of panic, while the rear forces were reduced to chunks of flesh by the aerial bombing. The chain of command meant nothing in this situation. Not to mention, their tightly packed formation was a poor move.

It wasn't long before the Merinesburg defensive line collapsed. All it took were twenty riflemen attacking with machine guns and some aerial bombs from our harpies to annihilate a military force of one to two thousand troops in a matter of minutes. It was something else. And gruesome at that.

"Should we rescue the survivors?" I asked.

"Hrm, good question," Sylphy replied. Her sharp gaze was pointed toward Merinesburg. She was wary of something. "I did not see their mage squad out there. What if they strike while we're in the middle of healing the survivors?"

"Ah, good point."

We couldn't yet afford to mindlessly put ourselves in the line of fire. Their forces were stationed fairly close to the walls of Merinesburg—about a hundred meters or so. Normal magic probably wouldn't reach us, but the type of chorus magic the Holy Kingdom used could hit us no problem.

As I puzzled over what to do, I saw multiple white flags rise from the city wall, and the gates opened up. This sudden turn of events caused a bolt of tension to run through everyone on the airboard.

"What's happening?" Sylphy used the golem communicator to contact our recon harpy and the rifle squad.

A rifleman got back to us, but they sounded confused.

"Um... A group of church clergymen have emerged from the gates waving white flags. What should we do?"

Clergymen, eh? Given the timing, was this Elen's doing?

"What's the move?" I asked.

"If they're waving white flags, we can at least hear what they have to say," Sylphy said with a shrug of her shoulders.

And with that, our battle for Merinesburg ended abruptly... I guess Elen had worked her magic behind the scenes.

Anyhow, all we could do was keep our guard up. If we weren't careful, we could still have the rug pulled out from under us.

The rifle squad ahead of us made contact with Elen and her people first. They reported via golem communicator that she wished to surrender and expressed her desire that we treat the injured.

"Leonard, Melty, and I will negotiate the terms," Sylphy said. "Kousuke, you will build the location for us. Let's see... It looks fine over there. All we need is a stone table and some chairs. Put the field back to normal after we've finished, please."

She pointed to a field off the side of the road, a location out of range of the city and its bowmen. The field certainly belonged to someone, but either it hadn't been seeded yet or was currently not being used, as there were no crops growing on it.

"Roger that," I replied.

"Understood," said Sir Leonard.

"Zamil, you stay with Kousuke. Ira, use the rifle squad as security and tend to the injured."

"Understood, Your Highness."

"Mm, okay."

Under Sylphy's direction, everybody got to work. It was then that another voice rang out.

"And myself? I have grown quite bored."

It was Grande, who had spent this entire time napping, eating snacks, and looking at the battlefield with a bored gaze.

"Hm, there's nothing really for you to do..." Sylphy mused. "If you could go back to your old form, we could use you to apply some pressure, but you have no interest in the conflicts of man, right? You don't have a reason to lend us your aid."

"That is indeed true. However, I am rather bored, so I shall tag along with you, Kousuke."

"The more security around Sir Kousuke, the better," said Madame Zamil.

With everyone's next move decided, we all disembarked the airboard and I stuffed it back into my inventory before Sir Leonard met up with us from the rear. We were all walking in the same direction: toward the city gate. Of course, not all of us were going all the way...

"Take care."

"Yeah, no worries."

Madame Zamil, Grande, and I were the first to say goodbye, as I had building work to do.

"Now, then, let's get this done."

I dug up a reasonable area with my mithril shovel, then started stacking stone blocks. Finally, I pulled out a long table and ten chairs. It all took a few minutes max.

"Your power really is rather mysterious, Kousuke, my dear," said Grande.

"Tremendous, even," agreed Madame Zamil.

"Ha ha ha, all the compliments in the world won't get anything out of me!"

I wondered if there wasn't more to do. Perhaps I could make drinks? But if the wind blew, sand and dirt would get into our glasses. There were no walls, after all. That prompted me to think about how useful bottles really were as a tool. As long as you closed the cap, you had nothing to worry about.

"Think I should prepare drinks?" I asked Madame Zamil just to be sure.

"I do not believe that will be necessary. I highly doubt they will think to drink them…"

"Good point."

Madame Zamil felt they'd be too wary of being poisoned.

"Kousuke, I am famished," Grande complained.

"Really?" I replied. "We're about to have an important meeting here. Can't you hold on a little longer?"

"Boo, boo, no, no, no! I'm hungry hungries!" Grande began to whine in the fakest voice imaginable.

"Aaah, young lady, young lady! You must stop at once! You're destroying the stone blocks I made with that tail of yours! Aaaah!"

She was just trying to annoy me at this point. I wasn't sure if she just wanted my attention or if she was plotting something else. Either way, she'd end up destroying the stone floor I made if she kept going. In fact, chunks of rock were already flying all over the place. She was so powerful!

"Okay, fine!" I relented. "What do you want? A hamburger?"

"A pancake! With lots of cream and jam!"

"Is that so? I don't think you can eat that while standing up."

"There is a table right there," said Grande with an innocent—well, innocent-*looking* smile that betrayed the thoughts in her head.

She was absolutely planning something.

"We'll be using that table for important business in a moment."

"Aaah, suddenly I feel like going on a bit of a rampage. Like I kind of want to destroy the floor and the tables and the chairs here!"

Grande opened and closed her sharp claws—the claws that possessed the strength of a grand dragon. If she wanted to, she could cut through 100mm steel armor, the table, or the stone floor here like it was nothing.

"Okay, okay! I get it! Does this work for you?"

I pulled out a single person table, but Grande shook her head.

"No. I want to sit there." Grande pointed at a single position at the meeting table: the very head. The birthday seat. *Jeez.*

"Miss Grande?"

"I have been super bored over the last few days. Can you not allow me this much?"

"C'mon..."

I looked to Madame Zamil for help, but she averted her eyes. Why was she doing this to me? Why wouldn't she help me? Was it because of her religious beliefs? I suppose there was nothing I could do about that. And if Grande got serious, we wouldn't be able to stop her. Although...maybe Madame Zamil could?

My compromises were rejected, and Grande refused to budge on the birthday seat, so I pulled up a chair for her and prepared a pancake. If she finished eating before Sylphy and the others came, there'd be no problem!

"Seconds."

"Coming up."

There was no way Grande would ever be satisfied with a single pancake. She had some way of storing the food she ate, too, so she would eat a shocking amount every now and then. Was her stomach connected to another dimension or something?

And so, as I begrudgingly served Grande, Sylphy and the others returned, along with Elen, her attendant sister, and a clergyman.

Sylphy narrowed her eyes at me. "Kousuke?"

"I had no choice."

I simply pointed to the busted-up stone flooring. Sylphy silently turned her gaze toward Grande.

"Oh, come on," said Grande. "It is fine, no? I am, um, what do you call it? An observer!"

Sylphy didn't remove her gaze from Grande even after she blabbered that excuse. Eventually, however, she gave up with a sigh and sat at her own chair.

"Members of the church, please, take a seat," Melty said.

At her guidance, Elen and the others sat across the table from Sylphy. I was only familiar with Elen and Amalie. There was a middle-aged clergyman who must have been high-ranking, judging by his ornate robes, and another middle-aged man adorned in warrior's armor, making for a total of four individuals.

Across from them were Sylphy, Melty, and Sir Leonard. Melty notwithstanding, the other two were fully equipped and projecting oppressive auras.

"Who is that young lady?" Elen turned her crimson eyes toward Grande and narrowed them as if she were looking at something bright. Did Grande also have that radiance thing? "She does not appear to be human..."

"She's a grand dragon with the power to turn into a form very close to a humanoid," Sylphy explained. "Her name is Grande.

She is not a direct member of our Liberation Army. She's here with the man named Kousuke over there due to their personal relationship."

"I am Grande. Consider me an observer of sorts, or as another object in the room," Grande proudly explained with white cream and red jam all over her mouth.

The present members of the church seemed to have no idea how to react to her, and I understood their confusion. How could you possibly believe that this little girl was a grand dragon? If I was in their position, I certainly wouldn't have.

"This is no lie." As soon as Elen spoke up, the confusion among the members of the church hit a whole new level. They put absolute trust in the Saint of Truth's abilities, and if she was saying Sylphy was not lying, then there was no lie. Yet even still, it was clear from their reactions that they found it all too hard to believe.

"Pay her no mind. As she said, she is nothing more than an observer. Shall we continue our discussion?" Sylphy suggested, causing our "guests" to adjust themselves to face her.

But Elen, well, she was focused on Grande. Or more specifically, focused on the pancake the dragon was eating. As soon as she noticed me looking, she began to stare back at me.

How could I possibly bust out pancakes at a time like this? I shook my head, but she simply let out a sigh that screamed "you are so useless." I wish she wouldn't ask the impossible of me.

"If you would have us pay her no mind, then we shall do as such," said Elen. "Shall we begin our discussion?"

Elen turned her crimson eyes to Sylphy, who responded in kind.

I probably wouldn't get in a word here, so I simply wiped Grande's mouth clean while watching over the meeting.

"Let us begin with our demands," Sylphy said. "We request that the Holy Kingdom release Merinesburg to us, the Liberation Army. Additionally, we want all soldiers within Merinesburg to disarm immediately. We will also be confiscating all weapons being stored within the city."

"Is that all?" Elen asked.

"More or less, yes. Our objective is to take back the territories of the former Kingdom of Merinard and rebuild. We do not treat demi-humans or humans differently in our nation. We are all humanoids. That's why we will not chase out or execute anyone simply on the grounds that they believe in Adolism. However, we will also not allow any violence to be enacted against demi-humans in the name of Adolism. If anyone cannot accept that, they will be exiled," Sylphy explained, her amber eyes locked on Elen.

"I see. I understand your demands. Then can I assume that you will not be killing or stealing from citizens en masse?"

"Correct. However, there are those who treated demi-humans horrifically, and they will suffer the consequences. We understand that citizens of the Holy Kingdom have abused demi-humans and refer to such acts as 'enlightenment.'"

"Not all citizens of the Holy Kingdom have performed such acts," Elen whispered, furrowing her brows.

"Enlightenment" was another word for the act of violence toward a demi-human. They simply tried to make it sound like something nice.

According to the teachings of the main sect of Adolism, demi-humans were born sinners. As such, the faithful and just followers of Adolism had to give a helping hand by punishing them. *Supposedly.* No matter how they tried to gussy it up, it was just physical abuse. Kicking and punching, working them to the bone while depriving them of food or water, and all kinds of other unspeakable horrors. Not that I had seen any of this firsthand.

"We are more than aware," Sylphy replied. "We also know all too well that the primary offenders are nobility and those from wealthy merchant families—people with power. Them, and high-ranking clergymen of the church who should supposedly be pure of spirit. Additionally, we know that the reason the Holy Kingdom invaded our lands twenty years ago was because they wanted elves to help them increase the population of magic users within their own borders."

"..." Sylphy's ironic tone caused Elen's expression to darken even further.

"But there's no point in saying that to such a pure saint. I am simply informing you that despite being aware of these atrocities, we will not commit any unnecessary violence. I will not allow the soldiers of our army to steal or commit pointless murder. If I did, we would be just like all of you."

"Your Highness."

Sylphy was on the verge of saying more, but Melty raised her voice from the side and cut her off. Even then, it looked like she was about to say something else, but managed to stop herself and closed her eyes.

"The anger and rage that has built up inside of us over the last twenty years is no small thing," Melty said. "However, that is that, and this is this. Let us hash out the terms of your surrender."

And so the discussion switched gears as Melty began to talk about the disarmament of the Holy Kingdom's soldiers, how the temporary government would work, its defenses, and safety measures throughout the city.

For now, the church's military would be disarmed, and we would confiscate their armaments. As for the guards in charge of protecting the city, they would be allowed light armor, batons, and sticks. If we were to eliminate the presence of guards entirely, it was very possible the city would become unsafe.

Some of the Liberation Army's infantry would join with Merinesburg's guards to work together. I also thought it would be a good idea to have some harpy scouts dispatched into the air to make sure nothing was happening from up top. With golem communicators, they could act without having to wait for civilians to report things.

Additionally, we would instate temporary curfews for nighttime and make arrangements to keep the economic damage to a minimum. All kinds of small details were decided upon.

"How will we be handled?"

After the talks had settled somewhat, Elen asked an important question. It was not just herself she was referring to, but also the church members in positions of power within Merinesburg.

"As I said earlier, we have no intention of taking lives simply because you are clergymen of the church," Sylphy said. "I would take no joy in making your heads fly, and all it would do is scare the inhabitants of the city, which I also do not desire. For the most part, you will do as you have been doing, but under our supervision. Though I imagine you will have to adjust to our way of doing things."

"Will your people really be satisfied with a punishment as light as that?" Elen asked.

"That is my concern, not yours," Sylphy replied quickly and stood up. "First, we must disarm your men. If you do not wish for any more blood to be spilled, make sure you convince your soldiers to lay down their arms promptly. Leonard, bring half of the riflemen and infantry and take the city."

"As you wish."

"I will also head for the castle, along with Zamil, Kousuke, and the remaining riflemen. Lady Saint, you and your retinue will be coming with us. Chief Guard Gustaav and Leonard will be accompanying us."

"U-understood."

"Right."

The armored middle-aged man was named Gustaav, and he was captain of the guard. Instead of accompanying the Holy Kingdom's forces to the battlefield, he and his men had taken up a defensive position on the city walls. As a result, not a single one of his men was killed. Had he come out with the rest, they would've been reduced to nothing. The fact that he chose to follow Elen's words and surrender was a wise decision on his end, and one that saved many guards' and citizens' lives.

"We'll also come with you," said Melty, referring to the group of civil servants she had brought with her. They'd had nothing to do up until now, but this was their battlefield.

"Right," said Sylphy. "Could you also tell Ira and her mage squad to join us there once they have finished treating the wounded? We'll assign some of the riflemen and infantry we have with us to guard them. Also, tell the harpy recon squad to keep an eye on the city outskirts, and the aerial bombing squad to monitor Merinesburg." Sylphy nodded in response to Melty while also issuing out orders.

"Oh, finished already?" said Grande. She had been watching the meeting unfold with a bored expression after finishing her pancakes.

"Yup."

"Hrmph, why do you humanoids glare at each other so? I still do not understand after listening to everything said."

"Because it all traces back to the war twenty years ago," I told her. "There's a lot of context you're missing."

"Huuuh, humans cannot even live a hundred years, yet they meaninglessly go to war with one another." Grande stood up with an exasperated expression on her face and spread her wings wide. "You are going into the city, correct? There's nothing for me to do there, so I shall return home for a time."

With that, Grande launched herself into the sky, leaving the members of the church wide-eyed in shock. Maybe they had finally recognized her as the dragon she was. I understood their doubts, considering what she looked like. While she had dragon features, who would ever assume a petite-looking girl like her was a real dragon?

"Let us get moving," Sylphy said. "You lot are coming with us. Kousuke, ready the airboards."

"Roger that."

The unit heading into Merinesburg to take it over was one thing, but we couldn't afford to walk to the castle on foot. It was quite the distance away, after all.

I pulled out the necessary number of airboards from my inventory, and we began making our way to the castle.

On my airboard was Sylphy, Melty, Madame Zamil, Elen, Amalie, and Ira, who we picked up on our way over. The rest of the church folk were riding on another airboard. Guard captain Gustaav was walking with Sir Leonard to the castle.

As soon as I started driving, Elen began to speak, her face as expressionless as ever. "I was quite surprised, you know. If I am to be honest, I was rather concerned when I saw the numbers you arrived with."

Er, Amalie was with us, so was it really such a good idea to show concern for us and not the Holy Kingdom's forces?

"With the power Kousuke has been given, those numbers were nothing," Sylphy told her. "But are you really sure you should be speaking like this?"

"I cannot keep hiding the truth forever."

I glanced at the backseat through the back mirror to see Elen nodding her head as if she had no concerns at all. Next to her was Amalie, who looked extremely lost and confused. She turned her head to stare at me through the back mirror.

I don't know what Elen told her about me, but I imagined it was that she was cooperating with me, the Fabled Visitor.

I doubt she expected that I belonged to the rebel forces.

"U-um, Lady Eleonora?" Amalie asked. "What is going on?"

"I've been cooperating with the Liberation Army."

"Wha...?!"

"Kousuke brought us the old scriptures, but he himself has always been a member of the Liberation Army. He saved me by complete chance, and as I cared for him, he revealed his allegiances to me. I've been communicating with them ever since through the slimes that live in the castle."

Amalie was so pale that she looked like she was on the verge of passing out. I understood the feeling. Amalie was a pure and virtuous citizen of the Holy Kingdom and a follower of Adolism, and she had just discovered that the saint she served had been cooperating with the enemy. This must have been a nightmare to her.

"But the reason I have sided with the Liberation Army—or, more specifically, with Kousuke—is because of a divine revelation. I told you about what our Lord told me, right?"

"Th-then, you mean the murders of Captain Balto and the others..."

"Well, that wasn't intentional," Elen said. "Though I suppose I did taunt them a bit."

You did?!

"It was a truly fortuna—hmm, an *unfortunate* fate he met."

I wish she'd at least try to pretend she felt bad. She clearly looked like she was guilty! She wasn't acting the part of the saint whatsoever! Amalie was on the verge of collapse!

Sylphy glared at Elen. "You're supposed to be a saint? Are the followers of Adolism blind?"

Sitting next to her, Ira had also narrowed her large eye. Melty, on the other hand, was all smiles. I had the feeling she and Elen would get along great.

"In an organization of only a few thousand, perhaps everyone can get along," Elen said. "But in an organization of tens of thousands, maybe even hundreds of tens of thousands, people break off into different sects, individuals are driven by their own desires, and the reality is that it's much harder for everyone to cooperate."

"Horrific." Sylphy let out a sigh. "This is why I cannot handle humans and the way they dehumanize one another..."

"Demi-humans aren't any different in that respect," Melty pointed out. "Get three people together and you have a sect."

"Mm, Master told me about how they struggled with that," agreed Ira.

Sylphy looked as if she had been betrayed. Elen, on the other hand, smiled gently at her.

"I have been thinking this for quite some time," she said, "but for someone called the Witch of the Black Forest, you have quite the pure heart."

"Please don't look at me like I'm a child." Perhaps sensing her disadvantage, Sylphy went quiet.

Was it okay for me to be paying the backseat so much attention while driving? It was. Thanks to Ira's shock-absorbing barrier, if we hit anything, it'd feel very soft. It would also stop any incoming arrows or magic attacks.

"Um, Lady Eleonora?" Amalie spoke up again.

"Yes?"

"What exactly did your divine revelation show you?"

"Ah, well, I suppose there is no need to keep it to myself any further. My Lord said as follows: I would come face-to-face with death. However, upon overcoming that darkness, I would have a fateful meeting. I should then stay with them and live on. When that white pig bastard—"

"Lady Saint, language, please," I interrupted.

Elen cleared her throat. "Ahem. When the former archbishop nearly had me assassinated, I saw that as my coming face-to-face with death. Then I was saved by Kousuke. In other words, my fateful meeting. And that brings us to now. Since I have yet to lose my eyes of truth or my radiance, I can only believe that my interpretation has been correct."

I had been certain Elen must have already shared her divine revelation with Amalie, but that didn't appear to have been the case.

Sylphy and the others hadn't known the specifics either, as the expressions on their faces were intrigued—especially Ira's.

"Fascinating," she muttered. "Kousuke's appearance in the Black Forest also tracked with elven legends. According to those, he was guided to this world by the spirits. But the being known as Adol led Kousuke to meet the saint via divine revelation, and in Adolism, Adol is the one true God. This concept is the same across ancient and modern Adolist scriptures. And yet, Adol has granted the saint a vision that seems to recognize Kousuke's existence, a being that was guided here by the spirits. That said, Kousuke's powers are very close to being miracles, so—"

Ira's observations were whispered at high speed. Hah, she was steadfast, if nothing else.

"Anyway, I believe my actions fall in line with the Lord's desires," said Elen. "As a result, we have acquired original scripture and proved that modern Adolism is a violation of the original beliefs. I am sure our Lord will roast the corrupted upper echelons of modern Adolism, as they so deserve."

"A-are you really certain of that?"

Amalie was pale in the face, quivering. The difference in their depths of belief, or perhaps sanity in this case, had never been clearer. Since Elen had not lost her powers, she did not doubt that her actions were just and true. As a result, she appeared as though she felt no fear over the nearly two thousand lives that had just been lost. The power of belief was amazing...and also a little scary.

"We also took a look at the original Adolist beliefs," Sylphy said. "As far as we could tell, there was nothing within them that the Kingdom of Merinard could not accept. If nothing else, I have no intention of actively driving it out of the country."

"I...see..."

Amalie had lost all the strength in her voice. From her perspective, they'd been invaded by the enemy, had most of their protectors annihilated in a matter of minutes, nervously followed along with Elen's surrender, been brought straight to an important meeting, and then found out on the way home that the woman she served had actually betrayed the Holy Kingdom. Were I in her position, I'd probably have ulcers. I should give her a life potion later.

With that in mind, we continued toward the castle on our airboard until our destination came into sight.

"We're almost there!" I called back to them.

The backseat had quite the awkward atmosphere around it at this point.

But it had been some twenty years since Sylphy left this castle, and now she was finally back home.

"It would appear that Lord Dekkard is aware of what we've been up to."

I turned my gaze to the youth. He didn't need to say the obvious. Paras, the captain of the 3rd Order of the Holy Knights, acted as though he hadn't noticed. He was obviously ignoring me. This guy was a real pain in the ass.

A robed middle-aged man, the captain of the second mage squad cleared his throat and burst through the awkward atmosphere to report directly to his king. "Ahem... So, what shall we do?"

Hrm, I was being a bit immature. Paras was a youngster who had only just come of age, so as the older man, I needed to be more mature.

"We have no choice but to continue onward," I said. "It is annoying that the supplies have been decentralized, but if we send a messenger ahead, we can prepare what we need ahead of time..."

Dekkard, that damn apostate. Since he hadn't formally been excommunicated from the church, he'd used his authority to move military supplies. In order to move a massive military force without issue, one needed a detailed plan and a proper supply train, which were now in tatters.

Needless to say, the anti-rebellion subjugation forces were under my command, and I had the perfect supply plan. But that damn sly bastard... I would catch up to him and slit his throat.

"Would you like us to go ahead and take out Lord Dekkard?" asked Paras. "I do believe that would put an end to any further disruptions."

I shook my head. "No, that would be too dangerous. We do not know how powerful the rebels are, and Dekkard can use high-level miracles. I do not doubt the power of the Holy Knights, but it is entirely possible we could lose some of our fighting power. As the Holy Army, we cannot afford defeat. That's why we need to use our forces smartly."

Half of this was just for show. Paras's 3rd Order was nothing but the dogs of Cardinal Krone. Cardinal Benos had strictly prohibited me from allowing them to earn accomplishments on the battlefield. We couldn't let them overtake us.

"I see. Then I suppose that is that."

Paras gave up fairly quickly. I wondered what dark thoughts he harbored under his careful guise. This was why I could never trust a mixed-blood. I wouldn't have been surprised if someone told me he was connected to Dekkard or the rebels. After all, he was a filthy half-demi-human.

CHAPTER 6

Elven Royalty

THE CASTLE was still and quiet.

That made sense. The army that was sent out to defend the city from us had been annihilated in minutes, then we had made our way to the castle with their saint, along with approximately three hundred soldiers. They must have been scared. *What's going to happen to us now?* they were probably thinking.

"What's the play?" I asked.

"Our first priority is to calm everyone down," Sylphy replied, grabbing the airboard mic connected to the speaker.

I'd made sure that the mithril alloy cable had a bit of length to it, so that someone could use the speaker so long as they were relatively near the airboard. Not being able to use the thing unless you were actually on the airboard itself would've been a drag, so I was glad I'd lengthened the cable!

"We are the Merinard Liberation Army, and I am its commander, Sylphyel Danal Merinard," she announced. "We have defeated your Holy Kingdom army, and your saint has surrendered. We have accepted and do not wish to spill further blood. If you put down your weapons, we promise to do you no harm. However, should you resist, there will be no mercy. That is all."

Sylphy returned the mic to the airboard, then began to deliver orders to the infantrymen. First, they would put all of the confiscated weapons in the courtyard. Meanwhile, the civil servants would work on taking control of the administration within the castle, with the help of the rifle squad protecting them.

"And us?" I asked.

"We'll need you to put the confiscated weapons and goods into your inventory," Sylphy said, "but first, let us make for the royal family's living area. Ira, come with us."

"Mm, okay."

Ira nodded, and the mage squad responded in kind. Elen would also be coming with us.

"I too shall accompany you," she said. "Amalie and the others, please guide the civil servants."

"O-of course. Um... Will you be going alone?"

"Yes. It will be fine." Elen nodded her head expressionlessly to the worried sister and stood next to me. "Should things go sour, my destined partner will save me."

"..."

"..."

Elen pushed herself up against me, prompting Sylphy and Ira to narrow their eyes at her. *Eek!* I could feel the fireworks going off between them.

We made our way up several sets of stairs amidst this awkward atmosphere, eventually walking down a hall toward our destination. The furnishings in the castle were quite plain. Was this Elen's sense of style at work?

"How nostalgic," Sylphy murmured. "Memories from twenty years ago are coming back to me."

"Mm, it's been a long time," said Ira. "A lot of the furnishings have changed, but the castle itself is as it was. That candlestand is the same, for instance."

Ira looked at a candlestand on the wall shining a dull golden light. It was probably made of brass. I guess the Holy Kingdom's guys wouldn't go out of their way to pull a brass candlestand off of the wall, huh?

"Is it just me, or is it cold in here?" I asked. The further we walked, the colder it seemed to get.

"That means we are close," Sylphy replied, a rigid expression on her face.

Ah, right. Her father had used his powers to freeze the entire area. Normally, a person would die if they were frozen, but he must have used some kind of magic to keep his family in a sort of stasis. I decided not to think too hard about it. Trying to scientifically approach magic here was a fool's errand. Especially in matters of life and the soul.

If we were talking about purely physical phenomena, of course, that was different. Wind magic had all kinds of interesting applications. I'd also like to take a look at explosion-and-light magic as well. I bet we could make magic that shot out powerful beams of light, or even a laser weapon.

"This is as far as we go. Any further, and Lime and the others will stop us," Elen explained as we stopped midway through the hall.

At this point, we could feel the frozen air on our skin clearly. It was like we were in a fridge.

"Is it okay to keep going?" I asked.

"It will be fine," Sylphy assured me. "I'm sure they're watching."

She proceeded forward without a care in the world, followed by me, Elen, Ira, and the mage squad. The cold grew harsher, and it felt as though our skin was being rapidly stabbed. I could handle this, but poor Ira was shivering.

"Ira."

I reached out for her, and she took my hand in both of hers tightly. I used both of my hands to try and warm hers.

"So warm..."

"Only a little further. Hang in there."

"Mm."

Ira nodded, having regained some of her usual pep. Sylphy and Elen looked on jealously.

"Want me to hold your hands?"

Sylphy tried to play it casually. "Sure."

But Elen was as direct as could be. "Yes."

Both girls grabbed on to one of my hands each. I literally had a flower on each arm.

"Considering the serious situation we're in, I must look ridiculous."

"I don't think it matters," Sylphy said as we walked further down the frozen corridor.

Elen and I followed after her, almost like she was pulling us. Behind, I could hear the footsteps of Ira and the mage squad.

After walking for a bit, we eventually arrived at our destination.

"This is crazy."

The whole room was frozen over.

The fancy furnishings, the couches that were likely once soft, the beautiful princesses sitting on them, the king lying on the floor with the queen by his side—it was all frozen over. A single moment frozen in time.

A strange light enveloped the area. It was extremely similar to one I had seen before... Yeah, the second day...no, the morning of the third day after I had come to this world.

"Spirits?"

"Yes. Ice spirits," Sylphy explained.

Her gaze was set on the five individuals in front of us who were frozen asleep.

The king lying on the floor looked like he was in his late twenties or early thirties, and he was handsome as all hell. The queen was frozen with a sad expression on her face, letting him rest his head in her lap. Her facial features bore a strong resemblance to Sylphy's.

In the center of the room were the frozen princesses, two on the large couch together and the third on a smaller couch. They all resembled Sylphy in their own unique ways. Were they her little sisters?

"These are spirits? But..." Elen wore a troubled expression on her face, prompting me to tilt my head in confusion.

Meanwhile, Sylphy let go of my hand and stood at the entrance of the frozen room. With both feet planted firmly on the stone floor, she began to sing.

The song probably had no real words. So far, I'd been able to understand all the languages of this world, spoken and written—if there had been words, I should have been able to understand the lyrics.

But the effects of her music were astounding. The ice spirits that floated freely through the room while giving off a light blue glow suddenly began to circle the center of the room, almost as if they were dancing along to Sylphy's song. Their numbers gradually began to decline, and as they did, the frozen air started to warm up. Time within the room was beginning to move again.

The first person to open their eyes was one of the elven princesses who had her eyes closed and had been leaning next to the beautiful princess beside her. She was the smallest of the bunch, not much different from Ira in that respect.

"Mm... It's cold in here."

She shivered for a moment while rubbing her sleepy eyes, before casting her gaze upon Sylphy at the entrance, then the rest of the room.

Her blueish hair shook a bit, and her aquamarine eyes surveyed the scene.

"Who are you? If? Dori...?" The princess called out the names of her sisters, then began to try to shake them awake.

"It's cold..." The next princess awoke, the one who had been sleeping next to the first. Was she If, then? "Aqua...? Dori, and Mother, too? Father...?"

The young lady clearly wasn't entirely awake yet. She rubbed her eyes and shook her head a few times. She had red hair that shone brilliantly in the light. It was a color that could never exist naturally on Earth, yet, for some reason, it suited her perfectly. Her eyes were like emeralds, and she was thin, with long legs. "Slim" was perhaps the best way to describe her.

"Hm...?" The next person to awaken was the blonde-haired princess with the...filled out body who was sitting on the smaller sofa. She looked to be a little shorter than Sylphy, but she was... uh, yeah, bigger than her in other ways. Incredible. She destroyed the concept I had that elves were all slender.

The young lady seemed to have a headache, as she clutched her head with both hands and slowly looked around the room. Eventually, she turned toward Sylphy by the entrance.

"Sylphy...?" she said.

"Wha?"

"Whaaa?!"

The other two princesses raised their voices in shock, turning toward Sylphy. Apparently, they hadn't recognized her.

"Ix..."

The last person to wake from their slumber was the queen, and she whispered the name of who I could only assume was the king. She turned her sad gaze toward Sylphy, crimson eyes just like her daughter's locking on to her and opening wide.

"Sylphyel...?"

"Yes, Mother." Sylphy just barely managed to squeeze out a response with her near trembling voice.

"My word... I see you are still quite the crybaby. Come here." She smiled warmly as Sylphy slowly made her way over to her and collapsed to her knees, hugging her tightly. "Thank you... You must have gone through so much."

Sylphy cried quietly while digging her head into her mother's chest. Her mother simply kept caressing her.

While Sylphy let her mother dote on her, I crouched down next to the king and took his pulse. His body was cold as ice, and I couldn't feel a heartbeat. Just as Lime and the others had said, in exchange for his life, he froze time for his entire family.

"Lime."

"You caaaalled?" Something fell from the ceiling, immediately took human form, and tilted its head. As expected, she'd been keeping an eye on us.

"Can the king be saved?" I asked.

"Impooosible. He used all of his magic and life force twenty years ago, so his soul has shattered."

"I see..."

I was hoping there was a chance, but the world wasn't so kind.

"Either way, we can't leave him here like this..."

I peeked over at Sylphy, and she was still crying into her mother's chest. I couldn't just put her father's body into my inventory without her permission, so I decided to speak to her sisters first.

I stood up and approached the three princesses. The first princess to wake up had been called Aqua, and she had blueish-silver hair; the second princess was If, with brilliant red hair; and the last princess to wake up was Dori, the oldest of the three, and she had gorgeous golden blonde hair.

Apart from Dori, the other two had hair colors you would never have seen naturally on Earth.

"Hello," I said. "My name is Kousuke, and it's a pleasure to meet you all. In the Black Forest, Sylphy... Lady Sylphyel took me in and saved my life. Since then, I have been working alongside the Liberation Army to take back the Kingdom of Merinard from the Holy Kingdom."

"Is that so...? My name is Doriada Danal Merinard. I am one of Sylphy's three older sisters. The one with the red hair is Ifriita, and the other girl is Aqual."

"I see... Then the woman over there, the queen? Is it safe to assume that she is your mother?"

"Correct," said Doriada. "Seraphita Danal Merinard. The wife of King Ixil Danal Merinard and mother to the four of us."

"So there are four of you in total?"

"Yes." Doriada gave something of a troubled smile. I could only assume this was because of how much Sylphy had changed. In appearance, she looked about the same age as Doriada, or perhaps even older. She was likely taller than her, and she'd filled out in the same way Doriada had as well. On the other hand, even though Doriada had a smaller build than Sylphy, she was, um... just as explosive. I honestly didn't know where to look without being disrespectful. She was something else.

On the couch, Ifriita and Aqual had huddled together and were staring at me. Ifriita had a slender build, while Aqual was flat

like Ira. All three of them were truly beautiful. To some degree, I could understand why the Holy Kingdom was so desperate to get its hands on them. To the enemy, each one of them was a strategic material capable of producing mighty warriors. It was enough to make me want to throw up.

"First, I know this is all a bit disconcerting for you, but please do not worry," I told them. "We have come here together with Sylphy to save you all and fight to take back the Kingdom of Merinard. And that battle is reaching its end, I believe."

"Is that so...? How long have we been asleep?" Doriada asked.

"Approximately twenty years. I know waking up after such a long slumber must be hard on you all, so we can explain everything once you've rested."

"All...right." Doriada opened and closed her hands before standing up. "Ah."

"Er."

As soon as Doriada rose, her clothes evaporated, resulting in her two large fruits jiggling in front of my very eyes.

Oh, marvelous.

The air in the room froze, just like the way it had before Sylphy broke the spell earlier.

For the time being, I closed my eyes, covered them with my left hand, and then pulled out a pure white sheet from my inventory. I held it out in Doriada's direction. Needless to say, I made sure not to touch her when doing so. I knew just how far apart we were!

"Can I open my eyes now?" I asked, once I felt her take the sheet from my hand.

There was silence for a moment. Then I heard "Of course" in a low, embarrassed tone. I opened my eyes to find her now sitting on the small couch, her face bright red and her body wrapped in the sheet.

"So, um, my apologies," I said.

"N-no need to apologize. It was an accident, after all," she replied in a voice so quiet I thought she might disappear.

Not surprising considering she'd just been seen buck naked by a man she was meeting for the first time. In no world was there a man who wouldn't freeze up in that scenario. If anything, I wanted to be praised for how quickly I recovered and gave her something to cover up with.

"Um..."

"D-don't look over here!"

I turned my gaze toward Ifriita, who had pulled Aqual into her arms as if to hide her, her face bright red. She then held her palm out toward me.

Moving like that would obviously...

"Eeek?!"

"Hiyah!"

Just before their clothes could fail on them, I whipped out a second sheet and tossed it over their bodies.

"Wha?!"

The white sheet spread perfectly in the air, slowly falling over the girls. Heh, I was a man capable of learning! I wouldn't repeat the same mistakes twice.

"Melty."

Without turning to Sylphy and the others, I called for Melty, who quickly took the third sheet I had on my shoulders.

"Right," she said. She would handle the rest.

"Um, I imagine the low temperature probably damaged their clothes over the long years," I said.

"Mm, yeah," Ira said. "I didn't even realize."

"For now, I'll dump out a bunch of outfits in their size. Sorry, but could you carry me out of the room, Lime?"

"Roooger that!"

I pulled a bunch of women's clothes out of my inventory, then covered my face with both hands. I then felt something soft begin to carry me. Lime was so very convenient.

I didn't mean that in an insulting way, mind you. I just meant that she was very dependable.

Once I heard the door close behind me, I opened my eyes and found that Lime and I weren't the only ones to have left the room—Elen was here as well.

"I doubt they could relax and talk things over with a saint of Adolism present," she said. "I am nothing if not considerate, after all."

"Gotcha. Well, I'm glad Sylphy got to accomplish one of her primary objectives. Families should stick together if they can, huh?"

None of that really meant much to me. My parents were divorced, and my mom died of an illness. My old man and I weren't exactly on speaking terms, either. I was sure I had some happy family memories buried somewhere deep down, but if I did, I couldn't recall them.

"Do you not have any fond memories of your family?" asked Elen.

"I wonder," I hummed. "It's kinda complicated. Not something I can explain quickly, I guess. My sense of what it means to be married differs pretty hard from how it is in this world."

Unless a couple were devout followers of religion, the Japan I knew treated marriage more casually. You went to city hall, filled out some paperwork, stamped some things, and that was that.

I knew things weren't *actually* that casual; when you got divorced, I knew you had to pay certain fees and child support, and that it was all kind of a pain.

I had seen all sorts of things on the road to my parents' divorce, so to me, marriage and the very concept of family felt a long way removed. Like I was watching something through a monitor. I could watch and observe them, but I could never reach out and touch them, nor did I want to.

"I do not have many fond memories myself," Elen said. "Both of my parents were firm believers of Adolism, so when my powers came to light, they immediately handed me over to the church. In exchange for gold, I should add."

"Well, that's an unpleasant story."

"As the saint, they handled me with the utmost care, making sure I was raised and fed well. Meanwhile, my parents probably lived a good life thanks to the gold they received. Nobody turned out for the worse."

"Give me back my sympathy."

"You would request the return of something without a physical form?" Elen narrowed her red eyes at me as a thin smile formed on her face. She held her body like she was protecting herself. "Then I imagine you will request all manner of vulgar things from me, won't you?"

"Oooh, Kousuke is a schemer?" said Lime, watching us with great excitement.

"You've got it wrong. I'm a gentleman."

I could feel myself growing exhausted just talking to these two. But I had to say, I appreciated the lighter atmosphere.

"Well, either way, this is an emotional reunion for Sylphy," I said. "When they're done, the real struggle begins."

"Sounds like you have quite the struggle ahead of you. Hee hee." Elen made it sound like it had nothing to do with her, but little did she know, she was going to be doing a whole lot of helping out. As for what I planned to make her do, I hadn't figured that out yet. But I would!

"Can I help toooo?" asked Lime.

"Good question... If we find something you can help with, do you mind?" I asked. "For now, I'd like you to focus on protecting Sylphy and the royal family."

"'Kaaay!"

Lime was so earnest and adorable.

Just as the thought crossed my mind, I noticed thick red and green fluids emerging from the corners of the hallway. Bess and Poiso were here.

"Ah, I'm sooo exhausted!" I raised my voice. "If only Bess and Poiso were here to make me feel better!"

"I suppose I have no choice, then," said Bess.

"You called, and I'm here!" Poiso chimed in.

The two slimes emerged and combined with Lime to lift me up and begin vibrating. I felt like a portable shrine one might find at a Japanese festival.

"You really *do* have a broad strike zone, don't you?" Elen remarked. "Humans, demi-humans, monsters. It doesn't matter to you at all."

"Lime and her sisters are more like spirits than they are monsters, I'll have you know," I replied. "For some reason, faeries and spirits are drawn to me even though I don't have a lick of magic energy in my bones. More importantly, these slime girls make the comfiest bed in the world. You should give them a try."

"I suppose I will. Just for a moment."

Elen had her guard up, but, seeing that I was having no issues, she decided to try the slime bed. Heh, she was going to experience a comfort so amazing that she'll never want to do anything else!

"Kousuke, sorry to keep you—what is going on here?" Sylphy cut herself off as soon as she saw us.

I totally understood where she was coming from. After her emotional reunion with her family, she came in here only to find Elen and I half submerged in the slime girls, enjoying a moment of bliss. Our bodies were being massaged, and on top of that, Poiso was producing the most refreshing of aromas.

The combo of massage and aromatherapy was something else. Both Elen and I had been through a lot physically and mentally, so this was all extremely effective. In fact, it felt so good that nothing else seemed to matter.

Sylphy covered her mouth and nose with a piece of cloth and glared at Poiso. "You better have not mixed any dangerous elements into that aroma of yours."

Aaah, this felt amazing.

"Nothing addictive!" Poiso insisted.

"Release Kousuke and the saint at once," Sylphy demanded in a serious tone, clenching her fists.

Heh heh, yoooo, Sylphy! Don't be such a hardhead! This aroma makes you high as hell!

"These two were so stressed that I had to go this far, you know," said Poiso.

"I'll keep that in mind, but I can't have these two like this right now," Sylphy insisted. "Get them back on their feet."

"You sure treat us spirits roughly." Poiso sighed, and a tremendous scent suddenly shot through my nose and straight to my brain.

"Buah?!"

"Nngh?!"

It was like when you had too much wasabi or something! *Ow!* It hurt!

"Nnnngh..." Elen was gripping her nose, tears flowing from her eyes. This was way too much just to get us back at attention. She did look adorable, though.

"Back to normal?" Frowning, Sylphy grabbed my nose and turned me in her direction. "Kousuke?"

"Kerblaaah."

When I tried to shoot a look at Elen, Sylphy forcefully pulled me back. She looked cute with a frown. How could such a creature be so adorable? Was this jealousy? Was she jealous? She was reacting more intensely than ever before! In fact, this might've been the first time she let it show so clearly.

"Here I cooome!" chirped Lime, putting her hand around Elen's nose to do...something.

"Nngh?!"

Actually, I knew exactly what she was doing, and depending on her methods, Elen might require a psychiatric checkup. Give the girl a break, Lime.

"I cannot believe you would be so violent against a holy saint..." Elen had been released from the slime bed and was on all fours, trembling. Having one's nose blown the slime way was apparently a bit too much for her.

As for me, well, I was currently having my clothes adjusted. Sylphy had pulled me out of the slime bed a bit forcefully. At times like this, I was best off going with the flow and letting her take care of me. I had learned this over my time here, if nothing else.

"They are ready to... I mean, we're ready to begin the meeting," Sylphy said. "Come in."

"Understood."

"All right."

Elen switched to her expressionless saint mode in an instant. Behind her, Lime was using one of her tentacles to fix her clothing. I couldn't help but find the sight kind of heartwarming. In fact, it seemed to me like Lime was growing rather fond of Elen. When Bess became a bed for her and Poiso a blanket, I felt no animosity from them toward Elen. If anything, it seemed like they had some affection for her.

Had they grown close while working together to communicate with the Liberation Army? Or did Elen possess something that drew the spirits to her? Either option seemed likely.

With that in mind, I returned to the once frozen room...

...And I managed to resist the urge to raise my voice.

All right, Aqual was fine. Sure, her outfit was a little bit frilly—she was wearing the magical girl outfit I'd made for Ira—but that was fine. Depending on your perspective, she was just wearing a cute dress.

But Ifriita, well. She was wearing a red tracksuit for some reason. Sure, it kept you covered up entirely, but why a red tracksuit? Because her hair was red? An elven princess wearing a red tracksuit just felt all sorts of off to me.

She glared at me. "What?"

"Oh, nothing."

I averted my gaze only for my eyes to settle on Doriada and her no-sleeve knit sweater. Oh... Excellent. I remained puzzled by her choice, but she looked great in her new attire. Large breasts and sweaters with vertical stripes were the perfect combo.

"Ow!"

"You're staring too hard."

Sylphy had pinched my thigh, but I didn't *think* I was staring that hard... And now Doriada looked all embarrassed because of what she said.

"I must apologize for the trouble we have caused you, Sir Kousuke... No, Lord Kousuke."

I turned in the direction the voice had come from.

How could I best describe her...? She was stunningly beautiful. She had the same amber eyes as Sylphy, and each strand of her hair was like a beautiful, shimmering silver thread. Indeed, this woman had both Sylphy's eyes and her hair. Her features resembled hers as well. They were undeniably mother and daughter.

She wore a black dress, and she directed a smile ever so slightly tinged with melancholy at me. I knelt before her and lowered my head. Regardless of how she would be treated going forward, right now, she was the wife of the deceased king of the former Kingdom of Merinard. I felt I should show her the utmost respect. I would put aside the fact that Sylphy and I were intimate, or that her daughters were all sending me unfortunate looks.

"I am undeserving of such words, Your Highness," I said. "Since I was born and raised in another world, I am certain I might come off as rude or unbecoming at times, so I only ask for your mercy."

"Please, there's no need to be so formal," she assured me. "Sylphyel has told me that it would have been nigh impossible for her to come this far without your help. And that you are indeed a visitor from another world. A Fabled Visitor. Is that correct?"

"Um, yes."

"Then that's even more reason for you to drop the formalities. Real Fabled Visitors hold rights and powers equivalent to royalty in many ways. And as far as I have heard from Sylphyel and Melty, you are in fact the genuine article."

"Is that how this all works?" I asked.

"It is. And more importantly, you are Sylphyel's husband, are you not? I do not particularly enjoy making my son-in-law kneel before me." Seraphita gave me a slight smile. Was this her way of joking around? I had no idea how to react!

"Quite frankly, I would prefer if you had the time to speak to my mother and sisters and get to know one another," Sylphy said, "but we do not have the luxury of time."

"You can still call me 'Mom' you know?"

"Kousuke, I'm sorry, but could you put my father's body in your inventory? He's safest there until we can give him a proper burial."

"Sylphy ignored me!" Seraphita gasped. "Oh, gosh. Dori, Sylphy's hit her rebellious phase! What am I going to do?"

"Mother, I think Sylphyel is a bit preoccupied at the moment..." Doriada was doing all she could to comfort her mother, who was raining crocodile tears. Hrm... I could only imagine this was a front, locking up the deep sadness of losing her husband in her heart and doing her best to act cheerful for her daughters.

"I'm going with Sylphy," Miss Red Tracksuit suddenly cut in.

"If?" Aqual, still in her light blue frilly magical girl outfit, looked up at Ifriita next to her.

"Before we all fell asleep, I only backed down because of Father," Ifriita said. "But I haven't given up on the fight against the Holy Kingdom. I'm going to join the battle."

Miss Red Tracksuit was breathing heavily. The problem was that I didn't know her well enough to say anything one way or the other about her combat potential. Going by her name and appearance, it seemed like she'd have an affinity with fire spirits, which came with the image of highly destructive power, but was that actually the case? If this was just a misguided sense of entitlement coming from her position as a princess, she'd be nothing but a burden.

"My dear sister, If. I'm sorry, but I want you to stay back for now," Sylphy told her. "If we're going to take control of the entirety of Merinesburg, we can't afford to waste any time."

"I see your body *and* your attitude have gotten bigger since I fell asleep, Sylphyel. Listen, just leave this to me." Ifriita puffed out her chest. "I'll roast those Holy Kingdom fools with my magic!"

Yeah, this wasn't good. I shot a quick glance at Melty and Ira, but they simply closed their eyes and shook their heads with troubled expressions. Ah, okay. Got it.

"Sylphy, we'll handle getting Merinesburg under control," I said, "so you guys should spend some time together as a family."

I glanced at Ifriita, who quickly wrapped her arms around her body as if to protect herself. She was like a cat trying to threaten me.

"Hah."

"Hey, wait! Where were you looking when you laughed?! I'm gonna kill you!"

"Sylphy, I'm counting on you," I said.

"I know."

"Hey, wait a minute—gah! You're so strong?!" Ifriita yelped. "Wait, Sylphyel, when the heck did you become an ogre?!"

"Hee hee, my dear sister, shall we play for a bit?"

"Now's not the time for—hey, wait! Ow, that hurts! Aaaagh!"

I could hear Miss Red Tracksuit's screams from behind me until they were shut out by the thick door closing in front of her.

"Lime, Bess, Poiso. Protect this place, okay?"

"You gooot it!"

"Fine, I suppose I will."

"All righty!"

"Ira, Melty, Elen, Madame Zamil. Let's get going."

While Sylphy kept the berserker occupied, it was our chance to finish up everything we could.

Taking control of the castle itself went swimmingly. Melty gave the orders, Elen backed her up, and we got not just the Liberation Army but the folks who worked in the castle to work. It probably helped that the people here were afraid of our soldiers. After all, a force of thousands had been pretty much annihilated. For the people of Merinesburg, we probably looked like a terrifying force of nature.

The first thing we did was disarm everyone in the castle. We were going to have the rifle squad and special forces guard the castle, so we didn't need the Holy Kingdom's men. Obviously we didn't want them starting an uprising, so we made sure to take every last weapon and piece of armor they had.

Next we began taking currencies and foods. For currency, we took actual money, jewels, gems, precious metals, and even handwritten notes. We left behind the bare minimum in terms of art and furnishings, while the rest vanished into my inventory. We weren't planning on turning this stuff directly into money; I was collecting them so I could confirm their details directly. I would then pass that info on, a record would be written up, and tomorrow, we would return it to the nation's vault.

The same went for food. The stuff stored at the castle was there in the case of an emergency, so it wouldn't help to leave the shelves empty. If I monitored things myself, we wouldn't have to worry about stolen goods or things going bad, but then I'd be stuck on storage duties, so it was decided that we'd log it all up before returning it to the storehouses.

As for why we were doing this, it was because simply accepting the Holy Kingdom's materials as fact was risky. In the name of safety, the Liberation Army had to check everything anyway, so it made more sense to do it all together like this. Plus, if we found any inconsistencies due to shoddy management, it let us smoke out those who were responsible.

"So much... So much to do!"

Either way, after finishing things in the castle, I'd have to go around all of Merinesburg, hitting up barracks, lodgings, weapons storage, food storage, and collecting all their things. Then I'd have to visit the major power players in the city to take their stuff as well. In order to send things to the right places in the right amounts, we needed to confirm the total quantities of everything we now had.

Needless to say, my inventory was perfect for this. The fact that I could get an accurate number without doing much of anything was extremely useful since we were dealing with massive quantities. Tons of swords, spears, arrows, etc. And when it came to emergency food, I discovered we had tons that were no longer edible or usable. I also found plenty of cases where the Holy Kingdom's recorded numbers were totally off. One particular example was the flour— they supposedly had plenty in stock, but upon actually checking, they barely had anything at all. The management here was dire.

Every time we found an inconsistency, Melty wore the biggest smile on her face. She looked like she was having sooo much fun!

She was terrifying! Whoever was in charge, apologize! Before it was too late!

Once I'd wrapped that all up, it was time to hit up the facilities where we kept the prisoners of war. Most of the Holy Kingdom soldiers who went to battle were killed, so we didn't have many in captivity, but we did have a fair number of folks who had been wounded pretty terribly. They needed clean places to sleep and constant medical attention.

This was less of a prison and more of a hospital, to be honest. A hospital with very heavy security.

It was built after I'd demolished the mansion that was originally here. It had belonged to powerful people who had fled after they found out the Liberation Army was approaching.

I'd taken what little furnishings were left and tossed them into my inventory, then used my mithril pick to destroy the place and reduce it to base materials, which I then used to build this hospital-slash-prison. The fencing was tough and quite tall, so I left that the way it was. After I built a lookout tower, it was pretty much done. I also built a water tower in the center of the facility that used an unlimited water source. That was maybe the only thing that was worth special mention.

Oh, and when I was destroying the mansion with my shining pick and shovel, flattening the earth, and then building a stunning block of tofu... Er, I mean, a stunning prison, I was spotted by a few citizens. Honestly, there was no way I could have hidden the entire process. The area was so wide that trying to clear a space like that of all onlookers was near impossible.

After finishing things up, I had the aerial bombing squad carry over the prisoners.

Um, what was next again? Gah, there was so much left to do!

"I'm dead," I groaned.

"Weakling," said Ifriita. "Seconds."

"The heck is your problem?!"

"The fact that you actually served her seconds despite her being irritating speaks to how kind you are, Kousuke," Sylphy chuckled.

Despite saying I would return the emergency food to storage tomorrow, I ended up squeezing it in at the end of the day after wrapping up my other hellish tasks. As you might expect, I was dead by the time it got dark and I was finally freed from my personal hell. More specifically, it was Sylphy that saved me from Melty's clutches under the pretense of wanting to properly introduce me to her family and serve them Earth dishes. Sylphy was legit an angel. Melty was a demon.

So now I was in the middle of serving Sylphy's sisters and mother a variety of different Earth dishes. Aqual loved the desserts, Miss Red Tracksuit was super into the pasta and meat, and Doriada was enjoying some fried chicken and other junk food. Sylphy's mother seemed to be a light eater, so she was nibbling across a bunch of different dishes and enjoying the mead I'd put out.

"Amazing," said Aqual. "There are so many treats I've never seen before. It's like a dream come true."

"It doesn't taste half-bad," said Ifriita.

"It's all delicious," Seraphita told me.

I honestly couldn't handle Tracksuit's attitude, but she seemed to be enjoying her food as well. If I just considered her dumb comments to be the words of a young girl, it didn't bother me that much. Even though I got the feeling she was older than I was.

"You have so many talents, Kousuke," Doriada said with a smile, her cheeks puffing out.

It was a little unfortunate that such a pretty face was covered in pizza sauce, but I couldn't dislike a woman who enjoyed good food.

"I'm not really talented at all," I insisted. "This is just my power."

"I would argue that the ability you possess as a Fabled Visitor

is a talent," Seraphita said. "It's one that you learned how to properly use on your own, is it not?"

"I wonder, sometimes. I hope so."

Had I really mastered my powers? I wasn't actively trying to
unlock achievements or anything, and because I'd mostly just
been going with the flow, there were lots of things I still hadn't
unlocked. Quite frankly, I still hadn't entirely reached the depths
of this power of mine.

"You're surprisingly spineless."

"No, just objective. I don't have the confidence that I'm making full use of my abilities. I've killed a whole lot of people to get
here, you know."

I might've been able to reduce some of that bloodshed. But
I didn't think my actions were wrong, generally speaking. I may
not have taken the best path, but my goals were virtuous. After
all, we succeeded in freeing Sylphy's family.

"My apologies," I said. "I shouldn't have mentioned this during such a happy occasion."

"Please, as you are," Seraphita assured me. "We have to accept
the reality we have awoken to."

"Mother is right," Doriada added.

Twenty years had passed since these women were forced into
slumber. In that large span of time, countless demi-human lives
were lost or made miserable under the rule of the Holy Kingdom.
Not only that, but in order to save these women, the Liberation
Army had to kill countless Holy Kingdom soldiers. Right now,
the royal family was standing atop a mountain of corpses.

"We have to decide what to do going forward," I mused.

It wouldn't be an exaggeration to state that the reason the Holy Kingdom invaded Merinard was due to the existence of these women. They desired their blood, even if it meant going to war. Now that they had awoken, the Holy Kingdom might once again invade.

And even if we took back all of the Kingdom of Merinard's territories, what place would Sylphy's family have in it? The de facto leader of the Liberation Army was Sylphy, so of course they would be treated well. But was there a place in the upper echelons of the reborn kingdom for them? I wasn't sure.

Obviously, they were family, so it wasn't hard to imagine them being treated properly, but in terms of governmental positions or roles of power, I couldn't come up with any good ideas. I was no good with this kind of thing.

"Well, let's leave difficult matters to the side for a moment and just enjoy the fact that a family has been reunited," I decided.

"You're the one who brought this up," Miss Red Tracksuit pointed out.

"Ah, my apologies! Here, take this instead!"

"What is this... It's hot?!"

I thrust some takoyaki at her. Ha ha ha, after she was done eating it, I would tell her what the ingredients were. I was sure she'd end up needing therapy once she found out what kind of indescribable creature she had just eaten.

After our meal, we had the royal family take a break so that the heads of the Liberation Army could gather for a meeting.

Seraphita and Sylphy's oldest sister, Doriada, wanted to participate, and since the request came from the former queen, it was allowed.

"We won't say anything. We just wish to listen in."

"Mother, Sister, are you not tired after your long slumber?"

"We're fine, though If and Aqua have reached their limits."

Both women simply waved off Sylphy's concerns with a smile. They had a completely different aura. There was something inherently cultured and classy about them. Every move they made was refined, something Sylphy...lacked. Her education as a member of royalty was never completed, so it wasn't exactly her fault.

"What is it?" she asked me.

"Nothing at all! So, um, first, reports from each division, yeah?"

"Correct. Let us proceed."

Melty turned her gaze down to her memo pad, the one that I crafted and gave to her. These had been distributed to all the domestic affairs officers, along with ball pens. They, along with the vendors, had given them rave reviews. In fact, they'd said they could never return to parchment, wood, or quill pens.

"First, regarding the Holy Kingdom prisoners of war," Melty said. "We have a total of 168 people in captivity. They're all injured as well."

As far as I had seen, over three hundred soldiers had survived, though not all of them with limbs intact. There should've been soldiers held captive in Merinesburg, too. The numbers didn't seem to match.

"Those who had no hope of being healed and those who had injuries that would lead to critical aftereffects were granted mercy."

I shuddered at Melty's cold explanation. Mercy... In other words, they were euthanized. So everyone couldn't be saved? Potions made from Grande's blood could be used to restore lost limbs, but getting enough for hundreds of soldiers wasn't realistic.

"Did the church have anything to say?"

"Yes. In fact, this was a proposal from them and the critically injured themselves. Nobles and disabled commoners with no magic are often incapable of finding work, forcing them to suffer in poverty forever," said Melty with a shrug. "Though we don't ever intend on abandoning our own."

This was one of the many differences between the Holy Kingdom and the Liberation Front. In our case, since we had life potions, none of our troops would ever have to worry about those kinds of aftereffects. Even if they did, we could send them to the rear, where it was safe, and have them work as logistical support personnel. Obviously, we wouldn't be able to use potions made from Grande's blood on all of them, but we'd do what we could.

"Continue," said Sylphy.

"Yes, Your Highness. As for the prisoners, noblemen and those with magical power have been given magic sealing restraints and are being monitored. Civilian soldiers who suffered no serious injuries are being treated as they were up until now. When diplomatic negotiations begin with the Holy Kingdom, they'll function as our diplomacy card."

Sylphy nodded.

"We still have plenty of space for more prisoners, so we should be fine if we capture anyone from the incoming subjugation forces. However, considering the number of heavily wounded enemy soldiers from battles up until now, we are going to need more medical personnel if we hope to save their lives. We will also need Kousuke to mass-produce more medicine."

"Understood. Approach the saint tomorrow about the subject. We can arrange for medicinal herbs, yes? Kousuke, I want you to make life potions from the herbs that Melty gathers."

"Wait a second, Sylphy," said Ira. "I know Kousuke's medicine works wonders, but we also need normal medicine. If we forcibly requisition the herbs on the market, medicine prices in Merinesburg will skyrocket, causing discontent among the citizens."

Sylphy tilted her head. "Hrm... Then what should we do?"

"We should proceed with cultivating herbs," Ira replied. "With Kousuke's power, we should be able to mass produce them no problem."

"I see. Do we have a means by which to acquire seeds and seedlings?"

"Kousuke has some. Plus, we can order them from pharmacies and alchemists in the city. We could also have adventurers gather them from the local forest."

"I see. Melty, work with Ira to quickly get the medicinal herbs we need."

"As you wish," said Melty. "Next, I would like to report on the goods we requisitioned in Merinesburg."

To summarize Melty's report, we had acquired about two months' worth of food. *Two months.*

"In other words, we can remain here indefinitely?"

"Correct."

"Yeah."

"Mm-hmm."

"Indeed."

"Huh?"

"Whu?"

The only ones to react confused were Seraphita and Doriada.

I mean, it was true. If we had two months of leeway, I could reorganize sections of the city and build a large field rather easily. With enough time, I could even build fields that would quickly give way to crops on the roofs of all the houses. Of course, I would have to remake those roofs so they functioned properly, but two months would be more than enough time.

"There are materials we can't get within Merinesburg, so we couldn't hole up entirely," Sylphy said, "but our enemies would definitely fold before we had to. That being the case, I have no intention of just waiting out a siege."

"Um, Sylphyel? What is going on?" Doriada asked with a confused expression on her face.

Sylphy went quiet for a moment. Then she said, "With

Kousuke's powers, we can harvest crops in a very short amount of time. In fact, if he leads the process from beginning to end, it would take him three days to produce wheat."

It was easy to tell what Doriada was thinking. What on earth was she talking about? She turned her gaze toward the people around her—Melty, Ira, and Sir Leonard—but they all simply nodded.

Doriada looked even more confused.

"It's true," I said. "Even if I don't control the process, if it's farmland I prepared, another person could sow the seeds and see a full harvest in about two weeks."

Doriada looked at me, so Sylphy explained further.

"Doriada, I know this sounds like madness, but Lord Kousuke is a Fabled Visitor," said Seraphita. "If they say he is capable of such acts, then it must be true. You mustn't make any unwanted remarks."

"Y-you are right. I apologize."

"Believe me, we all know full well that Kousuke's powers lack common sense," said Sylphy. "It's completely fair that you would find it unbelievable."

"Mm. He's a mass of absurdity," Ira agreed.

Ira was constantly experiencing whiplash from my skills, and she was currently giving Doriada the gentlest of gazes. Even now, she would occasionally stare off in the distance after being faced with one of my absurdities.

"Next is...public order in Merinesburg. Leonard."

"We have taken control over all Holy Kingdom facilities in the city. The city guard has been cooperative. We have already finished

223

announcing a night curfew in order to curb crime and chaos. We have races with night vision patrolling the city and apprehending anyone who seems suspicious."

"You'll mostly be dealing with humans. Be gentle."

"But of course." Sir Leonard nodded with an extremely serious expression on his face. He could be very hard on members of the Holy Kingdom, so Sylphy must have been worried about him going too far.

"All that's left is...how to deal with Adolism."

The atmosphere in the room instantly grew heavy. Yeah, this was certainly an unsolved problem. I was personally against any overly cruel treatment.

"I see. That is a fair line to draw," Elen said, quietly nodding her head.

It was the next day, and we were in one of the reception rooms in the castle. She had just been told where yesterday's meeting had settled.

"If you think that all makes sense, you would be helping us greatly," Sylphy said, letting out a deep sigh from where she was seated across from Elen.

The conclusion yesterday's meeting came to was simple: maintaining the status quo.

Members of the church would obey the orders of the Liberation Army going forward, but any church property or fortunes seized would be returned to them. In exchange, they would strive to provide their visitors and those faithful with a sense of calmness and safety.

We would have the church work toward permeating their teachings with the original beliefs from the old scriptures we discovered, rejecting the demi-human bigotry that had been taught up until now. Since changing things all at once would only cause the people to distrust the church, we would be having them do this gradually.

As for the budget allocated from the Liberation Army (aka the government) to the church, after investigating how their current budget was being used, we would reevaluate the amount of funding they received. Elen wanted to use this opportunity to purge the greedy priests within the system. Those types mostly belonged to the main sect, so she wanted us to come up with some crime they might've committed and either exile or execute them. When discussing this particular subject, Elen had a great smile on her face. She really couldn't stomach the main sect's priests.

And so talks had come to a close for no—

"Sylphy! How can you even think to play nice with our invaders?! We should take them all, string them up, and light them on fire!"

Miss Red Tracksuit had been silent next to Sylphy this entire time, when suddenly some violent ideas burst out of her mouth. Sylphy simply covered her eyes with one hand and let out a sigh.

Elen, who was next to me, shot me a look that screamed, "And who is this idiot?"

I understood where she was coming from.

"If, didn't you promise not to say anything?" Sylphy said.

"I did. I did, but this is all so wrong! They're the ones who instigated the Holy Kingdom!" She pointed her finger at Elen, shouting loudly. "It's their fault all of this happened to Merinard! How can they just get away scot-free?!"

"Twenty years have passed since you fell asleep," Sylphy told her. "A whole generation has gone by in Merinesburg, and many followers of Adolism live there. If we, the de facto rulers, begin to massacre members of the clergy, public order would obviously deteriorate rapidly. Besides, Eleanor's faction of Adolism, the Nostalgia-sect, believes in the old scriptures, extols harmony with demi-humans, and they are very close to the ideals of our old Kingdom of Merinard. Joining hands and cooperating together can only benefit us both."

"But Adolism is the enemy!" Miss Red Tracksuit sputtered. "And you! Why are you next to that woman?!"

"Er, I mean, it'd look like we were ganging up on her three on one if I sat over with you," I said. "It'd be intimidating."

"Aren't you on Sylphy's side?!" She sat down again, pointing at me, then smacked the cushion. "Sit over here! What the heck are you doing?!"

"Hey, Sylphy?" I asked. "Is this really your older sister? Like, is she legit a princess? She's completely different from what I thought princesses are supposed to be like."

"If is, well, impulsive," Sylphy replied.

"Quite the considerate way of describing her."

"It must be quite rough for the Witch of the Black Forest to have such an unfortunate older sister."

"Why are you all ganging up on me like this?! Grrrr!" Miss Red Tracksuit glared daggers at us as she screamed loudly. Man, she was annoying.

"Okay, look here," I said. "Say we eliminated all of the clergy. What would we do if the followers started rioting? Would we kill them too? There are tons of believers in this kingdom now, along with the clergymen to match those numbers. You want to burn all of them to ashes? Who benefits from that?"

"W-well, I..."

"If we did that, there would be no reconciling with the Holy Kingdom. Are you telling us to wage war until one of us is completely annihilated?"

If we used the new bombs I'd developed without holding back, we could probably turn the Holy Kingdom into a wasteland, but I had no intention of ever going that far.

Miss Red Tracksuit went silent. If she was gonna get all teary-eyed after someone barked back once, I wish she would've stayed quiet to begin with. Dummy.

"Kousuke, I think that's enough for now," Sylphy said. "If is, well, still young."

"Young? Isn't she your older sister?"

"Sure, but as an elf, she's still a child. And since she was asleep for twenty years, there's basically no age gap between us anymore," Sylphy explained, looking at Miss Red Tracksuit with a caring gaze.

Miss Red Tracksuit... Ifriita held her head low, tears dripping from her emerald eyes.

Whoa, whoa, whoa! Why was she crying?! Now I looked like the bad guy!

"You made her cry-y! You made her cry-y!" Elen jeered, pointing two index fingers at me with the usual expressionless look on her face.

"Shut up!" I hissed.

"If, look... We're long past being able to just defeat our enemies," said Sylphy. "We need to be looking toward making them accept our terms, so we can end this war. And in order to negotiate with them, we need Adolism, because they have a pipeline to the Holy Kingdom. So we can't just do what you say, If."

"Though there are sections of Adolism you're more than welcome to burn to a crisp," Elen added. "Particularly, the rotten priests drinking during the day and bringing in women during the night."

"She's trying to talk sense into her, Elen, so please don't muddy the waters..." I sighed. "Actually, what happened with your boss? Shouldn't she have arrived by now?"

"She's running late because she's been trying to slow the subjugation army down as best as she can. She will be arriving tomorrow."

"Hrm, then she should get caught in our recon and security net," Sylphy said. "As soon as she's spotted, we'll be in touch. Let us prepare to welcome her..."

"Understood."

Sylphy left the room with the still-tearful Ifriita in tow.

"Are you not going with them?" Elen asked me.

"I made her cry, so..." I shrugged. "That said, I can't really hang for too long."

I had to sort out some fields for medicinal herbs and craft life potions using the herbs gathered from the marketplace—without hurting the economy too much. And if I was going to be making fields for medicinal herbs, I might as well grow crops as well. Potatoes and beans could be stored easily, and they wouldn't go to waste. If we had too many, we could sell them or distribute them as necessary.

"You are quite the busy man," said Elen. "Funny, considering my image of you is as a man constantly lying in bed."

"That's just because of how we met one another. I'm actually quite the hard worker."

I tried to flex, but Elen suddenly fell toward me. She placed her body down in my lap and turned so she was looking up at me.

"Well, I do not want to work. Everyone keeps coming to me, Lady Saint this, Lady Saint that. It is terribly exhausting."

"That sounds rough. You're doing a great job, though, Elen."

She stared up at me as I gently rubbed her forehead, and those red eyes narrowed happily. She looked like she was feeling great, and she was also adorable. I wanted to skip work too, but before long, a horned demon appeared to drag me off.

CHAPTER 7

The Calm Before the Storm

231

"**T**HE HARPIES seem to be moving quite frantically," I whispered, looking up to the sky.

I was in a corner of the large castle courtyard and was about to use my mithril shovel to dig up some dirt to make a medicinal herb garden.

"Really?" The beautiful girl who responded had gorgeous blonde hair like gold threads, blue eyes, and pointed ears that made it all too clear what race she was.

"Yeah. It's possible they've spotted Elen's—I mean, the saint's boss. Though this is later than scheduled."

The blonde beauty, Doriada, nodded her head in response.

When it came to long distance travel in this world, horse and carriage was pretty much it. But moving via carriage brought with it all kinds of problems. While they were typically built with magically enhanced materials that wouldn't break as easily, the axles apparently *could* break, so sometimes the wheels would come off. When monsters or bandits attacked, it wasn't just time lost but lives as well.

Therefore, people being late in this world was par for the course. In this case, because Elen's boss was a ringleader in the Nostalgia-sect, her position within the Holy Kingdom had suddenly worsened, so the main sect was probably trying to get in her way.

"You know, you are quite the fascinating individual, Kousuke," Doriada mused.

"I'm fully aware I've gone all-in on being 'fascinating.'"

How could I argue when I was able to dig up a giant area of land with one swing of my shovel?

"Were you given that mysterious power from the spirits?"

"Honestly? I have no clue. I just suddenly found myself in this world one day. I don't have any memories of speaking to God or any spirits. In order to survive, I wandered into the woods, suddenly awakened to my skills, and then met Sylphy right after."

"I see... Ah, how exactly did the two of you meet?" Doriada's cheeks lit up with excitement. "I am so very curious."

How the two of us met, eh...?

"It was so early in the morning, I couldn't see a thing. And that's when she knocked me out of my bed."

Doriada gave me a puzzled look.

"While wheezing from the sudden fall, I tried to grab my weapon, but she stabbed her knife into the palm of my hand, like this."

Now she looked even more confused.

"The pain was so intense that I fell into a state of confusion, and then she kicked me in the face. With the bottom of her boot."

The only word I could use to describe Doriada's face was "baffled."

"Then she stepped on me while I was on the ground. Her boot to my head. I could feel my skull cracking."

"Um, this is the story of how you met Sylphy, right?"

"Indeed."

Just thinking back on that time sent a chill down my spine. If Sylphy had truly intended to kill me, she could have snapped my neck before I even woke up.

"Our first meeting was extremely violent."

Doriada must have been expecting a more romantic tale, because she covered her eyes and let out a deep sigh.

"Then after that, well, I managed to not get murdered and succeeded in exchanging info with her," I went on. "She took me to the elven village, which is where the refugees, not even members of the Liberation Army, tried to lynch me. That was when Sylphy saved me and put a slave collar on me, turning me into, well...her slave."

Doriada turned away from me. "I'm going to go talk to Sylphy."

"Ah, aaaah! It's fine! Really!" I stopped her. "Sylphy made me a slave to save me from the refugees who all hated humans! She was kind to me, for real!"

Doriada had a horrifying aura about her. Something awful would happen if I let her go find Sylphy right now.

"Our first meeting was rough, but as we spent time together, she showed me all sorts of sides of herself," I explained. "That violent side of her really was just that one day. After that, the whole slave thing was just to protect me, so it was inevitable!"

"If you say so, then I will keep quiet. I won't say a word to her about it."

She didn't look entirely convinced, but I at least persuaded her not to go to Sylphy. Thank goodness.

"Can I ask you something?"

"What is it?" Doriada replied.

"Why are you out here watching me work?" I asked while designating a spot to place down farming blocks.

"I wanted to know what kind of person Sylphy fell for," Doriada answered earnestly. "She's physically grown quite a bit, but to me and Mother, she's still a child."

"I see."

To them, Sylphy had yet to come of age. Because of the way elf biology worked, her body had fully matured, and since she grew up in such a harsh situation, she was mentally mature. However, from an elf's point of view, she was undeniably still a child. It made complete sense that her mother and oldest sister would want to know what kind of man I was, if I was acting as her companion.

"Well, I can't really objectively assess myself," I said, "but I can state with all certainty that I love Sylphy, and I believe she feels the same. As for Ira, Melty, Elen, Grande, and the harpies, well, they all gave their consent."

I couldn't help but vacantly stare off into the distance. Saying it out loud really put my accidental infidelity into perspective. I had no excuses at this point. They were all important to me. In my old world, words like that would make me the worst man imaginable, but ethics were different here.

"Hee hee hee, it's incredible that you're so composed while dealing with so many women," Doriada giggled. "Have you considered adding one more?"

"Eek... You'll have to ask Sylphy and the others."

Since coming to the castle, the insatiable slime girls had been making moves on me. If I added more women, my life would be in danger. My survival instincts were telling me that Doriada was dangerous.

"Understood. I shall do as such."

With that, Doriada left, her feet light as feathers. What? Seriously? She was going to ask? How could I turn her down? What could I do?

"I'm counting on you, Sylphy."

After thinking so hard that steam began to erupt from my head, I abandoned all thought and decided to focus on work instead. I had to make a medicinal herb field, after all. It was necessary to keep casualties to an absolute minimum. I also wanted to make some other fields, while avoiding overproduction. Fruit trees would be nice. Yeah, and grapes might be a good idea. You could eat them as is, turn them into wine, dry them and make raisins... All right, it was time to get to work!

I completely emptied my mind of the unknown future rapidly approaching me and put my back into my field work.

Heya, folks! It's me, Kousuke. Things in the castle seem chaotic, but for some reason, nobody's calling for me! I mean, sure, there's no need to have me there to greet Elen's boss. After all, Sylphy is the de facto leader, and having Melty and Sir Leonard there as her aides is more than enough. I personally think I'm pretty much the number two in the Liberation Army, but when it comes to official positions, I don't actually have a title like Ira, Melty, Sir Leonard, Danan, or Madame Zamil do.

So, even with things in the castle being a bit hectic, I quietly focused on my work.

"Staaaare..."

"..."

"Staaaare..."

All the while dealing with the extremely oppressive staring coming from a certain elf princess in the shadows. Ha!

The way she was actually saying her actions out loud was pretty damn cute, actually. But her stare was anything *but* friendly! Ha ha ha!

I glanced toward her...

...And then she immediately ducked back into her hiding spot! The problem was that every time this happened, her blueish-silver hair would fall behind her, so it was easy to tell who she was at a glance. She was short as well, meaning this was undoubtedly the third sister, Aqual... Honestly, I wasn't sure how to refer to her, since she was technically older than me. But it was definitely her.

I'd finished with my digging work and spreading farming blocks, and I was now thinking while planting medicinal herb seeds.

Why was she watching me? It was reasonable to assume it was because I was closest to Sylphy. The whole family, herself included, seemed convinced that I was a Fabled Visitor, but she probably still found it difficult to trust me, as a human. Humans from the Holy Kingdom had cornered her entire family, forcing her father to sacrifice himself to save his daughters and wife. All of this had only happened a few days ago, from her perspective. And now one of those humans was calling himself a Fabled Visitor and currying favor with her little sister.

Little sister... Yeah, that was right. Sylphy was her little sister. Physically, Aqual was about the same as Ira, which meant that her, um...ahem, were similar to a young girl's. But even so, she *was* Sylphy's older sister.

"Dessert!" I called out.

Her long ears shot out from the shadows at this simple invitation, and yet she was still older than me, and Sylphy's big sister. Maybe it was less that she was monitoring me out of concern for her sister, and more that she wanted food.

I could feel the doubt rising within me.

I looked up into the sky, where the harpies had calmed down a bit, and decided based on the sun's position that it was just about snack time. Roughly half a year had passed since I came to this world, which meant half a year of living without clocks. Even I'd learned how to figure out the time of day based on the position of the sun, if only approximately.

Anyhow, I'd wrapped up my planting at a good point, so it felt like the right time to take a break. From here, I basically just had to set up an infinite water source. I would have to consult with Ira regarding the water supply. If I was going to automate it, I would need her to make the magic tools.

It made sense to take a break. I pulled a moist towel from my inventory and cleaned my face off, then set up a wood table and two chairs in a spot where I hadn't laid down any farming blocks.

It was time to face off!

Actually, no. I placed a sweet treat down on the table and gestured her over with a smile. More specifically, it was my brand-new creation: a strawberry parfait. Quite the masterpiece, topped with cream and strawberries in a most artistic fashion.

"Let's both have some!" I said.

Her eyes widened.

Of course, I'd prepared two parfaits. Given our relationship, sharing a single parfait was out of the question. Plus, since most people knew that I could make more than one of almost anything, nobody would ever fall for that tactic. But also, in this world, the concept of sharing a parfait and picking at it while giggling and getting all embarrassed didn't even exist.

Aqual emerged from the shadows after looking at me and the desserts but soon stopped in her tracks. "Uuugh..."

Apparently revealing herself to me was taboo, or at least that's how she made it seem.

"Well, I suppose there are some things you just can't expect people to get without talking it out," I said.

I wasn't sure if she agreed or not, but she nonetheless

approached her chair while remaining cautious of me. She sat down and took the parfait I passed toward her, said her thanks in a quiet voice, and then began to nibble at it.

Her face lit up.

"Mm, delish," I said. "Not bad if I do say so myself."

The sweet and sour flavor of strawberries, the sweet cream, and strawberry sauce spread throughout my mouth. The three flavors reached perfect harmony, filling my heart with joy. The balance was excellent. Even someone who wasn't big on sweet things could enjoy this.

"So, why exactly were you watching me, Your Highness?"

Aqual stopped nibbling at her parfait and turned her gaze toward me. It wasn't as hostile as before, but I could tell it was anything but friendly.

"Um, did I do something to upset you, Your Highness?"

She remained silent for a moment before finally saying, "You bullied If."

"Oh..."

I unconsciously looked up at the sky. I had in fact made Miss Red Tracksuit cry, but that was because of her insistence on an absurd plan. Sure, maybe it wasn't the most mature way to deal with a princess who had little worldly knowledge, but what she was saying had been absolutely unacceptable. I had no intention of taking back my words.

Aqual was watching me in order to figure out the truth of the situation. She must be quite logical. Hrm.

"Your Highness, I have no way of knowing just how much you

have been made aware of, but I can at least offer you my perspective on what happened."

"I will hear it."

Aqual nodded, so I politely explained the events leading up to me driving Miss Red Tracksuit to tears: that our Liberation Army and Ifriita's thoughts had diverged; that Ifriita had been saying things that could lead to a bloody battle not just with the clergy but between followers of Adolism, the Liberation Army, and the people of Merinard. I explained that the Nostalgia-sect of the church was a necessary pipeline to the Holy Kingdom and the main sect, so that we could end the war.

"And that about sums it up," I concluded. "As it stands, and given the state of things, if we did as Ifriita wanted, the sacrifices would be far too many. I am well aware that this decision goes against how she and Your Highness feel, but we simply cannot execute such a plan."

"I see," Aqual said. "I understand now that If had insisted on something very violent and off the mark."

"Thank you for your understanding."

"But could you not have explained as much to her without making her cry? Like you did for me just now?"

"Mm..."

I didn't have an excuse. I'd be lying if I said I didn't pick up the fight she laid down. I might've looked down on her for speaking like she knew what was going on.

"If can be short-tempered and intense, but she also has a very delicate heart," said Aqual. "Please be a little kinder to her."

"I understand. I shouldn't have been so harsh."

It was hard to turn down her request when she stared at me with such beautiful aquamarine eyes. Her body was so small, yet she had a sense of presence that didn't allow you to say no to her. Was this charisma part of being a member of royalty?

"You are an honest and kind person. Just the sort of man I would expect Sylphy's husband to be," she said with a smile before picking up her spoon again. The aura she was projecting a moment ago was nowhere to be found. Now she was just an adorable girl enjoying a parfait.

"Hrm..."

"Is something the matter?" she asked.

"No, not at all." I shook my head at the befuddled Aqual and started picking at my own parfait again.

Royalty was on another level. She looked young but was not to be underestimated. Unfortunately, that just made Miss Red Tracksuit stand out even more.

"Thank you for the treat," Aqual said after she'd finished her parfait. "I am quite glad we got to talk, and I hope we can get along going forward."

She elegantly bowed to me before leaving. That was like a curtsy or something, yeah? So if Doriada was the big sister type, then Aqual was the logical and courteous princess.

My first impression of her was as a timid princess who hid

in the shadow of her older sister, but... Actually, maybe that *was* her true nature, considering she had only just awoken from her slumber back then. Now that things had calmed down and she had some composure, she was able to behave differently, changing the kind of impression she gave others. I'd have to keep watching her to confirm one way or the other.

I certainly wasn't expecting her to rebuke me for my actions, though. I'd apologize to Miss Red Tracksuit later on. I got too emotional and went too far.

But I couldn't just abandon my farming work. I'd apologize after I wrapped up things here. I had to be the one to handle this in order to get the fast results we needed.

And so I quietly continued to swing my shovel into the dirt, setting down farming blocks and tilling with my ho. Since I could process a whole area in one go, the work itself was super easy.

Once the farmland was ready, I had to plant seeds and seedlings block by block, so that was the most time-consuming task. I could use my command action to plant while moving backward, though, which allowed me to quickly move around without actually moving my legs at all. It looked terribly awkward from the outside, resulting in all kinds of horrified stares, but it was very useful.

"Guess that's about it."

After planting seeds and seedlings in about half of the medicinal herb field, I ran out. It would stay like this until Ira and Melty got me more to work with.

"All that's left is..."

I worked my brain to see if there was any work left to do. I'd made a facility for the prisoners, I'd finished dividing up weapons and ammunition ahead of the arrival of the Holy Kingdom's subjugation forces, and all that was left was to mass produce more arms and munitions.

"Hrm..."

The rifle squad's machine guns would probably finish the enemy off, and I had made plenty of rounds for those guns, so I didn't think I had to worry about running out. Even the Holy Kingdom wouldn't be idiotic enough to push ahead when their front line gets annihilated by a wall of machine gun fire.

But also, this was a religious force we were talking about, and those were the types to disregard casualties and just come charging forward. I was pretty biased when it came to this kind of thing, so it was hard to say one way or the other. If they did come charging like that, we'd have to show them something more terrifying than their beliefs were strong. Hrm, what about the automatic grenade launcher? Was it time to finally put it to field use? It could fire forty-eight rounds at a distance of 1,500 meters. A terrifying beast, for sure. The multi-purpose projectiles it used had a kill radius of five meters and a damage radius of fifteen meters. If it made direct impact with a target, it could pierce even 50-millimeter armor. I didn't know how powerful the Holy Kingdom's beloved mage squad was, but surely even they stood no chance against a barrage of high-explosive projectiles.

Perhaps this was overdoing it, but I decided to make the rounds anyway. If I made use of this thing from atop the castle walls, I could cover an exceptionally wide area. But if I did that, there was no doubt that I'd be formally recognized as an enemy of the Holy Kingdom. Hell, they'd basically see me as the demon king... Not that this was the time to worry myself with such things. First, we would ask for their surrender, and if they kept coming, we'd simply smash them to dust. Then we could ask for their surrender a second time, and things would most likely end there. At least, if our enemy had rational minds.

"I need iron, copper, and powder," I mused.

We had a decent stock of all three, but it was best to get as much supply as quickly as we could for the future. Manure, which was required to make powder, was abundant in the sewer, so the problem was iron and copper. If I wanted to get my hands on some quickly, it would be best to have Poiso accompany me into the sewers so I could gather swamp ore. It felt kind of wrong referring to it as such, but I digress.

"Poiso, you there?"

"You called?"

With no walls nearby and the ground made of dirt, I didn't expect her to appear, but she had zero issues coming to the surface. How the heck did she do that?

"I need iron and copper stat, so I wanted some of that sewer metal," I told her.

"Got it. Where would you like me to bring it?"

"I was actually thinking of coming along."

Poiso thought for a moment, then shook her head. "You would have to walk quite a bit, so I'll bring it here. Who knows when you might be summoned? It would be best for you to not travel too far."

"Hrm, really? I guess you're right." It was true that I might receive impromptu summons. I had valuable skills, which meant I could do a lot of different things. It'd be unfortunate if someone couldn't get in touch with me when needed. "The problem is that I have nothing to do."

"Then how about going to the reception room?" she suggested.

"The reception room?"

"Correct."

The reception room was a sort of lounge located in the royal quarters. It was where Sylphy's family had been frozen.

"I'm sure good things await you there."

I couldn't read her intentions, but I knew I could trust her. If nothing else, she truly believed something good awaited me, and she had no reason to want to trick me. In fact, it would be far easier for her to crush me and bury me in the darkness. She had the power to do it.

"I don't get it, but okay," I said.

"The way you listen to others is a wonderful trait."

After parting ways with the slime girl, I headed toward the reception room. I already knew its location, so I didn't get lost. I watched the maids and sisters who were stationed here hurriedly run about as I made my way toward the royal quarters. The whole frozen area was known to be untouchable to the staff, so as I got closer, it got emptier and emptier.

I continued down the single hall, and eventually I couldn't hear any of the frantic footsteps from before. It was kind of lonely.

I opened the reception room doors.

"Huh?"

Despite Poiso's cryptic message, the room was empty. I mean, that was fine. I didn't quite get it, but sure.

I scratched my head. Turning around and wandering the castle at this point would be boring. Since this place had a nice sofa, maybe it wouldn't be so bad to spend some alone time here. (The sofa had been brought from one of the non-frozen quarters. The stuff that used to be here had been frozen for twenty years, so it had all basically crumbled to dust.)

I approached the sofa in front of me to sit down but nearly cried out in surprise.

"Mm..."

Ifriita was lying there, not in her usual red tracksuit but instead in a dress befitting a princess. She was sleeping, so I hadn't noticed her until I drew close.

"Hrm."

Looking at her sleeping quietly like this, I couldn't help but recognize her as the princess she was. Her facial features were dignified, as expected from Sylphy's older sister. And when she was this quiet, she really was gorgeous. The word existed for people like her.

"Nn..."

Was it really okay for me to see her like this? What were Poiso's intentions? It was obvious what would happen if she woke up. She'd call me a beast for looking at her sleeping face without her permission, then probably pummel me with magic.

Exiting before that happened seemed like the wise choice. Indeed. I stepped back to leave the area, when...

...Her emerald eyes met mine.

We stared at each other in silence.

If she had still been half-asleep, I could have quietly faded out, but her eyes were wide open. She was a fast riser.

What options did I have here? What could I do? Since I'd made the prison facility the other day, I still had stone blocks on my shortcuts. If things got bad, I could block an attack.

What was my move?

We just continued staring. Kousuke is watching carefully!

"Say something," she finally demanded.

"You look adorable when you sleep."

"What's with the stiff tone? Your whole performance is acting like royalty isn't royalty, no?"

"My *performance*? Who do you think I am?"

Ifriita sat up, entirely unconcerned with my words, then yawned. Was it proper for a lady to yawn like that in front of someone?

"So? What is it?" she asked. "Are you here to violate me, like you did Sylphy, Melty, and countless others?"

"Nah, I'm not into girls who wear red tracksuits."

"I don't follow, but I am certain you're making fun of me."

I let her glare wash over me as I sat across from her on the other side of the table. Now that we were sitting, what next? If nothing else, she responded way more peacefully than I had anticipated.

"Uh, right," I said. "Um, me violating you? Not happening. For multiple reasons."

"What is that supposed to mean?"

"First of all, and this is embarrassing to say, but I don't have the courage to make the first move on any woman. And I certainly wouldn't do anything to anyone while they were sleeping."

"I do not think the former is anything to brag about," she snorted.

"Additionally, I want to clear up a misunderstanding," I added. "I'm not going around violating them. They're the ones violating me. Consensually, anyway."

"R-really?"

Ifriita seemed to sense the seriousness in my eyes, as she began to flash me a sympathetic gaze. There were certainly times like the first, when I essentially leapt into open arms or was drawn to the affection I'd been given, but after forming proper relationships, it was fair to say I was simply being devoured night after night.

"As for how I ended up here, Poiso told me something good was waiting for me here," I explained. "I'd just finished all the work I could do right now, and it didn't seem like anyone was here. Confused, I was going to sit down and relax when I saw you asleep. You looked adorable like that, so I couldn't help but watch you for a while. However, that doesn't change the fact that I looked without your permission, and for that, I apologize."

"So you're capable of earnestly apologizing?"

"When I think I'm in the wrong, of course. Also, I went too far before. I don't take back what I said, but I could've picked a better way to say it. Sorry."

I then bowed my head once.

"I see," Ifriita replied quietly, casting her eyes downward. She was acting so meek... Maybe she couldn't get into character without her tracksuit?

"Ah, um, so...look, I owe you twice now," I stammered. "For watching you sleep and for taking things too far."

"So?"

"That means I'm willing to listen to any two requests you might have. If they're within my power, anyway. This is my way of apologizing."

I didn't like seeing her so dejected, so this idea was born from that.

"Two requests?" she asked.

"Yup! If there's a food you want from before, name it. Pretty accessories, clothes—hell, I could make you a sword, spear, or a set of armor if you'd like. Though I guess maybe that would be kinda strange for a young lady such as yourself."

"You'll listen to any request as long as you can fulfill it?"

"Sure. Of course, it's gotta be something sensible. I'm not taking you to battle the Holy Kingdom, murdering everyone over there, or taking my own life."

"In that case..."

Ifriita chants a mysterious spell!

"Pardon?"

I wanted to go back in time ten seconds and tell myself to stop before it was too late.

"Kousuke?"

"Yes?"

"What's going on?"

"Um... Honestly, I'm not sure."

"I can tell you are not lying, but you are also not telling the truth."

Cursed Saint of Truth!

"Fine, I can explain how this came to pass, but not why. She won't tell me."

I could feel Sylphy and Elen's cool gazes looking down, targeted at Ifriita who currently had her head on my lap with a calm expression on her face. Indeed, my lap was serving as her pillow.

"Then explain. You know what will happen if you try to trick us, right?"

Sylphy glanced at Elen, who continued to stare down at me with her crimson red eyes. The message was clear: If I lied, they would know. Just like a moment ago.

"When I finished my tasks in the courtyard, Poiso told me I should come here," I told them. "When I did, I found the princess asleep on the couch. I couldn't help but stare because she looked so cute."

"I have a name," said the princess from my lap. "Use it."

"I thought it was rude of me to stare at Ifriita's face while she slept, so I apologized. I also apologized for my tone and how I worded my position during our conversation before. Since Ifriita still seemed kind of down in the dumps, I told her she could make two requests of me, one for each apology."

Sylphy and Elen both narrowed their eyes. I mentally apologized for my careless actions.

"When Ifriita heard that, she said, 'Then become mine.' I had no clue why it had come to that, and I told her that I was already Sylphy's, so that would be impossible. I couldn't be only Ifriita's."

"Hrm." Sylphy's cold, sharp gaze softened.

"But then Ifriita said, 'Didn't you say you'd do whatever was in your power? Do the work so I can join your harem.' That's when I called Lime and had her get the two of you. I initially thought that maybe I should go to you myself, but for her second request, she asked me to let her lay in my lap... My bad."

Since that second request wasn't impossible, I had to comply. Hence why I had Lime call them over.

"He is not lying," Elen said.

"Is that so?" Sylphy nodded and cast her gaze toward Ifriita. "Then it's your turn to explain, Big Sister."

"There's nothing to explain. There's no grand reason behind my actions."

Elen stared at the princess and immediately negated her answer. "She is lying."

"I was jealous that you went and found a husband before me," Ifriita admitted.

"This is the truth."

"Then you acted simply on jealousy, and you don't actually have any special affections toward Kousuke?"

"Of course not!" Ifriita laughed. "Since meeting him, have I had a single reason to form any affection for him? I don't think anything of this guy."

I'd assumed as much, but hearing it said so directly put cracks in my glass heart.

"She is lying."

We all fell silent.

WHY?

"She is lying."

It was important, so Elen went and said it twice, her face as expressionless as ever while she shook her head.

Ifriita sat up at once, her face bright red, and screamed. "It's no lie! Could you not mess around?!"

Elen shook her head. "She is lying. I swear upon Adol Himself." She made the cross sign with her fingertips. I would later hear from her that this specifically meant that she was telling the truth with God as her witness.

I looked at Sylphy, who folded her arms and put a hand to her chin in thought. She really didn't have to take this so seriously.

"Wh-what's with you and this whole lying thing?!" Ifriita protested. "You're the only one lying!"

"I swear that I only speak the truth," said Elen. "I swear to these eyes that my Lord gifted me."

"I had yet to tell you this, If, but she is a saint of Adolism," Sylphy added. "According to Ira, she has a type of mystic eyes with the ability to see if someone's statements are true or not. After testing them out, we confirmed they have a 100 percent accuracy rate."

Ira was experimenting with Elen's eyes without me even knowing? I suppose that made sense. Sylphy and the others weren't followers of the church, so that would've been necessary for them to trust her.

"Uh..."

"'Uh'?"

"UWAAAAAHHH! Sylphy, you big dummy!" Unable to bear the shame any longer, Ifriita suddenly stood up and ran out of the reception room in tears. She was incredibly fast.

"Um, should I go after her?" I asked.

"Leave her be. Once she's calmed down, she'll come back on her own." Sylphy sat next to me, with Elen on the other side. I was stuck between the two of them. "Now then, it's time to discuss how we handle this fool and his thoughtless proposal."

"Indeed we do," Elen agreed.

"Forgive me!"

Locked between the witch and the saint, I resorted to my last option: a complete and total surrender.

"And anyway, how could you make a pass at other women when you have yet to even take *me* to bed? I heard you even made a move on a dragon girl? Plus, you met her *after* you met me, and you have already taken her to bed?" Elen, now in a foul mood, had started lecturing me. Wait, she hadn't met Grande yet, had she?

"Wh-who did you hear that from?" I groaned.

"Poiso."

"That evil bubble slime!"

I could see her sticking her tongue out in my mind. When it came to being wicked, the three slime girls always had one up on me, but Poiso was the only one to stir up a situation like this.

"You haven't yet taken her to bed?" Sylphy cast a tepid look at me. I wish she wouldn't look at me with those eyes. "Saint, Kousuke can be quite the coward."

"I am aware."

"Once you have been to bed with him, it's different, but he needs a push for that first move. You either need to taunt him until he loses all reason or push him down yourself."

"I see. Well unfortunately, I did not have the physical power to push him down." The saint turned her red eyes toward me, an unfittingly sadistic light in them.

"H-hey, wait!" I sputtered. "Sylphy?!"

"Kousuke, this is your fault," Sylphy said. "You've had lots of chances to make a move on her, have you not? Do not keep her waiting for so long."

"Look, I know, but Elen is at the top of the Church of Adolism! She's a saint! I can't just take her to bed willy-nilly..."

"I'm the head of the Liberation Army and royalty, am I not? Ira is the head mage of the Liberation Army and the court mage of old Merinard, formally recognized as a prodigy. Melty may not have had a special title, but she is a rare overlord charged with secretly protecting the royal family. The harpies are elite members of the Liberation Army's combat forces, and Grande is considered the princess of the grand dragons who reside deep within the Black Forest, no?"

I had no response.

"In what situation would you be ready to lay your hands on the saint? Would you require a grand wedding? When would that happen? After the war is over and we're at peace. Do you plan on making her wait that entire time?"

"W-well..."

"Well, what?"

I turned toward Elen, and her crimson eyes met mine.

"I guess, um, it's up to whenever...she's ready?"

Elen's gaze turned scornful. "Coward."

"Kousuke..." Sylphy sighed, exasperated.

"C'mon, what do you want from me?! How could I possibly make the first move on someone as beautiful as Elen?! Plus, in my world, trying to get with multiple women at the same time is extremely taboo! Sure, my sense of ethics has changed a bit since coming here, but that's still a major hurdle for me! My morality was built up over years! I can't just go and change it on a dime!"

Plus, I had reasonably high moral values! I wasn't the kind of dude to join a team and play multiplayer games with people!

I didn't have high communication skills. I was always the introverted type who played survival games that required knowledge and technical skills.

"I see... So your world's ethics are important to you, then?" Sylphy said.

"Of course!"

"Well, this world has its own ethics."

Elen casually leaned into me, putting her body weight against me. Oooh, she felt so nice and soft!

"As far as I can tell, you appear honest to your desires... The wall preventing you from stepping over the line seems thin, but it is actually rather tough."

"Agreed," Elen said. "I believe they call those types secret lechers."

"Miss Saint, where did you even learn that?" Anyway, I wasn't a secret lecher. I wasn't pretending I had no interest in the lewd. "Anyway, I get it, okay? I apologize for making Elen wait and vow to do something about it as soon as—"

"Tonight, then," said Sylphy. "I'll make it happen."

"Understood," Elen agreed.

"Whoa, wait, hold on! Isn't that a little soon? How about we calm down."

"Nope. That is how you usually stretch things out."

I was left totally helpless. I turned to Elen for any kind of olive branch, but she was expressionless, her cheeks bright red. Her eyes were oddly unfocused. Yeah, she was long gone.

"No, but seriously," I said. "Are you sure?"

"It is no problem," Sylphy insisted. "Everything has been discussed. The scriptures have been passed over to Archbishop Dekkard. All that's left is for you to prove yourself after dinner via the Crown of Radiance thing. Ah, right... Tonight's dinner will be with my mother, sisters, the saint, the archbishop and his people, and us. Three parties. Sorry, but could you handle the menu?"

So Archbishop Dekkard was the name of Elen's boss? She must have arrived around the afternoon when things seemed busy. Sylphy and Elen had to have come here after things calmed down over there.

The reason I was asked to handle dinner was both to show off my powers and to prevent poisoning. Anything I took from my inventory was 100 percent certain to be clear from poison. We took care of the main sect folks in the castle, but there was no guarantee we didn't miss someone.

As I thought it over, Elen suddenly stood up swiftly.

"I am going to go take a bath," she announced.

"You are getting way ahead of yourself."

"If I remember correctly, among the things confiscated from the main sect's corrupt priests were aromas that put people... in the mood. Melty oversees requisitioned goods, yes? I shall speak to Ira about it."

"Stop that," I argued. "Let's do this the normal way!"

Elen exited the room whispering something to herself. Ah, man. This was gonna be real bad. I had to hope that Ira and Melty had their consciences in order. Unlikely? Unlikely. If push came to shove, I'd have Lime save me. She would help, right? Sure.

"You are rather considerate of the saint." Sylphy looked a little displeased. Ah, jeez...

"If I'm being honest, she's a little dangerous, okay?" I said. "Not unstable, but, like, her mood fluctuations can be extreme."

"I get that. She reminds me of myself before I met you." Sylphy's expression shifted to a more serious one. I guess she wasn't really angry to begin with.

"Before you met me? Have you really changed that much since I came into your life?" I wasn't familiar with that version of Sylphy, so it didn't feel real to me.

"I have. The reason I can let myself be doted on now is because of you. I've changed," Sylphy said, leaning up against me and resting her head on my shoulder. Her smooth silver hair brushed up against my cheek, tickling me.

"Before I came of age, I lived my life as the Witch of the Black Forest, throwing away my dependence on others and focusing everything toward taking the kingdom back and getting revenge. But after meeting you, I managed to take back my heart as Sylphyel, instead of just the Witch."

"I see..."

I sort of understood, but not entirely. I never got to know Sylphyel the witch. Or maybe the woman who beat the everloving shit out of me at first was her?

"I am certain she is even more hardcore than I was, though," she added. "Born with mystic eyes and sold by her parents to Adolism before she could even think for herself. As far as I've heard, the inner workings of the church are filled with trickery and the worst of humanity. And then on top of that, she is beautiful. She is a woman who had to live wearing the mask of the saint in order to protect her own heart."

I gave her a confused expression.

"In other words, as soon as she lets you dote on her the first time, there will be no end to it for some time. She will be attached to you around the clock."

"Seriously...?"

When Sylphy gave herself over to me, she basically turned into a child. And she was telling me Elen would be worse? What would that even look like?

"Ouch," I muttered.

"What exactly are you thinking?" She had clearly seen through me, as she was glaring and pulling at my cheeks, her face bright red and adorable as always.

"Elen of all people, huh...? I can't even imagine her like that."

That arrogant—okay, maybe that was too harsh. That haughty, expressionless joker, Elen the saint, coming at me even harder than Sylphy when she was in one of her moods? I couldn't picture it. All I could imagine is her cracking a smirk as she stepped on me or something. She seemed like a stone-cold sadist to me.

Suddenly, Sylphy started pushing me, so I went with the flow and let myself get pushed to the edge of the sofa.

"There we go," she said in a satisfied voice, then put her head in my lap.

This girl, I swear.

"Since you allowed If to do this, I do believe it is only fair that you let me do it, too."

"Very good point," I said. "And I'll even give you a special head-rub bonus."

"Mm, no objections here."

Sylphy's smug satisfaction was similar to Grande's as I petted her head. Since she was probably super busy today, I wanted to let her get some rest on my lap.

And so we stayed like this in the reception room together until Melty came calling to prep for dinner.

"Greetings. It is a pleasure to make your acquaintance. I have heard about you for some time now—a Fabled Visitor from another world, the witch's collaborator, a dragon's partner, and of course, our own savior. My name is Dekkard. I have had the excessive title of archbishop forced upon me, but I am ultimately just an insignificant old man."

He was a gentle-looking older man, with gray hair and a full gray beard. He had a firm body, with no excessive flab anywhere to be found. His back was straight as well, making him the image of a healthy older man. In fact, I wouldn't have been surprised if he was a former temple knight.

"I see. Well, the pleasure is all mine, sir. My name is Kousuke."

"Ho ho ho, no need to take on such a serious tone with an old man like me!" The white-robed man laughed merrily.

His clothing had no excessive decorations. It was the bare minimum, with only a cross on it to identify him as a member of the clergy.

"I just can't get used to these new robes," he added. "Old timers like me are fine with the same old stuff."

"Father, even if you are, that would be rude to those you deal with," said the crimson-eyed saint sitting next to him, with a resigned sigh.

The old man seemed to find her dejection amusing, as he smiled merrily. "Ho ho ho, well put."

"Sylphy, he's nothing like I expected," I whispered.

I expected an archbishop of the church to have a certain manner of speech and be all about alcohol, money, and women. But this man looked nothing of the sort. To put it positively, he seemed like a benevolent, good-natured older man. To put it straight, he just seemed like a nice old dude. He didn't strike me as the sort of guy involved in internal power struggles.

"I'm as taken aback as you are," said Sylphy. "But I suppose, well, he is who he is."

She then directed her gaze to the priestess with the severe expression who sat on Dekkard's other side.

She was entirely focused on me. One would never mistake her gaze as friendly. I felt like I was being evaluated.

She looked like she was approaching old age. Younger than my mother, but close, at least. Her chestnut-colored hair was mixed with grays, and she had tense, upward-turned eyes. Her thin, straight lips made her seem like someone who didn't believe there was a single fun thing in the world. Her robe, much like Archbishop Dekkard's, was devoid of decoration.

Having noticed my gaze, Elen stepped in to introduce her. "This is High Priestess Katalina, Archbishop Dekkard's right-hand woman. She's the boss I spoke of."

"I am Katalina. I am glad to find the Fabled Visitor in good health. I am a humble woman, but it is a pleasure to meet you."

Her glare from earlier had vanished. In fact, the woman Elen introduced wore a warm smile toward me. I wasn't sure why she must keep up appearances at this point, but maybe both this archbishop and high priestess wanted to appear as a kindly father and aide in front of Elen. With that in mind, I'd have to stay on guard with both of them.

"Other introductions were made earlier today, so I will move on," Sylphy said. "Sitting there is my mother and older sisters. In other words, the royal family of the former Kingdom of Merinard."

"I am the wife of Ixnil Danar Merinard, the former King of Merinard. Seraphita Danal Merinard."

"I am the eldest daughter, Doriada Danal Merinard."

"Second eldest daughter, Ifriita Danal Merinard."

"I am the third daughter, Aqual Danal Merinard."

"And I am the youngest daughter and head of the Liberation Army, Sylphyel Danal Merinard. Though I suppose you already know that."

Afterward, Sylphy turned her gaze toward Ira.

"I'm Ira. Court mage of the former Kingdom of Merinard.

Currently the captain of the Liberation Army's mage squad. I am also one of Kousuke's companions."

With all eyes on Ira, she introduced herself loudly despite her small stature. Was that last part really necessary?

"Who is left...?"

Sylphy's eyes were trained on the mannerless girl sitting at the dinner table greedily eating. She had demon-like horns coming out of her head, and strong and brutal clawed hands which were currently dirty with food.

"Hrm? What is it?"

"Grande, introduce yourself."

"How annoying... I am Grande the grand dragon. Just for the record, I do not belong to this Liberation Army or whatever they call it. I am simply accompanying my mate, Kousuke. Of course, should he request it, I would happily lend my assistance. But generally speaking, I have no intention of involving myself with the senseless wars between humans. Also, Kousuke. I want to eat a cheeseburger."

"Okay, okay..."

I pulled out a large wood dish from my inventory and put a bunch of cheeseburgers on top of it, handing it over to one of the maids so she could bring it to Grande.

The ones who had their introductions skipped were Melty and Sir Leonard. Madame Zamil was guarding the door of this dining room with the mithril alloy short spear I made for her during our dungeon excursion.

"Unfortunately, I was sent to the Black Forest before my

education as a princess could be completed, so I do not know the appropriate way to hold a proper dinner like this," said Sylphy. "As such, I welcome you to a traditional Black Forest elven banquet. Let us toast to new meetings and the future."

Sylphy raised her cup of mead, prompting both Melty and Sir Leonard to do the same, with Ira shortly after. I raised my own cup, followed by the queen, her daughters, and then Archbishop Dekkard and Katalina.

"To new meetings and the future."

"To new meetings and the future."

Everyone repeated Sylphy's words in unison, then proceeded to sip from their cup. The sweet aroma of the mead gently tickled the nose. As usual, this was on the stronger end of drinks. The problem was that it was also easy to consume, so if someone like me overdid it, I would end up unconscious sooner rather than later.

"Ho ho, so this is elven mead," Archbishop Dekkard chuckled. "It's so sweet!"

"Lord Dekkard," High Priestess Katalina scolded him.

"I know. Excessive luxury brings with it depravity, right? However, treating others' kindness with disdain also goes against the creed, am I wrong?"

Her complaints went in one ear and out the other as the sister who was waiting in the corner refilled his drink. Serving us were maids from the Kingdom of Merinard, castle maids who sided with the Liberation Army, and sisters from the Adolist side of things as well.

Our different camps were divided by the large table, with Grande sitting in the birthday seat as the neutral party. Since she was disinterested in our goings-on, it was more like she was in a different space entirely. I just felt bad for the maid who was busily taking care of her.

"Are these unfamiliar dishes foods from your homeland, Sir Kousuke?" the archbishop asked as he dirtied his white beard with pizza sauce.

The fact that he went straight for the pizza made him quite the gutsy older man. Everything on the table was some sort of junk food dish, though, so it wasn't like he had any other choice. Most of the survival games I played were made in other countries, so I guess all the food I was capable of making was also from abroad. I might be able to make rice balls or other Japanese dishes with rice, but I still hadn't found any rice in this world, damn it all.

"Not quite," I replied. "Though they are all foods from my world."

"Hrm, then it is safe to surmise that your world also consists of multiple countries?"

"Yes, actually. Maybe human development remains the same regardless of the world. It starts with a hunting society, then people gather together to cooperate, they start tilling the fields—"

"Then war begins. What a deeply sinful thing it is," Dekkard said sadly while finishing off his pizza.

Next, he reached for the fried chicken. This man was quite the glutton. Dekkard took a bite out of the chicken in his hands, chewed, swallowed, and then suddenly hit me with a deeply philosophical question.

"Forgive me. This might not be the time, but what do you believe peace to be, Sir Kousuke?"

Despite the suddenness of the question, I answered immediately. "Peace is the preparatory phase until the next war. I think I recall hearing that somewhere in the past, and I find myself agreeing with it on a general level. Peace is a fleeting thing that eventually collapses no matter what. To speak frankly, it's when equilibrium is preserved."

Dekkard nodded in response. "I see... That is certainly one truth. In this current warring period of ours, the equilibrium is deeply out of balance. And that unbalance is calling forth more chaos. Humanoids are feuding, scorning one another, and killing one another. This is not the harmony that God desires."

"Huh."

"I believe you were sent to us to bring harmony to our world and fix the unbalance of these troubled times."

"I think that's maybe a little bit of an exaggeration, no?"

As far as I was aware, the primary cause of the chaos in this world was the war between the Holy Kingdom and the Empire. If I were to take his words at face value, he felt my mission was not just to free the Kingdom of Merinard from the Holy Kingdom but to bring peace beyond that. In other words, to end the war.

"That all sounds like so much of a pain in the ass that it kind of makes me nauseous," I admitted. "No matter how you think about it, I'm just not the guy for that."

I still didn't really know just how large each nation's forces were. What I did know was that they were the sort of countries that could drop down tens of thousands of soldiers just to suppress an insurrection in one of their vassal states. Just thinking about it made me dizzy.

If I didn't care about optics, sure, it might not be impossible to annihilate both nations, but I didn't want to take any actions that would turn me into some sort of demon king. I also didn't think I could come up with a solution that would peacefully put an end to the bloody conflict between the countries. Hell, I wish people didn't expect that from a gamer like me. Honestly.

"Ho. A pain in the ass, you say? Indeed, it is truly a damn pain in the ass."

"Archbishop, language."

"Ho ho ho, my apologies."

Dekkard reached for a cheeseburger. For her part, Katalina was using a fork and knife to enjoy a steak, excellent manners and all. What was Elen up to? Her eyes were sparkling as she dug into pancakes and crepes.

"But I suppose we can take our time and have this conversation later," said Dekkard. "Sir Kousuke, if possible, I would love to hear tales of your world. I am deeply fascinated to learn what sort of world the Fabled Traveler has come from."

"Mm, likewise."

"Me as well."

Both Ira and Grande jumped in on this, and Elen shot me an interested gaze while chewing quietly. High Priestess Katalina

271

also seemed interested, as her fierce eyes were looking my way as well.

"Sure, that's fine."

I'd have to pick and choose what to tell them, but that was far easier than discussing peace, so I began to tell them the story of my world that I had once told Sylphy.

After dinner was finished, both Archbishop Dekkard and High Priestess Katalina were guided to their respective rooms. Both seemed satisfied by the food and my tales, so I'd call this a great success.

"Well done, Sir Kousuke. Tired of talking, I bet."

"Yeah, a little."

In the end, I didn't just talk about my old world but also everything that had happened to me since coming here. How many times had I told that story? At this point, I was mostly used to it. Maybe I could take narration lessons or something.

"I was fascinated indeed by the differences in perspective you brought compared to what Sylphyel saw."

"Um, well, thanks?"

Normally, after eating, I would take a bath and then drink with Sylphy and the others. Some quiet time. But for some reason I was drinking alone with my mother-in-law, in other words, Lady Seraphita. Sylphy, Ira, Melty, Grande, and the harpies were all gone.

What was this situation? What was I supposed to do?

Sylphy had asked me to spend some time with her mother, and before I could do anything, this whole scenario had been set up.

Sure, she was Sylphy's mother and essentially my mother-in-law, but we had basically only just met. Plus, she still looked young—around the same age as Sylphy. I had no idea how I was supposed to interact with her.

"Sir Kousuke—"

"Um, to be honest, it doesn't feel right, or very cozy, I guess, to have you refer to me as 'Sir,' Lady Seraphita. You are essentially my mother-in-law."

She stared at me blankly for a moment before giggling to herself like a young woman. Crap, she was adorable. My heart was racing at Sylphy's mother—someone who was already married, at that.

"Then how do you think I feel when my son-in-law and the Fabled Visitor refer to me as 'Lady'?" she replied.

"Er, but, I mean, you're the queen."

"And you are a Fabled Visitor, no? In that case, how about we both drop the formalities? Would that be fine?"

"Ugh... All right."

How could I say no to such a gentle smile? How could I even describe the overflowing gentle aura she had? Was it her inherent nobility? For some reason, I just couldn't say no to her.

"Now then," she said, "there is something I would like to ask you, Kousuke."

"What is it?"

Unlike just before, she wore a serious expression on her face as she turned her body to face me.

"What are you thinking of doing with us?"

"What do you mean?" I wasn't sure how to answer her. I personally had no intention of doing anything. I didn't have that kind of power to begin with. "I'm personally not going to do anything. If you're asking me what I want you to do, then I want you to stay close to Sylphy and support her. It wouldn't be an overstatement to say she's lived up until now so she could reunite with you. After dealing with such hardship, she deserves her happy ending."

This was my complete and honest thought on the matter. She was forced to leave her homeland at a young age, learned of its destruction from afar, and spent her youth lighting the flames of revenge against the Holy Kingdom. Then she found me, and she fulfilled her primary goal. Or I guess she was in the process of doing so. She deserved an appropriate reward for that.

"I'm not asking you to throw away your own ideals, hopes, or dreams so you can live for Sylphy," I added. "I just don't want you to do anything that would upset her, is all."

I hadn't spent much time with Seraphita, but there was a strange transience I felt from her. As if she might disappear if I touched her.

"What do you want to do, Seraphita?"

"Me...? Well..." She looked down silently at her cup. What was she seeing in the mead, I wondered. "What should I do?"

She raised her gaze toward me, though her eyes seemed some-what unfocused. How could this be the same person who'd shot me such an innocent smile only moments before? The woman before me had deeply exhausted, dispirited eyes.

"Is it truly okay for me to just...live? After seeing my country destroyed, losing my husband, and having countless citizens suf-fer and be driven to death... Should I not be punished?"

She once again went quiet and stared down into her cup. Ah... What was the right thing to say? How was I supposed to cheer up a woman who'd been through all that? It was beyond my pay grade.

"This might sound cold," I said, "but when it comes to who is responsible for the destruction of the old Kingdom of Merinard, I'm a complete outsider. I don't have the right to say anything to you. By the time I came to this world, everything was already over. I experienced no struggles as a result of Merinard being destroyed. That said, I am fairly intimate with the people who became refugees and those who suffered under the rule of the Holy Kingdom."

Quite frankly, this was all beyond me. I was certain Seraphita was expecting something from me. Like judgment. Sylphy would never punish her mother, especially because she dirtied her hands to save her. As such, she could never pass judgment upon her mother or sisters with those very same hands.

But what about her underlings?

Melty would never. She'd never said it directly, but I think the reason she was helping Sylphy was because of her personal feelings for her. She would never push something onto Seraphita and the others that Sylphy wouldn't want. Ira was probably the same in that regard.

Danan and Sir Leonard both had powerful feelings of hatred toward the Holy Kingdom. I had never heard either of them speak poorly of the former kingdom's royal family, but they were adults. It was possible that they were just keeping it to themselves. But even then, it was hard to imagine them holding the royal family responsible for the fall of Merinard.

Madame Zamil was a step removed from even their position. If anything, she felt responsible for not being able to protect the royal family. She had a deep fire burning within her—an obsession—to make sure that this time she would protect them until the very end.

Now I get it. Now I understand just a bit how Seraphita was feeling.

"So as an outsider, you think that makes me equipped to pass judgment on you all?"

She nodded ever so slightly.

That was a problem. A *big* problem. What was I supposed to do? What sort of punishment fit the bill?

They destroyed the country, drove many of their citizens to suffering and death. The ultimate failing on the part of the royal family. Generally speaking, the duty of a king and his family was to ensure the survival of the nation and protect the lives and safety of its people. That was everything. In that sense, the sins of the king and queen were grave.

In order to keep the Holy Kingdom from growing more powerful, the king froze his wife's life in time, even though it had meant the ultimate sacrifice. That plan worked, and he ultimately saved her and their daughters' bodies and souls until Sylphy could arrive at this point to release them.

However, his actions could also be seen as abandoning the people. The Holy Kingdom desired elven blood so they could produce magically powerful children. If the royal family had offered themselves up, perhaps they could have avoided losing the people.

Judging by Seraphita's reaction, this probably wasn't off the mark.

"What are you asking of me?" I said. "Are you seriously saying that you want me to tell Sylphy to execute you in order to take responsibility for the fall of the kingdom? Don't be ridiculous."

"You are the only one I can ask," said Seraphita.

"Not happening. The reason I fought this hard with Sylphy was to free you all, so I could bring happiness to her. Having you executed would destroy her, which is the exact opposite of what I want."

"Please, I beg of you."

"Sorry, but no. Don't wrap Sylphy up in your sense of guilt. If you want a punishment, then how about going on living with the burden of those feelings?"

What Seraphita was grappling with was survivor's guilt. People who miraculously made it home from horrific wars or catastrophes sometimes felt guilt over being alive. Depending on how bad the situation was, they even required psychological treatment.

As I considered what to do, Seraphita began to sob.

"Please... Please, I beg of you... I... I do not know what to do..."

"Aaah..."

Her crying was a big problem. A huge problem, even.

Sylphy! Ira! Melty! Lime, Bess! Even Poiso would be fine! Someone come and save me! Grande... Actually, maybe not Grande. Not right now.

Unfortunately, my thoughts reached no one. The heavens had abandoned me, so I stood up and brought Seraphita's head to my chest like I did when Sylphy threw a fit. I gently stroked her head while patting her back with the palm of my hand.

"I think maybe it's time you relaxed those shoulders of yours and let someone dote on you. I hope you don't take this the wrong way, but the Kingdom of Merinard was destroyed once already. There is no royalty or queen. Leave the new Merinard to Sylphy. Would it be so bad to just live life as Seraphita from now on?"

In response, she wrapped her arms around my waist and nuzzled her head into my chest. Ah, she was just like Sylphy. Like mother, like daughter. She was probably *way* older than me, but when she acted like this, she was just like a child.

After a while, her tears finally came to an end and she released her arms from around my waist, pulling away. When she raised her face, her eyes were red, with dark circles around them. She must've been hiding them with makeup... It was entirely possible she hadn't slept at all since awakening from her slumber.

I pulled a clean cloth out of my inventory and wiped Seraphita's face for her.

"Nn..."

Despite the large dark circles and her red eyes, Seraphita was immensely beautiful. If anything, her vulnerable state made me want to protect her even—no, no, no. We were talking about Sylphy's mom and my mother-in-law. Bad boy. Stay.

"So, um, that's that, okay?" I said. "Instead of drowning in those negative thoughts, let's maybe enjoy life?"

"Ah..."

Realizing this wasn't a good look, I pulled away from Seraphita only for her to immediately reach out with a sad little sound. Crap, stay cool.

"I'm going to call for another woman," I told her, "so please wait here."

I steeled my resolve as best as I could, turned my back to her, and left the room, closing the door behind me.

I then let out a sigh.

"Haaah..."

"Not going to push her down?"

I stomped down at the green liquid by my feet. I knew she was watching! I bet Lime and Bess were here, too, keeping out of sight.

Come on out! I swear I won't get angry! Actually, that's a lie. I'm getting very angry. Get out here right now!!!

Lime didn't appear after that, but Bess did.

"I called for an attendant," she said with a composed expression, and so I decided not to punish her.

Thanks to her mediation, I eventually released Poiso and left Seraphita to them before heading to the room I'd been given. It was the office and reception room with the bedroom in the back that Elen had used to meet me. Apparently it was once a room for the person who once governed the city. Didn't sound to me like they were particularly well liked, either.

When I opened the door, I found Elen waiting for me, and the saint was less than pleased.

She trotted over, expressionless as ever, then embraced me before saying, "You smell like another woman."

She looked up at me with her crimson eyes, a dark glow flowing out of them. I thought I was going to wet myself.

"I have a super deep and justified reason for this," I said.

Elen began to dig her head into my chest as I stroked her back and told her all about what happened with Seraphita and how I was doing the exact same thing to her at this very moment.

"You should be ashamed for making a respectable saint such as myself wait while you went off to show kindness to another woman."

"But if I had left my mother-in-law there without doing anything, that would've been even worse, right? Worst case scenario, she might've committed suicide."

I thought back on Seraphita and her lifeless eyes. She must've been using every bit of energy she had to put on a brave front these last few days. I was more surprised that she managed to hold up in that mental state without sleep.

"That's... That might be true, but..."

The saint looked up at me with a dissatisfied expression, so I kissed her on the forehead and held her in my arms.

"The way you are trying to smooth this over is awful. I can tell you are used to this, and it is indecent." Despite what she was saying, Elen held me tighter and dug her face into my chest. Was she trying to overwrite Seraphita's scent with her own? "I shall deal with the queen starting tomorrow. Guiding lost sheep is the job for one such as I."

"Are you sure?"

When I thought about Elen as a member of the clergy, the first thing that came to mind was her using her eyes to disclose the injustices of bad priests. Guiding the lost? Not so much.

"Are you trying to make a fool of me?" she huffed. "I am the noble saint who sees through to the truth. With these eyes granted to me by God, lost sheep are shaved before me. I will see through to the truth of the matter that she struggles to say out loud."

That wasn't guiding lost sheep so much as it was terrifying and cornering them, but I opted not to say that out loud. If the issue could be solved, then I was fine with whatever tactics she used. Seraphita had dependable daughters, and if Elen's techniques didn't work, we still had other options.

"Now then, bonus time is over," she declared. "In other words, no more speaking about other women."

"Um, she's my mother-in-law."

"She is a widow with no blood relation to you. The marriageable age for elves lasts a long time. There is no telling what might happen, especially since you were kind to her in a moment of weakness. In fact, she might have already fallen for you."

"Surely, you're joking... Right?"

Elen sealed my lips with a finger.

"Like I said, no more speaking of other women. All right?"

I simply nodded.

The next morning.

Elen and I were walking to the castle cafeteria together. I woke up feeling great, and my body wasn't numb in the least. Elen's face was also looking smooth and shiny.

Hm? I seemed more energetic than expected? Of course I did. Elen might've been a saint, but she was still a normal girl. When it came to stamina, she was nowhere near Sylphy with her combat skills, the overlord Melty, or Grande the dragon. She didn't have the overwhelming numbers the harpies did, and she didn't use sketchy magic to break past my limits, like Ira.

It's not like she didn't use her saintly powers at all, but it was a very gentle night for me.

"I cannot help but feel a tinge of annoyance."

"That's just the difference in experience."

"Grr..."

She was entirely at my mercy last night, so she kept jabbing my side as we walked. These weren't the type of body blows Sylphy or Melty would give me that struck to the core of my being. Instead, they were merely adorable. The abs I had now were more than capable of deflecting her fists.

When we entered the cafeteria together, several pairs of eyes turned to look at us: Sylphy, Ira, Melty, Grande, Doriada and her sisters, and Seraphita as well. Archbishop Dekkard and High Priestess Katalina were there, too. Unexpectedly, it was basically everyone from last night's dinner.

"Hrm..."

Sylphy was sending Elen a rather impolite gaze. She was literally looking her up and down.

"Mm. You may call me big sister from now on," she decided.

"I refuse," Elen replied. "But since Sylphyel is rather long, I shall call you Sylphy."

"That works for me. Calling you Saint or Eleanora makes it seem like there's too much distance between us, so I shall call you Elen."

"All right, Sylphy."

Elen nodded expressionlessly while Sylphy smiled her first fierce and fearless grin in some time. I would have preferred to see her usual cute smile. I suppose they hadn't completely broken the ice between them yet.

"I'm Ira. Nice to meet you, Elen."

"And I'm Melty. It's a pleasure."

"Grande. Welcome, neophyte."

"Neophyte..."

Elen fixed her gaze on me, but there were others doing the exact same.

"How indecent!" Red Tracksuit called out. Although, I suppose calling her that when she wasn't wearing it anymore would be inappropriate.

Meanwhile, the High Priestess was sending me a terrifyingly cutting glare.

On the other hand, Doriada and Archbishop Dekkard were laughing mischievously.

"Oh my," Doraida tittered. "Being reliable is a good thing, no?"

"Ho ho ho, indeed," Dekkard agreed.

Were they eating meat? In the morning? With steamed potatoes and butter? How powerful...

Seraphita had been shooting a rather feverish stare at me since I arrived. Aqual was seated next to her and waved her hand in front of her mother's face, but she hadn't noticed her at all. I decided to pretend I hadn't seen anything.

"Now that everything's settled for the most part," said Sylphy, "we still have a lot of problems to deal with."

"Indeed." Melty started counting the many problems on her fingers. "We have to push back the subjugation force headed this way, then deal with post-battle conditions, take back Merinard's territories, deal with governance, settle discord between humans and demi-humans, work out how to treat the Church of Adolism, and establish diplomacy with the various foreign nations.

And there are countless other domestic affairs issues to deal with as well."

Fortunately, with the Liberation Army's weapons and supplies, we were mostly dealing with personnel shortages. This wasn't a problem for the government to deal with, so in that sense, I was pretty relieved.

"First comes repelling the subjugation forces... Honestly, I'm not really concerned, but..."

"Not concerned...?" High Priestess Katalina repeated in a stunned voice. "We are talking about an army of over sixty thousand troops."

Of course. Normally speaking, considering the fact we had five hundred troops at best in the city, were facing down a giant force of sixty thousand, and we had no clue how the Merinesburg guards would act in this situation, hearing someone say they weren't worried was lunacy at best. No matter how strong Merinesburg's walls were, our enemy was 120 times larger. It was said that in order to have the advantage in combat, one's forces should be three times as many as the enemy's. We were way out of that territory at this point. That said, when it came to a castle siege, the number of people who could attack at a time was limited by the breadth of the wall. Unlike a field battle, numbers weren't everything.

Ira shook her head. "No problem."

"No problem whatsoever," said Melty with a nod.

Grande shrugged as she reached for the next piece of meat. "Fear not."

Hold on, that meat on the bone...what part of what animal was it from? It was the kind of mystery meat you'd see in manga or anime. Man, I wanted some too.

"Where does this confidence come from?"

"In order to take Merinesburg from a defense force of two thousand, we sent in twenty soldiers," said Sylphy with a shrug. "They annihilated the enemy on the field of battle in minutes. Just wait and see... This is all thanks to Kousuke's power."

"Mm."

Ira nodded. Sylphy wasn't wrong.

I was going to have the harpies do bombing runs while we sent in the rifle squad on their airboards. Additionally, I'd place golem ballistas on the walls for the special forces to use while I used my automatic grenade launcher to pummel the enemy with multi-purpose projectiles. Plus, if we had time before the enemy attacked, we could plant as many traps as we wanted. There were only so many places the enemy could park sixty thousand men near Merinesburg.

I planned for this to be a one-sided theater of destruction. I loved over-prepping on the defensive end and just mowing down invading enemy forces. We had more than enough supplies and firepower to obliterate enemies equipped with swords, spears, and bows. We also had my trump card. There was no way we could lose. Magic was still a bit confusing to me, but from what I'd heard from Ira, while it was powerful, the range was no longer than a bow and arrow.

"Ho ho ho, I look forward to seeing this, then."

High Priestess Katalina shot Archbishop Dekkard a meaningful look, but then she sighed. For a person of common sense like her, this must've been nerve-racking.

No worries! Just watch! We're gonna totally dominate the enemy! Ha ha ha!

CHAPTER 8

Clash! Smash! Trample!

291

JUST FIVE MINUTES after Archbishop Dekkard said he was looking forward to seeing our work, we received a report that a large group, presumably the Holy Kingdom's forces, had been spotted. Had I jinxed it? Nah, probably not. Considering the info that Dekkard had sent us by horse before, they could've appeared at any time up until now.

The reactions in the cafeteria were divided in two. First were those who looked concerned. High Priestess Katalina, the sisters who were working as waitresses, the maids, and the royal family—with the exception of Sylphy.

This contrasted with the other group, who were completely unconcerned. Those who wore invincible grins on their faces. Those who had been waiting for this moment and bared their vicious fangs. Those who continued to eat breakfast like nothing was happening. None of them looked the least bit worried.

Needless to say, I belonged to the latter group.

"It is finally time," said Sir Leonard. "I just hope I get the chance to participate."

"If you do, it will be at the very end," Ira pointed out.

"I bet," said Sylphy. "There is no reason to intentionally risk casualties on our side."

"Hrm... Fine," Sir Leonard huffed. "But I still want to fight."

"Like Ira said, your elite squad will be necessary at the very end," Sylphy told him. "We're going to take control of their main camp."

While those three talked off to the side, I spoke with Melty concerning the day's schedule.

"Today you were going to plant medicinal herb seeds, yes?"

"Yeah. But I should probably prepare for our counterattack, huh? I can always plant seeds at night." I turned to Sylphy. "How far are they?"

"The foot soldiers will be here in about five days," she replied. "If they're marching as one unit, it'll be a week or more."

"I see... Hrm, what should we do then?"

With Sylphy's answer in mind, I began to think up ways to cook the opposition. If it was a forced march, they'd be here in five days, and if they moved at a normal speed, a week to ten days or so. Spotting them so far out gave us a massive advantage. No matter how quickly they moved, they would have to spend five days marching with their defenses wide open against gunfire, cannons, and aerial bombing. We couldn't possibly miss this chance.

"What do you mean?" Ira asked.

"If we know where the enemy is, there's no reason for us to sit here and wait," I said, shrugging my shoulders. "Our best move here would be to send out the airboard rifle squads and focus on bleeding them out."

Our machine gun equipped airboards were faster than cavalrymen, extremely powerful, and could attack the enemy from out of their range. The Holy Kingdom's forces would continue to suffer casualties, their marching speed would drop, and so would their morale. They'd be getting massacred by some strange weapon they'd never seen before without even being able to fight back. It would be unbearable for them.

"We could one-sidedly mow them down from even half the effective range. Plus, many of the folks on the rifle squad can see well at night, so they could attack both during the day and at night. I bet we could rout the enemy before they even arrived at Merinesburg."

One bullet box was 250 shots. Twenty guns firing at once meant 5,000 rounds. One round wasn't going to necessarily kill a single person, but if every gun shot through a full box twelve times, that would be 60,000 total rounds. In five days, we could theoretically annihilate their army of 60,000.

The effective range of said machine guns was a thousand meters, so half of that was five hundred meters. And these guns would be fired from airboards that moved faster than any cavalryman.

"Add our harpies and their aerial bombs to the mix, and we can't lose," I concluded.

"Kousuke, you're nasty," remarked Ira.

"There's no reason to use discretion right now," I said. "Sylphy, what do you think?"

Sylphy placed her hand on her finely shaped chin and thought for a moment.

"To cover supply, you'll have to be on the front lines, right?" she said.

"Yeah. I'll have to be able to supply the rifle squad and harpies with ammo and bombs. But don't worry. I'll be on an airboard, so even if we get chased, we can outrun the enemy."

I couldn't say for sure, but I felt I could fight back a hundred or so cavalrymen no problem. They couldn't chase me down. If they tried, I'd just set down a stone block in front of me, which would smash the charging enemy.

"Yeah, but if anything happened to you…"

"Then I can simply accompany him," declared Grande, after staying silent this entire time. "If necessary, I can fly him away."

It was true that Grande could carry me away with no issue.

"Haaah, fine," Sylphy sighed. "But I can't just send you, the rifle squad, and the harpies."

"Agreed," said Sir Leonard. "But right now, sending out any forces beside the rifle squad would be difficult. Our trailing main forces aren't set to arrive for another three days."

"Why—ah, right. Maintaining public order."

Sir Leonard nodded with a serious expression. "Exactly. Merinesburg's guards are cooperative, but there's no telling whether some fool might try to take advantage of the chaos. At the moment, we can't move troops."

Merinesburg was in disorder right now. Of course it was. The majority of the Holy Kingdom's forces defending the city had been defeated by a tiny military force, and now it was under the control of the rebellion, a group rumored to hate the church and its followers.

The guards had mostly been disarmed, and the castle was occupied by the Liberation Army. It all happened so quickly that the people were scared and nervous. If we sent out Liberation Army troops now, who knows what could happen in the city? Folks could use the rioting and chaos to break into homes and steal, and public order in Merinesburg would be at an all-time low.

"Hrm, three days, huh?" I mused. "Three whole days... If Grande is there as security, I think that's plenty. Twenty members of the rifle squad and the harpies would be more than enough to smash them. I get you being worried, but is now really the time for that?"

"Just as Kousuke says, we've used every hand available to us to fight up until now," Ira cut in. "There's no reason to change that strategy."

"Hrm, I suppose that is true..."

Ira's interruption had slowed Sylphy's momentum. She went on, "Let's say we waited three days to get our infantry together. They still wouldn't be much of a barrier against sixty thousand. Whether we go now or wait three days, our main fighting force will still be Kousuke, the rifle squad, and the harpies. What meaning is there in waiting?"

"I hate to admit it, but that is exactly the case," Sir Leonard agreed. "Our elite special forces may be skilled with crossbows and close-range combat, but against an enemy force just three or even ten times larger than our own, we will simply be run down. Even I stand no chance when surrounded by over a hundred soldiers."

Sir Leonard displayed his fangs as Sylphy looked at him and finally went silent.

"What do you think, Madame Zamil?" she asked.

"Me? Well, as far as I have heard from Sir Kousuke, the most important thing here is mobility. The greater the numbers, the weaker the legs. Using an elite few to confuse the enemy is the best tactic here, so we should keep the numbers small."

"But I do not think the rifle squad and Kousuke can end this battle alone," added Melty. "We will need someone who can officially respond to a cease-fire in order to tend to the wounded."

"Ah, that is a good point."

Ira, Sylphy, and I all agreed.

"Which is why I will also go," Melty said. "I can protect myself perfectly well, and if things get bad, I can grab Kousuke and flee just like Grande can."

"That is true, but you'll need an official position," said Madame Zamil.

"Hrm," said Sylphy. "In that case, I hereby order you to serve as the prime minister of the Kingdom of Merinard. Additionally, I give you the right to make temporary arrangements and treaties, including cease-fires, as far as this battle is concerned."

"Well, that was simple."

And so Melty was named prime minister like it was no big deal and given huge diplomatic powers. The members of

Adolism's Nostalgia-sect were at a loss for words as they watched us decide super important diplomatic matters over breakfast.

"Not every decision requires the bombast of a ritual or an event," Sylphy said. "Especially when time is of the essence. Ah, she'll need something that represents her authority as the prime minister. Kousuke, it's in your hands."

"Your Majesty, could you not just throw the responsibility at me?"

"It feels weird being referred to like that when I haven't had a coronation ceremony or anything."

"You'll get used to it in time."

"You've got a lot of nerve considering you just made someone prime minister like it was no big deal," Melty said with an oppressive smile, having suddenly had the position pushed onto her.

This was enough to overwhelm Sylphy, as she simply shrugged and let it past her. "If I must be queen, then I'm taking you along for the ride, Melty. Give up."

"Then Ira's the captain of the court mages," Melty suggested.

"Job titles are trivial," said Ira. "Our tasks remain unchanged. More importantly, what about Kousuke?"

Just when I was about to say that she was taking a farsighted view of things, Ira suddenly turned the subject toward me.

"Huh? I don't need some grand title," I protested.

"Hrm, you're not exactly the General Kousuke type. What about prince consort?"

"Describing Kousuke's position in a single phrase is rather difficult," said Sir Leonard thoughtfully. "If anything, he's the mastermind."

"That makes me sound evil. Couldn't we come up with something cooler? Like Kousuke the Fixer?"

"Doesn't that still just mean you're the mastermind?" asked Madame Zamil.

It was true that to the Holy Kingdom I was the mastermind or the root of all evil, but not to my own people.

"Anyway, enough about me," I said. "What's important is that Sylphy named Melty the prime minister and gave her decisive authority."

"Don't try to change the subject so blatantly."

"Silence."

The members of the church were dumbfounded by our casual back and forth. Anyhow, there was nothing to be gained just chitchatting here.

"Time to do some info collection, then."

"Right. I'll send out the harpies and confirm their numbers and infiltration route."

"Captain, what's wrong?" Hannes, a large man and my underling, asked in his happy-go-lucky voice.

I shook my head. "It's nothing."

"Of course it ain't, Captain!" Hannes looked around before

lowering his voice to keep things between us. "Whenever you make that face of yours, something's always wrong."

I swear... Usually this man acted on instinct alone, but occasionally he could be strangely sharp.

"Be ready to flee at any time," I told him.

"Huh? For real? But look how many people we have."

We were surrounded by clamoring Holy Kingdom soldiers. Elite squads that protected the borders, mage squads, and Holy Knights all over the place. Of course, if there were mercenary wannabes like my squad around, there were also those who protected the middle of nowhere towns and villages. Troop morale varied; this really was a makeshift force. But on the battlefield, numbers were power. In most cases, with the exception of exceedingly irregular scenarios, the side with the largest numbers won.

"The problem is where we flee to," I muttered.

"What do you mean?" asked Hannes. "Why not head back to the home country?"

"It's always been pointless discussing politics with you, but that won't work."

Something about the subjugation force was shady. It was put together in the name of ending the rebellion in Merinard, but the numbers didn't make sense. There were too many of us. No matter how much momentum the rebellion had, sixty thousand was too much. I felt that even half of that would've been overkill, and yet here all of us were. This meant that the people up top felt that even thirty thousand troops would be a dangerous gamble.

Plus, getting sixty thousand troops together went way too easily. I was curious, so I looked into it, and I found that the cardinals had worked together without issue, which was strange considering they were usually so hostile toward one another. However, that was all I had to go on. There was nothing about them tripping each other out, which was what usually happened. It was possible that this just meant they were taking this matter seriously, but if anything, I sensed that this was all according to their strategy and plans. Of course, this was all just a hunch.

"What is it?"

"Nothing."

Hannes had a dumb look on his—actually, he really was just dumb. I averted my gaze from him and mocked myself internally. Some three years ago, if someone had said they would mobilize their squad based on something as uncertain as "a hunch," I would have made fun of them or looked at them with pity.

But in my three years living on the battlefield, I'd changed. I realized that knowledge, theory, and information wasn't enough to truly see everything. Three long years had taught me this.

"To be honest," said Hannes, "I also got a bad feeling about this, if we keep going."

"Ha! Then be ready to move at any time."

If even this idiot sensed danger, then it was highly likely that death awaited us. Now then, what was our path forward? I looked up and saw a bird flying way up in the sky. When I started thinking about how high in the air it was, I felt a chill run down my spine.

"That's...not good."

If that was what I thought it was, then participating in this battle would be suicidal. How I moved from here onward would determine whether we lived or died.

"Those are their main forces?" I said. "That sure is a lot of people."

"What a spectacular sight," said Melty.

"It's like a swarm," Ira agreed.

After finishing breakfast and our discussion, myself, Melty, Ira, the rifle squad, and the harpies all left Merinesburg and proceeded east toward where the Holy Kingdom's subjugation forces were coming from. We were there to perform recon. While it would take their huge army a week to ten days to get here, they were just a skip and a hop away via airboard. We managed to spot them before noon arrived.

And, well, there sure were a lot of people. Folks suited in full armor every which way. There were also tons of carriages, likely holding supplies. We made sure we were far away and out of sight as they sent cavalrymen on recon, but we had eyes in the air, so dodging them wasn't remotely difficult.

"You know, when you think about it, going up against all those guys with only twenty people seems nuts, huh?" I remarked.

"You're only just now realizing that?" asked Melty.

"Only just now?" echoed Ira.

303

I sighed. "You guys are mean."

We had set up camp on a slightly elevated hill a little ways away from the subjugation forces. We were using the ridgeline as cover and using binoculars to keep tabs on the enemy.

"What'll we do?"

"Well, we'll declare ourselves, or at least suggest they retreat, before we launch our attack. It'll be dangerous, but that's our first move."

"Right, not that I'm big on the idea."

"If worse comes to worst, we'll just destroy them."

Since we confirmed the enemy's base camp, it was time to pull back and make contact with the enemy's light cavalry. If they attacked without listening, that was our answer.

"This is Kousuke. Aerial support, if you would."

"Roger that!"

Everyone boarded the airboards, and we began moving toward the front of the subjugation forces. Each of the ten airboards had two riflemen and two mages, plus two loaders and one driver, for a total of seven soldiers. The riflemen were our offensive forces, while the mages were on defense.

The folks riding my airboard were Melty, Ira, and Grande, for a total of four people. Grande was lying on the back seats covered in cushions, sleeping soundly. She really was something to behold.

"If you continue down this path, you'll reach their light cavalry soon."

"Roger that. Melty, if you please?"

"'Kaaay! But remember, I'm just a super weak young lady—"

"Oh, right. Right."

Even though I'd agreed with her, I felt her kick the back of my seat. If the driver's seat didn't have a seat belt or cushions, who knows what would've happened to my neck.

The task I asked of Melty was to raise Merinard's national flag. It had been constructed quickly—there was a mount for holding a flag on the roof of my airboard. It was so we could clearly display to the enemy that we were an envoy.

In all likelihood, our requests for their surrender would fall on deaf ears, and this would end in a battle, but this was also necessary for after the battle. If we got careless, it was possible their recon team could attack us without question. But we were ready for that: All the machine guns were fully loaded and could fire immediately.

"Jagheera, do not fire until I give the signal," I ordered.

"Roger that. On standby."

"Pirna, when the enemy's main forces get closer, go as high up as you can. If they have mages with them, they might start using antiair chorus magic."

"Understood! We can perform bombing runs from high altitudes no problem, so just give us the command when the time comes!"

"Will do. Let's go."

With my airboard at the front, eleven airboards in total drove down the road. This specific path connected Merinard to the Holy Kingdom, so it was wide and well maintained.

"I see their cavalrymen," Ira announced.

"Seriously?" I said. "You really do have amazing eyesight, Ira."

"My eye isn't big for nothing. Should we call out to them?"

"Probably, yeah. Melty?"

"On it."

Melty cleared her throat multiple times before picking up the magic megaphone set up inside the airboard.

"We are the official army of the Kingdom of Merinard. All invaders from the Holy Kingdom must return to their country at once! Should you fail to comply, we will begin our attack. I repeat: return to your country at once!"

Melty showered the light cavalry with her rather intense words. It was clear she had no intention of talking things over, but it was doubtful they cared to listen anyway, so it was what it was. We just had to make sure this wasn't a sneak attack.

"They're headed this way," said Ira.

"Do they look hostile?" I asked.

"Not sure yet. They don't appear to be holding their weapons."

"Gotcha. Then we should stay on guard. Jagheera, prepare to counterattack, just in case."

"Roger that. All units, horizontal battle formation. Odd numbers on the right, even on the left. Do not attack until ordered."

As Jagheera, captain of the rifle squad, spat out orders to her men, the airboards behind mine began to spread out to the right and the left.

"Looks like they're on guard after seeing us move. They've lowered their speed."

"Well, they've definitely never seen our vehicles before, so of course they'd be on edge."

The bigger issue was whether they'd charge us or not. Even I could see them now.

"Um, twenty of them, tops?" I said.

"Twenty-two, actually," Ira corrected.

"What a weird number."

Twenty-two cavalrymen could fight a force of infantrymen many times larger and still hold their own. In the face of the charging weight of a horse, your average foot soldier was weak and brittle. That wasn't a guarantee if you were dealing with demi-humans who had above average abilities, but still. Horses in this world were probably more powerful than the ones on Earth. They were a threat, either way.

"What should we do if they charge us?" asked Melty.

"Leave three alive and kill the rest," I said. "We need them to take information back to their camp."

As we talked strategy, the enemy began to spread out horizontally as well. They looked like they were going to charge us.

"Let's give them one warning," I told Jagheera. "If they don't stop, leave three of them behind and finish off the others. I'll leave the decision of who to keep alive to you."

"Roger that."

"Reinforcements?" I asked the harpies.

"None at the moment."

"Roger that. If you see any movement, let me know."

"Understood."

The spread-out cavalrymen were steadily approaching, but they had not taken up arms yet.

"Doesn't look like...they wanna talk."

"They've taken out their weapons."

About three hundred meters away, the cavalrymen had drawn their swords. Longswords, to be exact.

"Melty," I said.

"Warning. Stop at once! Should you fail to comply, you will be identified as the enemy and dealt with force. I repeat: stop at once!"

Melty's intimidating voice rang through the air, but the cavalrymen showed no signs of stopping. Welp, that was that.

"Jagheera, you have permission to fire. Don't waste any ammo."

"Roger that. All units, open fire. Leave three on the left alive."

The rifle squad's machine guns started firing upon the enemy in bursts to conserve ammunition, and, outside of the three on the left, all of the cavalrymen were thrown back off of their horses in a bloody mess.

"Overwhelming," said Melty.

"Guess the mage squad won't be doing much," Ira sighed.

"How noisy..." Grande was awoken from her slumber by the loud sounds of gunfire. I guess even she couldn't sleep through this.

"The enemy is fleeing... The three cavalrymen we left alive."

"Roger that. Well done. Jagheera, it's probably fine, but have all of your men check to make sure the guns are in working order."

"On it."

And so concluded our opening greeting: a total of nineteen dead. Honestly, I felt gross.

"I doubt there are any, but check for survivors," I ordered.

"Mm, important to check."

"Yeah."

I doubted anyone could take 7.92mm rounds and make it out alive, but I had to check anyway. It was possible that some of these cavalrymen had magic armor or arrow-deflecting amulets equipped. You know, some kind of magical item that prevented a fatal wound.

"What next?" Ira asked.

"The battle has begun. We'll wait a little after the cavalrymen get back to their base camp, then begin our attack."

I heard distant thunder as we marched forward. This was the beginning. Soon after, the three light cavalrymen who had fled the scene returned to base. Their explanation of events was incoherent.

"There were these weird carriages, and then there was a flash, then suddenly the cavalrymen next to us got blown away."

"Our arrow-deflecting amulets and armor didn't stand a chance! Our fellow soldiers were ripped to shreds."

"The sound of the air being cut won't leave my ears!"

The attack they fell under remained shrouded in mystery, but one thing was clear.

"They were the rebel forces, correct?"

"Th-they claimed to be the official army of the Kingdom of Merinard. They demanded the...invaders from the Holy Kingdom return at once, lest they begin their attack."

Official army? The thought was absurd. But the fact that their military strength had come this far meant that the old capital had likely fallen into their hands already. That was certainly unexpected. The plan had been to bunker down in the capital and exterminate these vermin, but now we had to retake the capital first.

"Eleven of these carriages, you say?"

"Y-yes. Extremely weird, junky looking vehicles."

"Hrm... That unknown attack is concerning."

"Could it be the crossbow we've heard so much about," my aide suggested.

I shook my head. "If the arrow-deflecting amulets and armor didn't work, it must be something else."

If we had gotten our hands on a corpse, we could have investigated ourselves, but it would have been unreasonable to ask the survivors to do that.

"Either way, there will be no retreat," I said. "The enemy is naught but eleven carriages. In that case, the rebel's weakness must reside in that number. In order to retake the capital in such a short time, they must have forced a castle siege and march. Their losses had to have been significant, and they likely used some kind of precious artifact to threaten the men in the city."

Artifacts capable of striking armored cavalrymen from afar were truly a pain to deal with, but they typically had a limited number of uses.

"I agree with your opinion on this, Sir Eckhart," said Mazie, leader of the mage squad. He looked up at the sky with an irritated expression. "However, that range is going to be a problem..."

Up high in the sky were those cursed shit birds. On the battlefield, they would often drop feces, muck, trash, and even rotting bodies down to the ground. They were detestable bird demi-humans.

"At that height, our chorus magic or attacks will not reach them. And that artifact of theirs has quite the range, correct?"

"Y-yes. Easily over two hundred meters."

"Two hundred! Now that is a problem. They have the range advantage!"

Mazie grimaced. No matter who used it, normal magic had a max range of about 100 meters. Elven spirit magic or magic performed by a group of mages in a ritual could push that number, but even then, 200 was the absolute max. Even the Holy Kingdom's mage squad's specialty, chorus magic, couldn't hit a target 200 meters away. At best, it was 150 meters.

"Anyway, they are few in number," I said. "Our best course of action is to bring things into a melee. We'll send forth the heavy infantry—with the mage squad's defensive magic, they'll be able to take the enemy's attacks. Then, once the enemy's run dry, we'll send our calvary at them. Those vehicles of theirs are likely a kind of war chariot. Those types of weapons typically become a weakness when relied on too heavily."

"This all sounds reasonable," said Mazie. "Sir Paras, what say you?"

"As good a plan as any. Should it prove necessary, my Holy Knights will obliterate them."

The leader of the 3rd Order smiled cheerfully. He wasn't yet a man, and his face still had its boyish features. He was a genius who had been selected to lead one of the five Orders of the Holy Knights at a tremendously young age.

"Actually, would it not make sense to send us forth first?" he asked. "I see no reason to waste the lives of our men."

"The Holy Knights are our trump card," I told him. "We'll use you when the time comes."

"Will you, now?" Paras stepped back without showing any kind of disappointment on his face.

The 3rd Order were part of Cardinal Krone's faction. Originally, Cardinal Benos's 2nd Order was supposed to accompany us, but they were sent out to the east to do battle with the Empire, so the sudden change was made. My Lord gave me strict orders to not give the 3rd Order any chances to prove themselves in battle. I could not send the Holy Knights out here and allow them to look good.

And more importantly, they were disgusting people with the blood of demi-humans flowing within them. I would not allow them to seize valor in my army.

"Heavy infantrymen, to the—"

Before I could finish giving my order, the thunder from before started up again... But this time, it was different. It was more like the unpleasant sound of fabric being ripped apart. Suddenly, the front line appeared to be in a panic.

"What happened?! Report!" I yelled to one of my underlings, but I already knew the answer. The battle had begun.

I could hear Eckhart shouting behind me as I returned to the camp where my Holy Knights were waiting. The entire subjugation force seemed shaken by the chaos on the front lines, but my men were different.

"Captain, how did it go?" asked my vice captain, who was the same age as me.

"He wants us to warm the bench until the time comes," I shrugged. "You know, as expected."

I could see Eckhart's ulterior motives. But things were designed to be that way.

"Eleven strange, junky carriages. An unknown weapon that, with a flash of light, simultaneously ripped through the air and through armor and arrow-deflecting charms. Sound familiar?"

When I shared the info with the advisor next to my vice captain, he brought his gloved hand to his nose—no, to his mouth, hidden by his deep hood.

"Hrm," he said. "It could be the bolt action rifle—or perhaps a new version of one? It sounds different."

"Bolt action rifle, you say... If I remember correctly, that's a weapon that fires arrowheads so fast the eye cannot track them, correct?"

"Yes. It has a range of over 1000 meters. With a 'scope' attachment, it can target enemies over 1,500 meters away. On top of that, it's powerful enough to pierce the armor of a heavy infantryman with ease. Arrow-deflecting charms would probably be useless."

"What do you mean by a new version?" I asked.

"The bolt action rifle I'm familiar with can't fire successive shots," he explained. "Judging by the sounds we're hearing, this thing is firing like crazy. If I remember correctly, that submachine gun he used could fire tens of shots at high speed. Maybe this is the bolt action rifle version of that?"

I ruminated on his words internally, carefully considering their meaning.

"In other words, you're talking about a weapon that can fire dozens of shots, all with the power to pierce heavy infantrymen armor from 1,000 to 1,500 meters away?"

"It's likely, yes. The fact that they're here in such small numbers means he's probably with them, so don't expect them to run out of ammo. Oh, and about those weird vehicles..."

"There were eleven of them."

"Ten of them are probably carrying riflemen, and then one of them is the one he's on. Sadly, I don't know anything about these new vehicles. I bet they're faster than cavalrymen, though."

"On what basis?"

"Riflemen are at a disadvantage in close-range combat. At least compared to an elite infantryman. If they're being carried by a vehicle, that means it's meant to cover for that weakness."

"In other words, either they're good at close-range combat, or they don't intend to let it come to that?"

The man hiding his face under a hood nodded. "Exactly. They can probably attack while moving around."

"So the enemy can endlessly shower us in armor-piercing attacks from afar while zipping around faster than cavalrymen?"

"That's probably their plan, yeah. And then you add the harpy aerial bombs on top of that. A direct hit is strong enough to destroy a wall, but on top of that, the blast sends metal fragments all over the place. It's like being showered in countless iron arrows at extremely close range."

I paused to think for a moment. "The Holy Kingdom can't win," I concluded.

"Captain?" said my aide.

"I mean, it's true, is it not? Our enemy can shoot speck-sized instant death attacks at us hundreds, no, thousands of times. It'd be one thing if everyone could learn the truth behind these attacks like us and simply bide their time, but the others have no way of surviving this. They'll be mowed down like autumn wheat."

I had already thought of countermeasures for the bolt action rifle. The mages would dig holes in the ground, and we could hide in those. There was no way to shoot an unseen enemy, and according to our advisor, the weapon's piercing strength would be diminished significantly enough that it wouldn't be able to pierce our armor. Plus, the effect of the harpy aerial bombs would be cut in half, and we wouldn't have to worry about metal shards—although a direct hit would still mean the end.

"Let's let the main forces do their job," I said. "That'll make things easier for us. If worse comes to worst, we can simply offer you up when we surrender for better conditions."

"Cut me some slack, boss man," said the hooded man. "Her Highness will rip me to shreds! Actually, Melty will probably strangle me first. Or Ira will roast me to death... God help me."

"You still refer to her as Her Highness?" I asked.

"She's worthy of deep respect. Talented in the martial arts, charismatic, and she has the will of heaven behind her."

"Explain."

"According to our priestess, any who stand before her as an enemy, even the Empire, will not come away unscathed. It's in everyone's best interests to get along with her."

"Then are you not in danger?"

"In my mind, I don't intend to become her enemy," the hooded man said with a shrug. "Though I did betray her, even if it was necessary."

He didn't even waver when I said I would offer him to the other side. If things got that bad, I had actually planned to do as much, but either he was certain he wouldn't be killed, or he was confident that we wouldn't be let free. Either way, he was definitely hiding something. I would have to save him as a final trump card.

"Anyway, just be careful of stray rounds or direct hits," he added. "If the wall of bodies grows thin, you had best make a thick wall of dirt."

"How would one presume to be careful of a direct hit?"

"Dig a hole. You've got plenty of energy, right?"

To think the noble and honorable Holy Knights' first move on the battlefield would be to dig holes. How miserable.

"Take care not to let the barrel and receiver heat up too much. This is black iron we're talking about, so they can handle some heat, but don't overestimate them."

"Roger that."

GAAAAAAAAAAAAN!

GAAAAAAAAAAAAN!

The sounds of intermittent bursts of gunfire filled the air of the battlefield, making it impossible to distinguish individual shots from one another. The machine guns our men were using could fire twenty shots in seconds, after all. Of course you couldn't distinguish them.

"Pirna, if you see any movement, let me know ASAP!"

"Got it! They're super panicked right now!"

That wasn't a surprise. They were being attacked at a distance out of their magic's range by projectiles that looked like specks. Obviously, the gunfire and sounds gave away our presence to them, but I doubt they realized we were attacking from so far away.

"They are all huddled together," Melty said. "Would it not be quicker to draw close and cut them down?"

"Sure, but it's not worth losing our range advantage," I replied. "Our objective is to one-sidedly attack them and annihilate their morale."

"They're being assaulted by unknown weapons, and their allies are dropping like flies. Plus they have no viable means of fighting back. Their morale is going to drop."

The atmosphere was light as we discussed the turn of events, but Melty was looking all the way at the front lines. At this distance, they all looked like specks to me, but an overlord like her could probably see things as clear as day.

"Pandemonium," Ira whispered, her one large eye pointed toward the front lines.

She could make out the horrors occurring over there.

"Their calvary squad has started to move!" she announced. "They're deploying to the left and right."

"Got it," I said. "Jagheera, the calvary is on the move. They plan on circling our flanks. Take defensive maneuvers while driving them back."

"Roger that. Proceeding to take out the odd numbers coming from the right flank and the even coming from the left flank. Let's shave them down while falling back."

On Jagheera's orders, the rifle squad airboards split off to the left and right, taking defensive maneuvers. I also began to pull back with my airboard.

"Aren't we going to fight, Kousuke?" Ira asked.

"Let's leave it to the rifle squad. If push comes to shove, we can equip the roof with a weapon. We have fixed armaments on board."

Right now, the roof was being used for the flag, but the frame itself was made sturdy enough to mount a heavy weapon on it. The problem was that I was the only one present who could use it and also the only one who could drive... Well, Ira could too, technically.

"If you want to drive for me, Ira, I can attack," I told her. "But that's probably not for the best, eh?"

"Mm, no. If their mage squad starts using chorus magic, I'm the only one who can defend against it."

The machine gun fire continued in the background as we spoke. Of the sixty thousand Holy Kingdom troops, about ten thousand of them were calvary. Meanwhile, we had approximately twenty riflemen fighting against them and ten airboards. In terms of range, speed, and firepower, we overwhelmingly had the advantage, but even then, doing battle with five hundred times our numbers was no simple task.

"Pirna, cut their momentum with some aerial bombs," I instructed.

"Aye, aye! Full force?"

"Full force. If we can take out their calvary, they'll lose their means of attacking us entirely. Try to get as many of them caught in the explosions as possible."

"Roger that!" Pirna responded cheerfully before cutting contact.

Soon after, the twenty harpies who'd accompanied us this far began their aerial bombing runs on the enemy. Having been showered in gunfire, the enemy was at a standstill, clumped together. And now approximately thirty harpy bombs were raining down upon them from high up in the air. They were probably equipped with tools or divine protection from arrows of some kind, but in the face of our bombs' explosive power, it was all meaningless.

"Talk about accuracy..." Melty observed.

"That is because those silly harpies practiced their bombing runs whenever they had free time," Grande said. "They would even put targets on the ground and race to see who could get the most points. Something about only those with the highest scores being chosen to go with Master."

"I see... So they really got into it."

"That's how they were training?"

Not that I had any room to complain considering the way their training had born fruit. I just had a more stoic image of their exercises is all. Though I guess, in a sense, this was pretty stoic?

"Let's put that to the side for now," I said. "We are literally in the middle of a life-or-death battle."

"That doesn't mean we have to approach things with a grim attitude," Ira argued. "If anything, being a little relaxed is good for us."

"Agreed," said Grande. "Those with strength should act as such. In fact, I would argue that directing one's attention to sensual pleasures on the battlefield is perfectly fine."

"I think maybe that's a step too far," I said with a wry smile.

But she and Ira were right in that it was probably best not to be too strung up just because we were in the middle of a battle. It was important to always be composed.

"Bombing runs complete!" reported Pirna. **"The enemy cavalry has lost their commander and is currently stampeding about!"**

"Got it. Get some height and resume information support."

"Okay! So we don't need to restock?"

"You'll do that after their cavalry is dealt with. Rifle squad, what's the situation?"

"They're running around aimlessly, which is a real pain," Jagheera replied. **"For now, it looks like they've stopped attacking in an organized fashion. Should we pursue?"**

"Please do. They won't be a threat to us much longer."

"Understood."

Now then, the only group left with the power to rush us were the Holy Knights. How were they going to move?

"Ngh, how could this have happened?!"

I gritted my teeth as I watched the cavalry stampede around in the aftermath of those accursed shit birds' attack. I had heard of their aerial bombs, but I didn't think they would be so powerful. That alone would have been bad enough, but the icing on the cake was the overpowering strike to our morale. The horses were terrified.

"Underestimating their small numbers was our downfall," I groaned.

"Also, not being able to spread out more to the left and right," Sir Mazie whispered gravely.

I had ordered our men to flank the enemy, but they couldn't spread out as wide as planned, and they ended up rushing them while crowded together. As a result, much of the vanguard was caught in those shit birds' explosions. With them gone, it was more difficult for the following units to push forward. In other words, their forward momentum was annihilated. And then you had that unknown weapon of theirs cutting our cavalry down.

"This is bad," I said. "They're stampeding! Have the heavy infantry move forward. Stop the enemy pursuit!"

"The mage squad shall also move forward to provide defensive support," said Sir Mazie.

"You have my thanks."

At the signal of drums, heavy infantrymen equipped with thick armor and shields began to march forward, taking on the attack for the fleeing cavalrymen.

"Their weapons pierce even the armor of our heavy infantry?!"

If nothing else, they could take on more than the average soldier, but it was a problem of degrees. This was still completely one-sided, and we weren't blocking those attacks. If this continued, we would either lose all of our heavy infantrymen, or they would run out of whatever weapon they were using.

Just as I was beginning to realize how bad the situation was, the enemy suddenly stopped attacking and retreated.

"Have they run out of artifact uses at last?" I asked.

"I believe that to be the case," Sir Mazie agreed. "Fierce relics like that are hard to come by. All that's left now is to draw them in."

"I can only hope so... But first, we need to check our damages and reorganize."

We had to deal with the wounded and our casualties. At this point, our entire army was stopped in place.

"Prioritize healing the wounded and providing aid," I ordered. "Notify all of our clergymen to provide recovery."

If the artifact attacks had stopped, there would be no further casualties. Fortunately, we had many clergymen and priest-warriors in our forces who were capable of healing miracles. Other nations would have had to abandon such wounded soldiers, but our miracles could bring them back to full health and return them to the front line.

But only thirty minutes had passed since we began to heal the wounded when they reappeared.

"You mean they can resupply their artifacts?!"

"Th-that's impossible!"

And so the massacre began anew. Indeed, this was no battle at all. They were staying the perfect distance away from us, showering us with fatal attacks.

Our infantry came under attack before the reorganization was complete, and the heavy infantrymen suffered grave losses trying to defend them. Our calvary's attempt at a counterattack was silenced. Any ambush we attempted was caught by the shit birds in the sky and crushed.

These attacks repeated themselves over and over again until the sun set. And by then, our Holy Kingdom army's losses were so bad, one had to avert their eyes from it all.

"Sir Eckhart, we can proceed no further."

"No, we must! If we have the knights perform a nocturnal assault, we—!"

"How can we do that when we do not know where the enemy is?"

Captain of the 3rd Holy Order of Knights, Sir Paras—no, Paras tilted his head as though he were insulting me. But what this youngster said was not wrong. The sun was setting, but we had yet to locate the enemy's base of operations. Every time we sent out light cavalry as recon, not a single man returned. They must have been located by those shit birds and annihilated.

"Our cavalrymen and heavy infantrymen have been massacred, 30 percent of our infantrymen are dead or near death, and our mage squad's magical energy is all dried up. Same with the clergymen and their miracles."

"I know, but...! But! I refuse to acknowledge a defeat or surrender! We are the Holy Kingdom's... We are Adolism's sword and shield!"

"Then what would you have us do? Fight a one-sided battle until all of our men are dead?"

"I do not fear death! I will not bend the knee to those disgusting demi-humans!"

If we surrendered or retreated against a middling enemy force of eleven carriages, I was ruined. My army of sixty thousand couldn't even get a single hit on them! Cardinal Benos would never forgive me. And it wouldn't just be me who suffered. If I failed here, the entire Melissenos House would—

"What do you think, Sir Mazie?" asked Paras.

Sir Mazie went silent for a moment. After having used all of his magic power, he was barely able to stand. "We have no choice but to surrender," he said. "We cannot afford further casualties in the mage squad."

"Wha—?!"

I was flabbergasted by Sir Mazie's words. Absurd! The noble Holy Kingdom's mage squad would never surrender to the demi-humans! They couldn't!

"We learned that making dirt walls could give us cover from the enemy's attacks. However, making a dirt wall large enough to protect the entire army is impossible, and simply hiding is not a feasible strategy," Sir Mazie said sullenly. He let out a sigh. "Even if it blocks attacks from their strange artifacts, it does not shield us from their aerial bombs. Our magic energy is running empty. We cannot attack them or defend any further."

"Then it is decided," said Paras. "Shall we raise the white flag?"

"Wha—?!" I sputtered in indignation. "You bastard! And you call yourself a Holy Knight?! You would surrender without ever raising arms—?!"

"Are you not the one who prevented me from doing so?" he retorted. "From the start, I recommended taking to the field as this army's blade. Sir Mazie was there to hear that."

Sir Mazie nodded. "Indeed."

"Yes, but...!"

"And how would you have us fight now?" Paras argued. "In half a day, half of our forces are dead. We have no magic or miracles to count on, and morale is at an all-time low. We still have our supplies, so the men are just barely hanging on, but if we lose those, I do not know what will happen."

"If we retreat temporarily, we can regroup and keep resisting!"

"Our enemy is faster than our cavalrymen and has weapons that can strike us from a far greater range than magic or arrows. How could we flee from them?"

Paras's cold glare settled on me. He wasn't hiding that he was looking down on me. My vision turned red with rage. How dare this disgusting half-demi-human look down upon me? Eckhart Melissenos?! Unforgivable. Absolutely unforgivable. This disgusting being was created as a disposable sword of the Holy Kingdom, and yet he dared look down upon me, a son of the noble Melissenos House?!

Fine. In that case, I would have him fulfill his duty as a Holy Knight.

"Then we have no choice but to have your order stop their attack."

The 3rd Order was under Cardinal Krone's watch, but I currently had the right to command as the leader of the subjugation forces. He would not be able to defy me.

"I see," he said. "You would leave that responsibility to my 3rd Order?"

"Yes. This is your time to shine."

"I understand." Paras nodded in acceptance, put his hand on the sword at his hip—then suddenly my entire vision rotated.

"Sir Eckhart has lost his mind. I will now take command in his stead."

White Flag

329

IT HAD BEEN a few hours of continued attacks by our rifle squad and harpy aerial bombing unit.

As the sun set behind the mountains, we received a comm from Pirna up in the air.

"Kousuke! The enemy base is flying a white flag."

"Oh ho, really? What do you think?"

Even in this world, the white flag was used as a sign of surrender or cease-fire. Knowing this, I shot the question toward Melty and Ira.

"It was a one-sided slaughter. They threw in the towel," said Melty.

"Probably," Ira agreed.

"Huh. Well, let's cease-fire then. Come in, Jagheera."

"What's up? We still have ammo."

"The enemy's flying the white flag. Cease-fire."

"Gotcha. Roger that."

The sound of gunfire came to a stop, and for the first time in a bit, silence settled over the battlefield.

"My ears are kinda pounding," said Melty.

"We have it easy," I replied. "The riflemen have to take life potions regularly, given how close to the sounds they are."

"That is an unfortunate flaw in your world's weapons," Ira said.

"That's just how it is. Now then, I guess this means we go into cease-fire negotiations. No choice but to head out, then."

"Mm, but don't let your guard down."

I earnestly accepted Ira's words of wisdom and called back the rifle squad. After getting them restocked, we made our way to the front lines. On my airboard was both the Merinard flag and a white flag, the intent being to communicate that we were an envoy to negotiate the cease-fire.

"They're coming up to meet us, too."

There were three cavalrymen heading out.

"Who should go?" I asked. "Me, Melty, and Ira?"

"Not you, Kousuke," said Melty.

Ira nodded. "Definitely not you, Kousuke."

"For reals...?"

I wasn't going to ask why. I was sure they were looking out for me, but also, compared to those with strength in this world, I was relatively weak. If I fought from a distance, sure, but at close range, I was worthless.

"He will be fine if I accompany him, no?" Grande said. "Worst-case scenario, I could carry him, and you could carry Ira, Melty. Am I wrong?"

"Er, yeah, I suppose that would work," replied Melty, a dissatisfied expression crossing her face. She probably didn't want to put me in danger, but all of my girls were being a bit too overprotective. I mean, I did get kidnapped that one time, so I suppose I didn't have room to speak, but I digress.

"Then let's not keep them waiting," I said. "Shall we?"

"Mm."

"Okay."

"Indeed."

We all disembarked from the airboard, and I quickly stashed it away in my inventory. The enemy's representatives were two knights wearing white armor and one older man with a staff. Then there was one infantry-looking guy holding a white flag.

There was still some distance between us, so I whipped out a small golem communicator and slung it across my body.

"Testing, testing. This is Kousuke. Can you hear me?"

"This is Jagheera. Loud and clear."

"This is Pirna in the sky! All good!"

"Okay! If you see anything out of the ordinary, contact me immediately."

Just in case of an emergency, I made sure to have some insurance ready. I checked that I had a weapon saved to my shortcuts. A handgun, shotgun, submachine gun, assault rifle, a machine gun (the same type as the one the rifle squad used), an auto grenade launcher, a large caliber machine gun and a sniper rifle: I had choices. My shortcut was revised for combat.

"Are you ready?"

"Yeah. I'll carry the flag."

I pulled the white flag from my inventory and shouldered it. Melty was going to handle negotiations, and Ira and Grande weren't tall enough to carry something like this. Actually, Grande could probably handle it with her insane strength, but she had to protect me if things got bad. It only made sense then that I carry the flag.

"Well, well. What beautiful women."

Was he forgetting me? I opted not to cut in. After all, it was best to lie low in these kinds of situations. The one to speak up was a super-hot, blond-haired, green-eyed knight. He looked pretty young, actually.

"Thank you very much," said Melty. "I never thought in my wildest dreams that a man from the Holy Kingdom would ever pay me a compliment. By the way, the sun is setting, so can we get a move on?"

"Right. Then how about a cease-fire of three days?"

"Out of the question. What merit is there for us? We have yet to lose a single soldier."

"Are three days not important for you as well?" he asked. "It is clear you are all strong, but you are few in number. Your weapons are powerful, but you only have eleven carriages. There's a reason you are not using them in larger numbers, no?"

He was right and wrong. Part of the reason we only had twenty riflemen was indeed an ammunition problem, but it wasn't an unfixable one if I made more golem workbenches. We had plenty of materials to make bullets and machine guns from, so if I really wanted to, I could build more.

"If only that were true. Is there any point in talking about what-ifs? Our current forces that are here right now are more than a threat to you all."

"That is true."

"We have no qualms about launching a night attack on you. We could also burn your supplies if you'd like?"

"I...am sure you could." The blond-haired hottie grimaced. "All right. Then we will perform a full retreat. In exchange, we ask that you do not pursue us. How does that sound?"

"Are you being serious? I hate repeating myself," Melty said in a troubled tone, tilting her head. "But I suppose if I must... What merit is there for us?"

"Would there be no merit in you not having to continue fighting us any further?"

"All so that you can reorganize and come attacking again after we let you go?" tutted Melty. "We might as well just slaughter you all now." The way she casually used the word "slaughter" was enough to make the young man's face twitch. "You are the ones who called us to the negotiation table. We have no qualms about continuing this battle. So I will give you one more chance. Choose your words wisely, okay?"

I could only see the back of Melty's head from where I was, but I was certain she had a wonderful smile on her face. Across from us, our enemy was as freaked out as could be. Um, kind guest, I recommend removing your hand from the grip of your weapon! Ah, kind guest? That's a bad, bad idea!

"Will you draw your weapon? I don't mind in the least."

GOOOOOOH.

A physical pressure washed over the area. Melty had likely released some of the energy that was stored within her as an overlord. It came with a tremendous physical pressure, but where did it stand relative to the rest of this world? I wasn't sure, but if even I could feel it, someone with no magic in his bones at all, that meant it was something else indeed.

"Melty, take it down a notch," Ira scolded her.

Melty frowned. "Aw, but he keeps looking down on us!" She looked adorable like that, but the air of intimidation was still rolling off of her. I shot a look at the young knight, and he was raising both arms in surrender, his face pale.

"Come morning, we will return to the Holy Kingdom," said the older robed man, leaning on his staff. "Additionally, we will take only the bare minimum of our supplies back with us, relinquishing the rest to you. We have enough materials to support sixty thousand troops. I imagine those will prove useful to you."

He just barely managed to squeeze out his words.

"It would be incredibly annoying if you ended up pillaging our territories for supplies as a result," Melty pointed out.

"We will not do that. I vow this on my name, Mazie Bonaparte, leader of the 2nd mage squad, reporting directly to the Holy King."

"I too vow this upon my name, Paras Iguodala, captain of the 3rd Order of Holy Knights."

Both the robed older man and the hottie young knight put a hand to their chests as they swore. Maybe that was their country's way of making an oath.

"Hrm... Well, I suppose that's about what we can expect as conditions," Melty conceded. "All right, we will not pursue you. However, once we are prepared, we will reinitiate our attack."

"I shall keep that in mind." The mage named Mazie nodded deeply. Um, in other words, if they took their time retreating, we'd kick their ass? Was that what Melty was implying?

"Then it is decided," said Melty. "Shall we shake hands?"

"I'll pass," Mazie said. "My withered hand would probably be crushed in yours."

"What a rude thing to say to a weak young lady."

Nobody said it out loud, but I was certain we were all thinking the exact same thing: She was no weak young lady.

"The subjugation forces have been routed. However, the 3rd Order of Holy Knights and the mage squad are alive. Eckhart is dead. Hm."

My eyes traced the floating text on the lithograph as I whispered to myself. This was not the best-case scenario, but it was still a fine result. As long as the 3rd Order came home intact. Eckhart's death was not a bad result at all. And considering the conflict with the Empire, the survival of the 2nd mage squad was also good.

"But there were so many casualties."

Both heavy infantry and the cavalrymen were annihilated. Half of our light infantry were dead, and morale was at an all-time low. Sending the surviving soldiers against Merinard going forward would be difficult, eh?

"The enemy had a mere eleven chariot-like vehicles? Is this a mistake?"

It was hard to believe, but then again, a Fabled Visitor had supposedly sided with the Kingdom of Merinard. According to that fox, while the man didn't have any fighting power to call his own, the effect he had on logistics, supplies, and the military was powerful. Did this report mean that he had perfectly demonstrated his abilities? The only way to know would be to ask Paras directly upon his return.

With that thought in mind, I heard a knock at the door. I urged them to come in, and a young man in white armor appeared before me.

"Lord Krone. Judgment has been passed on the apostates within the Holy City. However, Benos and a few other cardinals managed to escape. We are currently searching for them, but it is likely they used some kind of teleportation artifact."

"Hrm, Empire-made or perhaps excavated?" I mused. "No matter, this is all within the margins of error. They have no place in the Holy Kingdom. They likely fled to the Principality of Dehart."

"What should we do?"

"Leave them be. The Kingdom of Merinard will finish them off."

He would almost certainly make a move on Merinard in an attempt at penance. And when he did, he would be destroyed. God would make sure of it.

"Now we can return to the correct teachings," I whispered to myself, placing my hand on the sacred scripture bestowed upon me by the Holy King.

The same one filled with the original teachings from ancient times.

God was watching, and his works would arrange the world into its proper state. The texts that had been disfigured into evil works would be destroyed, and the world would know the true teachings. That was my duty as a devout follower of Our Lord.